# KATHRYN H. KIDD

## Foreword by Orson Scott Card

HATRACK RIVER
PUBLICATIONS

Cover art by Paul Mann
Cover design by James Fedor
This book was set in 16-point Glyphix Foundry "Oxford" from SWFTE International,
    using WordPerfect 5.0 and a Hewlett-Packard LaserJet II. It was then reduced
    and printed as approximately 12-point type on acid-free paper.
Printed by Publisher's Press, Salt Lake City UT
Sole distributor of books from Hatrack River Publications is:
    Publishers Distribution Center
    805 West 1700 South
    Salt Lake City UT  84104

First printing December 1989
10 9 8 7 6 5

Library of Congress Catalog Card Number:  89- 81620

ISBN 0-9624049-0-X

*To Clark —*
*cherished husband,*
*beloved friend*

## Hatrack River Books by Kathryn H. Kidd

*Paradise Vue*
*The Alphabet Year*
*Return to Paradise*

## Other Books from Hatrack River Publications

*Gert Fram*, by Nancy Allen Black
*Pray Away Pounds*, by Lisa Ray Turner
*Perfect Neighbors*, by DeAnne Neilson
*Home to Roost*, by Linda Hoffman Kimball
*Hand to Hand*, by Denise Tucker
*Out of the Woods*, by Scott A. Schulte

# Contents

# Foreword
## Orson Scott Card

I met Kathy Helms through a mutual friend. I was working as an editor at the *Ensign* magazine at the time; she was working for the *Deseret News*. She was engaged to marry Clark Kidd, a wizard computer systems programmer; I had proposed to Kristine Allen, my future wife, and was beginning my four-and-a-half-month wait for her answer. (Assuming the burden of marrying me was not something a wise woman undertook lightly.)

Kathy and I both harbored ambitions of being professional writers — I had just sold my first science fiction story, and she was secretly working on (or perhaps just thinking heavily about) what she jokingly called the Great American Novel. We didn't talk much about writing, though. Actually, there isn't that much to *say* about writing. Most writers' conversations about writing follow the same pattern: "Did you like my story/poem/ article?" "Yes. Did you like mine?" It gets very dull, except when the answer to the first question is *no*. But Kathy and I never talked about that, mostly because she never showed me anything she wrote, and I never asked her whether she had read anything of mine.

What we talked about was everything else — particularly the forbidden topics of politics and religion. With politics, we agreed remarkably often, considering the fact that I was becoming a Moynihan Democrat and Kathy and Clark were then Reaganites — back when that was still a somewhat daring thing to be.

But our best talk was about the Church. Not the gospel, usually — the Church. We shared Church Office Building and *Deseret News* gossip, but that wasn't half as interesting as stories about people in our wards and stakes. Mormon folkways and foibles. Good people, weird people. Strange customs that grow up in one ward or another.

Clark and Kathy got married. Since Kathy's father wasn't a member, they invited me to join Clark's father as a witness to the temple ceremony. They moved into a house on Princeton Avenue, and the three of us continued our friendship exactly as before. We would play board games and pinochle; we'd go out to restaurants and ice cream parlors. We watched each other change jobs, gain and lose weight, and step upward through various home computers.

Kristine and I moved to South Bend, Indiana, and then to Greensboro, North Carolina. Business took me back to Utah once or twice a year; I'd always spend at least an evening with Clark and Kathy, and often I'd stay overnight with them. Our friendship only grew, despite the distance between us.

When, as an editor at Compute! Books, I needed to find people to write computer books, I thought at once of Clark and Kathy. They soon signed a contract to write a series of books of computer games for kids. It was a simple matter for Clark to program educational games for the Vic, the Commodore 64, and the Atari; Kathy researched the games, composed the text, and wrote the articles and game directions. Nobody got rich, but it was fun.

Now Clark and Kathy live in Sterling, Virginia, where Clark is a high-powered software designer and Kathy writes for a fund-raising firm that primarily serves the pro-life movement. I visit there often, sometimes using their house for a week or two as a retreat from the incessant distractions that come when too many people know a writer's phone number. They also join me in some of the cities I travel to on business — Kathy gave me the tour of New Orleans, her childhood city, and we've done Philadelphia, Boston, Chicago, and, of course, Washington, D.C., which is beginning to feel like a second home to me.

Through all of this, Kathy has never changed. She has the same piercing, compassionate, yet hilarious view of her fellow Saints. I can always count on wonderful stories — true, even commonplace, yet always surprising and entertaining because they're seen through Kathy's eyes. Her faith remains unshakable; her love for the Church and its members never wavers. This is not because she doesn't see the weaknesses and failings of the people around her. Nor does she ignore them. I believe she loves people as much *because* of those foibles as in spite of them.

And even on those rare occasions when she finds people she can't enjoy, even with humor, she still treats them kindly and still watches them with the same piercing eye. They all become part of her memory, and then emerge again as stories. "You ought to write a book," I always said. "Someday," she always answered.

Then, this last spring, Kristine and I had the opportunity to start the Mormon publishing company we had long dreamed of. My brother Russell had always had the expertise and now had the time to help us start up the business. In short order he found us a fine, reliable distributor and a first-rate printer and was able to do all the legwork and paperwork in Utah. Kristine and I would do the editorial work in North Carolina. All we lacked was something to print.

What was it that we wanted to publish? Fiction for the Mormon audience. But what *kind* of fiction? How would it differ from what was already being published?

Mormon fiction as a commercial publishing category is very new — it began with the surprising success of Shirley Sealy's first novel back in 1977. Until she proved that Mormons would actually buy Mormon novels, Deseret Book and Bookcraft didn't publish fiction; once she proved it was profitable, commercial Mormon fiction grew by leaps and bounds.

But, like mainstream American fiction, LDS fiction had grown in two distinct categories. On the one side were the popular, commercial novels, which tended to be very simple-minded and presented a sugar-coated view of Mormon life. On the other side were the literary novels, which tended to be slow-moving, dull, and pretentious, and were often quite hostile to the Church. In both categories, of course, there were writers who transcended some of the limitations of their community. But they were rare.

LDS writers and publishers alike seemed to accept the notion widely believed in the world of American letters that popular novels *must* be shallow and badly written in order to be commercially successful, while literary novels *must* be self-indulgent, offensive, and impenetrable in order to be artistically successful. It was and is my fervent belief that both ideas are completely wrong, and that writers who believe in them invariably forfeit either their talent, their integrity, or their audience.

I think that the Mormon popular audience is ready for fiction that depicts Mormon life with every speck of power and truth that the best literary novels can offer. I also think that the Mormon literary audience would be grateful for stories that were actually entertaining, funny, moving, passionate. In other words, a book doesn't have to be dull to be good literature; it doesn't have to be dishonest to be an entertaining read.

After all, long before America learned to separate the readers of John Updike from the readers of Stephen King with an unscalable wall, America had Mark Twain, who managed to be highly commercial and literarily brilliant all at once. In that century England also produced Charles Dickens and Jane Austen, who, like Twain, told stories that made their readers laugh and cry — and yet their tales also stand as fine works of literary art. It is only in this century that the literary world has snobbishly refused to write for the audience of untrained, unscholarly readers who read, not what someone says they *ought* to, but what they *love*.

Another thing that Dickens, Twain, and Austen all had in common was a powerful awareness of their community. Their stories took an honest, often satiric look at the people they knew best. Yet they never wrote as outsiders, never took a hostile stance, because the society in their stories was the very society whose members they hoped would *read* their stories. Dickens's audience was the very England whose flaws he documented; Austen's readers were the same landed gentry and educated middle class she teased in the pages of her books. Twain's rough American characters were the same people who delighted in reading about themselves as the Connecticut Yankee, the common-sense river rat Huck, the trickster Tom Sawyer. The audience for these stories recognized the truth about themselves when they saw it, and laughed at their own quirks and failings in the pages of some of the finest and liveliest works in all of literature.

It seemed to me that Mormons longed for exactly the same thing — the truth, even when it stings or makes us look a bit ridiculous, as long as we know that the storyteller is one of us, as long as we can sense that he knows our strengths as well as our weaknesses, that he loves us even as he helps us laugh at ourselves. It seemed to me that Mormons were ready for an LDS Mark Twain or Jane Austen or Charles Dickens.

Why hadn't such a writer yet appeared? The talent is certainly available. The problem is that we keep getting distracted by issues of faith. Mormon writers kept concentrating on what I call "revolving door" fiction — stories about people gaining or losing their faith, joining or leaving the Church. Even at their best, such stories are not terribly interesting or illuminating, and they don't tell us much about what Mormons *are*.

After all, the people in Dickens's and Austen's novels never sit around worrying about whether they really ought to be English. Twain's characters never go through an epiphany when they decide to be American; nor do they decide, when things go wrong, that the only thing for it is to renounce their citizenship. In these great writers' works, the characters belong irrevocably to their community.

Mormon society, at its heart, consists of people whose commitment to being Mormon is as final and unquestionable as Huck Finn's commitment to being American. It doesn't occur to them that they could ever be anything else. There are those who scoff at such Saints, for from their perspective, leaning out the windows of a certain tall building, they think the committed Saint has surrendered his freedom or abandoned his intellect.

In fact, the mature Latter-day Saint doesn't have to go back and decide the same questions over and over again. The commitment, once made, is no longer negotiable. They have not lost their freedom but gained it, not abandoned their intellect but discovered it, for it is only with that commitment that a person first gains the freedom to learn and act within the Mormon community. Whatever they learn, whatever they choose to do in their lives, committed Latter-day Saints know they will learn and decide it from inside the Church. These people *are* the Church; they *are* Mormon society, and true Mormon fiction must deal with them, not with the people who stand on the fringes unable to decide whether or not to join or stay.

Some Mormons with intellectual pretensions imagine that committed, unquestioning Saints are all the same, and therefore that fiction about them would be like writing fiction about a herd of sheep. You can do it once, but how will your second novel be any different from your first?

In my experience, however, quite the opposite is true. The bleats of the doubters and complainers are monotonously similar, while among the committed Saints is an infinite variety of people, struggling with their own weaknesses while working together within their family and their ward to build the Kingdom of God. These are the people that Hatrack River novels are *for*, and these are the people that Hatrack River novels are *about*.

The most powerful and true stories of any people are rarely about faith, anyway. They are almost always about love and sex and death; about discovering each other, belonging to each other, and losing each other.

This was our vision for Hatrack River. Great LDS fiction must begin by rejecting the world's lie that there are two kinds of writer, one that tells stories that are "entertaining," the other that tells stories that are "true." The great LDS stories will be those that are at once fascinating and illuminating: stories that, in the old phrase, give their readers both sweetness and light — both entertainment and understanding.

So there I was, in the late spring of 1989, ready to publish a kind of Mormon fiction that was largely nonexistent. I had a novel of my own, *Saints*, which had attempted to meet these standards, and Hatrack River could — and will — bring out the first hardcover edition of that book. I had Susan Dean Smallwood's *You're a Rock, Sister Lewis*, a highly personal novel that also strove for entertainment and truth. I had plans for writing several novels of my own, and adapting some of my old plays to fictional form. But that was not enough. I needed more books, ones that did not yet exist, from writers who had not yet attempted to write them.

That was when I thought of Kathy Kidd. She had the deep understanding and love of Mormon society that was the essence of the kind of writer I was looking for. She knew the stories and could tell them in an entertaining way. She was a skilled writer of nonfiction, so she certainly had the ability with language. All that was left was for her to put all that into a novel.

I talked to her. I explained what I've just explained to you — what Hatrack River was looking for, what it needed to be. Kathy thought it was a great idea; what she doubted was her ability to write the book I was asking for. But she agreed to think about it, to see if a good idea came to her.

Almost immediately she began describing some of the story elements in *Paradise Vue*. It sounded great to me, and I encouraged her to go ahead. "I'll try to have it ready for you as a Christmas present," she said.

That was April. She started writing on May 16th. In June, she showed me the first few chapters — it was going much faster than she expected. I had some suggestions; she responded with enthusiasm and more hard work. By the end of July she had given me a finished manuscript.

I knew I wouldn't have time to read it for several weeks, but late one night I picked it up just for a moment, to see what she had done with those first few chapters we had discussed. At six in the morning I finally put it back down. I had read through the night because I couldn't stop, didn't *want* to stop. Kathy had not only written a publishable novel, she had written exactly the kind of novel that Hatrack River exists for. I loved the characters; the writing was bright and artful and clear; Mormon society was presented with truth and affection, with satire and sympathy. You hold that book in your hands.

I am tempted to say that now, with the publication of Kathryn H. Kidd's first novel, the Mormon people have their Jane Austen, their Mark Twain. But that would be false, because Kathy isn't "another" of anything. What the Mormon people have is their Kathryn H. Kidd. We couldn't know how much we wanted her fiction until she began to write it. But this is what we have been hungry for all these years. And good as this book is, I believe the best of Kathy's work is yet to come.

And because she turned in her manuscript so early, I won't be the only person who gets *Paradise Vue* for Christmas this year. So I'm hoping that one of the presents under my tree will be the manuscript of Kathy's *second* novel.

— *Greensboro, North Carolina*
*24 October 1989*

# 1
# Good Fortune

I learned about my new church calling from Carol Ann Little, the ward mouthpiece. Carol Ann wasn't a gossip, but she had one gift that set her apart from everyone else I knew. Without being told, she knew who was going to be called to a job before most people knew there was a vacancy. The woman was never wrong, unless you count the time she told the bishop who he was going to choose for the Young Women's presidency the week before the fact. When the callings were announced, Carol Ann missed every one. Ironically, the presidency Carol Ann picked was so much better than the one that was sustained, the whole ward just assumed the bishop had changed his mind to take her down a peg. Stranger things have happened.

If anybody else had told me I was going to be the new home-making counselor, I would have laughed. Education counselor, yes. But I was the only person I knew who couldn't even get butter to spread. I didn't have a Relief Society wreath on my door, and the only thing standing between my house and the Board of Health was the housekeeper that came in on Tuesdays. So even hearing it from Carol Ann didn't convince me.

Almost before I had my eyebrows raised, Carol Ann added, "Alex Roundy will be president, and the education counselor will be Bess Monson." She leaned back and took a sip of Diet Coke, looking pleased with herself, but I had my doubts. If Carol Ann was right on this one, it would be a coup even for her. Calling Alex to be a Relief Society president was about as likely as making her an apostle. And Bess Monson, education counselor? Bess was the Jell-O Queen of North America. She and her four little girls were always scrubbed and wearing dresses, and she never had so much as a hair out of place. But she had the I.Q. of a pencil sharpener. The only book she'd ever read was written by Mormon. Carol Ann was headed for major humiliation.

I'd almost forgotten Carol Ann's prediction two days later, when I opened my front door to find the bishop on the doorstep. He took one look at me in my pajamas — at 6 P.M. — and decided not to come in. Samson hissed at him malevolently, but I kicked him inside and went out on the porch.

"I've come to ask you to accept a position," he said, squinting in the sunset, and I knew Carol Ann was right. "This may sound a little unorthodox, but I've prayed about it and you're the one. I'd like you to be homemaking counselor of the Relief Society."

"With Alex as president and Bess Monson the education counselor," I said. I lifted my Pepsi in salute. "Carol Ann strikes again."

He sighed. "You know, Amy, half the fun in being bishop is calling people to outlandish jobs in the ward and looking at the shock on their faces. Carol Ann is a thorn in my side. Just once I wish somebody would pretend they hadn't talked to her first."

"You may be in luck on this one," I said. "Carol Ann didn't have any guesses for secretary."

Now that it was official, I had to talk to Alex. I usually went to see her several times a week, but the timing was tricky. She didn't get up until nine, but she liked to schedule appointments at 9:30. Then she was liable to go anywhere. But I had to catch her before the first of her soap operas came on at one. No true friend visited Alex after "Days of Our Lives" began.

I opted for a 9:30 visit and walked in the back door, grabbing a soft drink on the way downstairs. Alex was in her workshop, sanding the walnut case of a regulator clock. She had a lot of time for projects, with both her children grown, and she'd taught herself how to build clocks. I'd gotten her third clock, a big oak thing. It had a personality all its own, since the hour hand was Maltese style and the minute hand was serpentine. Alex was big on craftsmanship, but details escaped her.

I grabbed a chair and sat backwards. Alex said, "Hah!" It was her word for hello, and it was so uniquely Alex that half the ward had picked it up. People liked to imitate Alex. They did it so much that it seemed like she constantly had to invent new Alexisms to stay unique.

"Hah!" I said back. I was as guilty of imitating Alex as anyone. "Homemaking counselor? Is this a joke?"

"That's what the church is all about, Sweetie. We're put into these jobs to learn 'em. If you can do 'em already, what's the point? Besides, people surprise you sometimes. You may be cut out for this."

"I *won't* surprise you. I'm too old to learn how to make Jell-O."

"You're thirty-three years old."

"Thirty-five."

"Whatever. You don't have any children. You're rich. You don't even have a job, and you still keep a filthy house."

"I'm an artist. *That's* my job."

"Yep. You're an artist. Tell me one thing you've sold. You keep everything you like, and no one would buy the rest of it. You might as well put that energy somewhere useful."

"I put that energy into loving my husband." That sounded pious even to me, but Alex knew what I meant. We'd been friends a long time.

"Your husband's been dead for six years. You're not exactly picking up his socks."

She had a point, but the whole idea of homemaking counselor was still foreign. "And Bess as *education* counselor? This presidency's going to be a real funfest."

"You're just jealous of Bess. You'll like her when you get over it." She picked up a fresh piece of sandpaper and attacked a mitered corner. "It's the secretary who's going to kill you. Emma Austen."

She waited for a reaction, and she got one. Emma was a fingernail on the chalkboard of life. She'd been my nemesis for years. I didn't like to be in the same room with Emma Austen.

Emma was a real knockout, and nobody knew it better than she did. Her best friend was her mirror, and her favorite pastime was comparing other people to herself. No stranger on the street was safe from her eagle eye. With Emma as judge, everyone else always came up short. But for some reason, she seemed to have half the ward fooled. All her meanness was excused because she was pretty and she smiled. She had as many followers as Alex did, but the people who imitated Alex were not the same people who idolized Emma.

"Spiffy," I said. "The secretary from hell. Whatever inspired you?"

"It was an answer to prayer. Every time I prayed about it, Emma's name came up. She wouldn't have been my first dibs, either, but I didn't have a choice. You'll support her, won't you?"

"Not until I raise my hand on Sunday. After that, I'll do my best. For your sake, I'll try to keep my mouth shut. Don't ask for more than that."

Alex bit a splinter from the tip of her thumb and sucked on the wound. "It could be worse. She's in court all day, and that hot dating schedule keeps her busy at night. She'll probably be secretary in name only.

"By the way," she added, wiping a smear of blood from the clock cabinet, "leave Thursday open. Before we get sustained, I want to spend one last afternoon as a person. Let's take Bess and Emma out to lunch."

"Let me guess. Don Antonio's. You do know how to throw a party."

\*

Alex picked me up on Thursday morning. She didn't look like a Relief Society president. Her jeans were paint-stained and torn, but she was wearing three rings, her Rolex, and a ruby necklace. Even without all the jewelry, her *person* looked tanned and expensive. Compared with Alex, I was woefully inadequate.

We stopped by to pick up Bess. From the moment she got in the car she looked nervous. Alex and I were virtual strangers to Bess, who had always had jobs in the Primary, away from the body of women in the ward. I could understand how being in the car with two strangers would intimidate her, especially when one of the strangers was Alex.

Alex turned toward town, and Bess panicked. "Where's Emma?" she asked quickly. "Aren't we stopping for Emma?"

"Emma can't get off work," Alex said. "In fact, anything that's done in the daytime will probably have to be done by the three of us."

Bess said "oh" in a small voice, and settled quietly into the back seat. I caught a glimpse of her in the rear-view mirror, and she looked as trapped as a hamster in a cage. Nobody said anything, so Alex put some Scarlatti on the cassette player. We listened to the music the rest of the way to Don Antonio's.


Don Antonio's was going to be the official restaurant of Alex's Relief Society presidency, I could tell. She went there so often the owner once offered her a job as hostess. Alex said no. She didn't tell the owner, but she could have *bought* Don Antonio's if she wanted; she didn't need to work there.

Don Antonio's wasn't my favorite restaurant. I liked Cafe Pierpont or Marie Callender's or any one of a dozen other places better. But Alex liked the security of routine. Don Antonio's was like going to McDonald's without having to go to McDonald's. The food was always the same. Everyone recognized Alex and treated her like an old friend. She even parked in the back and walked through the kitchen to get there — a habit that did nothing to improve my appetite. But Alex said walking through the back door made Don Antonio's feel like home. It was part of the Don Antonio's experience.

When we opened the screen door to go inside, Bess blanched. It was then I realized she probably didn't even eat enchiladas. Suddenly I thought Bess was working just as hard to go to lunch with Alex and me as I'd have to work to teach a Primary class. It was a sobering idea.

The first thing Bess said when she looked at the menu was, "Don't they have anything besides Mexican food?" Alex's eyes widened. It obviously hadn't occurred to her that someone might not like Don Antonio's. I suggested a taco salad, and Bess looked relieved.

When the chips came, Bess wouldn't even eat those. "These are just tortilla chips and sauce," Alex said. "You don't like salsa?"

"I have an ulcer," Bess said apologetically.

Alex changed the subject by mentioning Relief Society, but that also went nowhere. We hadn't been sustained yet, and she didn't want to mention any specific ideas she had until then. When the talk flagged, I asked her how her husband was doing. She seemed grateful for the opening.

"I don't know if Ethan loves me anymore," she said. One thing about Alex I admired but couldn't emulate was that she wasn't ashamed to confide in her friends. I didn't consider Bess a friend, but Alex apparently figured we'd be working so closely that we shouldn't try to keep secrets from each other.

"That's ridiculous," I said. "He took you to Austria in April. He sends you flowers every month on your anniversary."

"That doesn't mean anything." Bess's voice came out in a squeak. She took a small sip of water, and her voice deepened again. "Outward displays like that sometimes cover up other feelings."

That was just what Alex didn't need to hear. For years she'd been telling me Ethan was stepping out on her. She never had any proof, and I didn't think she ever would have. But she was resolute in her suspicions, sure she was unworthy of Ethan's love.

"That's not true with Ethan and Alex," I said. "Alex just spends her lifetime in paranoia."

But Alex didn't want comfort. "I shouldn't blame Ethan," she said. "You can't stay in love forever. When you live with a person day in and day out, you see all the warts and the flaws. Little by little, the mystery is solved and the romance fades."

"So what if the romance fades?" I asked. "You're friends now. Friendship is better." Tim and I had been best friends, and I knew what I was saying.

Bess said, "I don't agree. There are different types of love. For most people, maybe you're right. But some people have something stronger, something different. For those people, passion never dies."

That annoyed me, and I didn't let it go unanswered. "Who's in love like that? Name one person. If you give me an example outside the movies, maybe I'll believe you."

"I can't name any names," Bess said. "But I knew of a case like that once. The love never went away."

I thought then that she was talking about her own marriage, and the comparison bothered me. It wasn't enough that her husband, Rick, was the handsomest man I'd ever seen. Now she was telling me the way he loved her was better than the way Tim had loved me.

I didn't believe Bess for a minute, but Alex reacted differently. Once she had a testimonial that other people had that kind of love, she immediately blamed herself. "Then Ethan needs someone better than I am," she said sadly. "He needs somebody who won't let the romance die out."

Alex and I had had this conversation a dozen times before, and it always made me angry. I gave the answer I always gave. "Ethan couldn't be looking for anyone else," I said. "He couldn't find anybody better than you."

After lunch, Alex drove aimlessly toward town. She seemed disturbed, and I thought she was still worrying about Ethan. But finally she turned off the tape player and said, "I'm not up to this."

"You're not up to what?" I asked.

"Being Relief Society president," Bess said, and Alex nodded. I felt annoyed that Bess had read my best friend better than I had, but Bess had annoyed me a lot today.

Alex turned left on Third South and continued, "It was one thing to work with the Young Women. We understood each other. We all had fun together. But I'm not Relief Society president material. Everybody knows it. I'm afraid all this is going to change me, and I don't know if I want to change. What if Ethan likes the new Alex even less?"

Bess said, "Has it occurred to you Ethan may like the new Alex even more?"

Alex thought about that for a minute. Then she shook her head as if dismissing it. "I don't know. I just feel so trapped. Everyone will be watching me to see if I slip up. I'll always have to be an example. That scares me. People shouldn't be looking to me for spiritual guidance. I can't even guide myself."

She stopped the car at a light and drummed her fingers on the steering wheel, waiting for the light to change. Then she eased the car across the intersection. "I feel so restless today. This is the last time, maybe for years, that we'll be real people. I want to do something wild and irresponsible today. I just don't know what it is."

Suddenly the car screeched to a halt. I'd been watching Alex, and I turned quickly to see if she'd braked to avoid an accident. But nothing was in the street. A driver behind us honked and then passed us when Alex didn't start moving again. She was staring at a storefront on the north side of the street. A sign in the window said, "palm reader."

"This is it!" she said, with more animation than I'd heard from her in days. "I've always wanted to get my palm read. Today we're going to do it." She parked her car right outside the store and started removing her rings. She hid all her expensive jewelry in her purse and then a found quarter to feed the meter. One infuriating thing about Alex was that wherever she wanted to park, there was always an open spot.

"We're not supposed to be doing this," Bess said, as Alex and I opened our car doors. "We *can't* do it."

Alex glared at Bess. "We're not the Relief Society presidency for three days," she said. "This is our last chance to do it." Bess didn't budge, and Alex got a pleading tone in her voice. "Nobody believes in fortune telling. It's a trick. It's done with mirrors or something. I just want us to do something crazy before we have to start serving Jell-O at funerals."

Bess looked at me for support, but I was silent. I'd never met a palm reader, and I wanted to see if she wore a bandanna and smoked filter tips. I also wanted to see if she took MasterCard. The official witch of Salem, Massachusetts, takes MasterCard.

With Bess lagging behind us, we walked inside. A bell above the door announced us, and a decrepit woman shuffled out from a back room. She hitched up her skirt when she saw us and flicked ashes off her cigarette. I'd been right about the filter tips.

The gypsy led us to folding chairs around a tilted card table, and I had a chance to look around. Other than the table and chairs, the room was bare. There was a threadbare carpet on the floor, and pet stains decorated it randomly. An obnoxious, yapping poodle appeared from the back and jumped on my lap, sniffing. I hate dogs — they're right up there on my list with children and cigarettes. But just like children and cigarette smoke, dogs always go for me first. As politely as I could, I pushed the poodle onto the floor. All dogs are bad, but poodles are the worst.

The fortune teller's name was Miriam. "Meer-iam," she said, with that hard Utah *r*. She discreetly looked outside, probably checking which car was ours. Little clues like that help a fortune teller. But a man in a beat-up Toyota had parked right after us, in the spot behind Alex's Jaguar. The gypsy wouldn't know which car had brought us here.

I'd always wanted to see a palm reader work, but watching this one in action was hardly dramatic. The fortunes were generic. I could have told fortunes like that — stuff about riches and travel and health and happiness.

Alex and I were disappointed, but Bess looked relieved. We shouldn't have brought her here. I knew it.

Meer-iam may not have been much on reading palms, but she could read our skepticism just fine. "As a little finale," she said when Bess's hand had been read, "I want each of you to put the first name of someone on a piece of paper. I'll tell you what you need to know about that special person." Great, I thought. Even fortune tellers use "special" when they live in Utah.

Alex went first. She rooted through her purse, discreetly pushing aside the Cross pen and pulling out a chewed stub of pencil. She also found a paper towel. Resolutely, she wrote the name Ethan. Meer-iam blew a smoke ring and read the name aloud once, then twice. She was earning her ten-dollar fee. "I see purple toenail polish," she said. "The woman who holds Ethan's heart will wear purple toenail polish. Ethan has a wandering eye, but purple toenail polish will hold him."

Alex waited for more, but that was it. She looked disappointed. What did she want? The purple toenail polish was a creative touch, but even Alex couldn't believe Meer-iam knew what she was talking about.

The pencil stub was passed to me, and I wrote Timothy on the towel. Alex gave Bess a meaningful glance I caught peripherally. So what if he's dead, I thought. It's just for fun. I grinned rakishly.

Meer-iam put her hand on Tim's name, theatrically waiting for psychic vibrations. I was not going to tip this woman. "I see a love that transcends the grave," she said. "Timothy's wife will never wed another."

Bess looked shocked, but I gave her a cynical look. That could be said about anybody. Tim could have been my son, and the fortune could have meant he'd grow up to be lucky in love. Tim could have been my *gerbil*, who'd been miserably celibate since Samson accidentally ate Happy last year. It was only coincidence that Tim was my dead husband, the true love of my life, and I wasn't going to remarry.

Bess didn't want to take the pencil, but Alex gave her a look that said, "I'm paying for this. Play it to the hilt." Bess wrote a calligrapher's *F* and put the pencil down quickly. Smart move. Meer-iam wouldn't know *F* stood for Frederick, Rick's real name. But the fortune teller wasn't fooled for a minute. In fact, she didn't even touch the paper before she started speaking. "This one's vibrations are strong," she said dramatically. "He'll give up everything for you. The two of you will be happy together all your lives." I couldn't believe Bess's luck. Even her fake fortune was perfect. She looked surprised and then blissful, forgetting for a moment this was all a bunch of garbage. Then she must have remembered, because she looked repentant and sad.

Alex paid Meer-iam $30 (Utah's witch didn't take a Visa gold card, but she did accept personal checks), and we laughed all the way home. Bess relaxed as soon as we were back in the car, and even she had a few observations about the fortune teller. By the time Alex dropped Bess off at her house, she seemed to have put the whole thing behind her.

I would have forgotten it too, if not for Alex. As soon as we got inside her house, she took off her shoes and inspected her toes. They looked like toes to me — purely functional. They were square and sturdy, and the big one on the left had a few squiggly hairs Alex had forgotten to remove. But the chief drawback was the color. Like the rest of Alex, her toes were that brownish yellow shade you get from tanning beds. They'd look putrid in purple nail polish.

Alex knew it as soon as I did. "This is ridiculous. I'd even wear the stuff if I thought it'd help, but it isn't me. I'd look like a fruitcake. Ethan doesn't notice colors. Pink is close enough." She rooted through her dresser until she found day-glo pink polish, the color she always wore. The chemical smell made my nose itch.

That was the end of the fortune teller, but it was not the end of Alex's worries about Ethan.

# 2
# Setting Apart

Sunday began ominously, when Samson knocked my sunglasses off the sofa and I stepped on them. In Paradise Vue Ward, you don't go to church without sunglasses. It's not that the ward is snooty — although maybe it's just a little snooty, too. But the logistics of the ward make church attendance a nightmare.

Paradise Vue is aptly named. Thirty years ago, a little old lady willed a prime piece of hillside property to the ward for a new building. The stake president gallantly volunteered his son as architect, and the Paradise Vue wardhouse was born. The building is a masterpiece. Behind the podium, the whole front of the church is an artful marriage of plate glass and stained glass. The stained glass depicts Christ, ascending. The plate glass surrounding it gives a panoramic view of the Salt Lake Valley. Ergo, people look behind the speaker and see Christ ascending over the Salt Lake Temple.

In theory, the architect had a great idea. When the speakers got boring, people could look downright attentive, even as they watched clouds move and planes coming in for landings at the airport out by the lake. But the architect forgot two minor details. First, Salt Lake City is a sewer of smog, especially in winter.

The second problem is worse: the vue itself has a western exposure. Morning meetings are no problem, but anything scheduled after the sun reaches its crest is agony. The sun blinds everyone facing the podium. Everyone in the congregation wears shades. Air conditioning bills are astronomical. The stained glass window would have gone the way of the Coalville Tabernacle long ago if the Utah Historical Society hadn't filed suit to keep it in place. There's a bright side, as any bishop will attest. In Paradise Vue, bishoprics have no trouble finding people to speak or pray or even sing in the choir. Everyone wants the sun at his back.

So when Samson broke my sunglasses, I was more than a little annoyed. I swatted him, and when it was time for breakfast I gave him the dry stuff instead of Fancy Feast. Samson sniffed disgustedly and sat on a windowsill to sulk.

My glasses were wearable. One earpiece was gone, and the frame bent upward a little on that side. But it was a matter of survival. I put them in my purse and went to church.

When I settled into a bench next to Alex, the bishopric was already sitting on the stand, lined up by seniority like ducks in a shooting gallery. Peter Swarthmore, the first counselor, sat at the bishop's right, looking as glum as usual. He was a nice man, but he just didn't look happy. Alex and I privately called him Brother Limerick, because the only time we ever saw him smile was when he'd write notes in his thick day-timer during Sacrament Meeting. Then he'd chuckle to himself. Alex and I pretended he was writing limericks in the notebook to stay awake, and when Sacrament Meeting got dull we'd try to imagine what kind of limericks an accountant would write.

Bishop Nebeker sat next between his counselors, with as cherubic a face as you'd ever want to see. He was one of my personal favorites, and my favorite Sacrament Meetings were the ones where he spoke. He had one particularly endearing quality I liked to watch: No matter how deadly the talks in Sacrament Meeting, the bishop always looked fascinated. I respected him for that.

Howard Carston, the second counselor, sat next, breaking the symmetry by being head and shoulders above everyone else. The bishop was just a little shorter than Brother Limerick, and symmetry demanded that Howard be just a little shorter than the bishop. But Howard was a former college football player, as beefy as a linebacker. I liked him because he waved and winked at people he recognized in the congregation, just like a Primary kid during the Christmas program. I usually got a fat wink, and it would make me smile for the rest of the meeting.

Sacrament Meeting began innocently enough. Brother Limerick immediately started writing and chuckling. The priests at the sacrament table looked restive, and the little kids squirmed in their seats. The little McKeown girl in front of us turned around and made faces at Alex. Alex made faces back.

There was a rumble of surprise when the Relief Society presidency was released. Delta Mae Eliason had been in for about a hundred years, and the little old ladies in the ward wanted to keep her there. Nobody knew there was going to *be* a change, excepting the intimates of Carol Ann Little. Come to think of it, that was everyone in the ward under age forty. The younger set wasn't a bit surprised.

The gasps were even louder when the new presidency was named. Alex was not your typical Relief Society president. Her maid came five times a week, not just once. She told R-rated jokes and read Harlequin romances, which is unusual on the East Bench. She said damn and hell, and sometimes even worse. She never wore less than $200,000 in jewelry, even when she went to Safeway. Alex always said you had to work hard to be eccentric, but I think it came more naturally to her than most.

But there was another side to Alex, one she kept pretty well hidden. She read scriptures for hours, and she did more praying than most people ever figured. I saw her cry more than once, but she never did it in public. She wasn't big on bearing her testimony, either, but she had more of one than a lot of people. Nevertheless, I've never met a person who was more generous — or who was more universally liked. She just wasn't your standard issue Relief Society president.

Nobody voted against Alex when her name was read. Of course nobody voted against Bess. It was a little more surprising that nobody voted against me, even though they must have been surprised to hear me called as homemaking counselor. Everybody who visited me made jokes about my house, so when my name was read I peeked around at the congregation surreptitiously. All the hands went up at the right time, and I felt a little better.

Nobody even voted against Emma. Without thinking about it, I rolled my eyes one last time as I raised my hand to sustain her. I was still on my feet then, so a few people on the stand caught my face and laughed. Howard Carston winked big, twice. Then it was all over and the four of us sat down again.

The rest of the meeting went pretty smoothly. The old presidency got up during Fast Meeting to talk, and Alex thought we'd better get up, too. None of us said anything earthshaking. Alex was brief, Bess was more eloquent than I expected, and I rambled. Emma mentioned something about the Lord calling her to "put her talents to good use," and I shook my head. Alex caught the movement and gave me a puzzled glance. She just couldn't see through Emma.

Brother Limerick wrote furiously at one point and chuckled until a tear scudded down his left cheek. Alex wrote "There was a first counselor named Pete..." on her program, but I laughed so hard she had to put the pen away.

I was a little nervous before Relief Society began. I stood at the back of the room, out of sight behind the closet door, surveying my charges as they wandered in and claimed their seats. The chairs might as well have had nameplates on them; I could pretty well say where people were going to sit before they walked in the door. The little old ladies sat square in the middle, with the Penrose Avenue crowd on the second row. The mothers with babies and toddlers sat near the door, ready for quick escapes. The others were on the right,

under the air conditioning duct. If the noise level was any indication, everyone was happy.

"*Look* at them! All those old blue-hairs look alike. When *I* get
old, my hair is going to be snow white. It's not going to be dingy
gray, and I'm *certainly* not going to dye it blue."

It was Emma, my nemesis. I didn't acknowledge her, but Alex
overheard what she said. "The older ladies think all the young
people look alike, Emma. Minerva Sorensen told me all the young
women have long hair and are pregnant."

"Well, *I'm* not pregnant," Emma said, tossing her long hair.
"And I *don't* look like everyone else." I looked up at her, and she
gave me a big smile. She put her arm around me conspiratorially
and in a low whisper said, "Amy, you may want to make a trip to the
bathroom. There's something wrong with your hair. It looks like
you combed it with your fingers."

"I did," I said cheerfully. "Lost my brush last month. I had
*hoped* no one would notice." She didn't even seem embarrassed.
When she looked away, I tousled my hair to make it look worse.


We got set apart after Relief Society. I really looked forward to
it, because I'd only had a few blessings in my life. I joined the
church when I was twenty and got two of them in a week — the
confirmation and my Patriarchal Blessing. Both of them were so
specific I couldn't have been more pleased, even though neither one
said I'd have children.

I didn't get another blessing for nine years, not wanting to
harass the Lord when He'd already given me two clear messages.
Finally when I was lying in a hospital bed, nearly dead with spinal
meningitis, Tim called the bishop for me. The blessing I got then
sounded like what Tim always called a hypochondria blessing: the
kind of priesthood blessing given to little old ladies who ask for one
every time the home teachers arrive, the kind of blessing meant only
to reassure, the kind that says, "You aren't really sick so there's
nothing to say but we love you."

So the only thing specific in the blessing during my meningitis was my name at the beginning. What I understood from the blessing was that the Lord wanted me to recover on my own, and I accepted that. Still, I couldn't help being disappointed. My first two blessings had been so individual and important to me that I guess I expected every one to be like that. It upset me so much I hadn't asked for a blessing since. Now I was curious to see if the Lord was speaking to me again. I was pleased to learn He was.

I was always interested to go in the bishop's office. It looked like an art gallery, because it *was* an art gallery. The bishop rotated paintings every two or three months when he wanted a change of scenery. I couldn't blame him for that. He spent an awful lot of time in that office.

The artwork was all expensive, and it was all beautiful — if you like that kind of thing. They were all landscapes of Utah mountains or scenery or cities, and several of them had temples perched inconspicuously on the horizon. Once or twice a year, one of them would be reproduced in the *Ensign,* with a cut-line crediting "the private art collection of Barton Nebeker." The bishop got a kick out of those cut-lines. I think it was why he kept buying paintings, and I'm sure it was why all his paintings were so pastoral and bland.

There was a new one today, hanging in the place of honor behind the bishop's desk. It was a dusty expanse of Utah valley, ripe for illustrating an *Ensign* article about the desolate landscape before Mormon pioneers made it "blossom as the rose." The Great Salt Lake glimmered in the distance, and from the placement of the lake in the picture I realized it had been painted from where Paradise Vue ward now stood. I remarked on it to the bishop, and he was proud I noticed. What I didn't say was the painting would be a lot more interesting with a sea monster floating placidly on the Great Salt Lake. The bishop and I got along fine, but he didn't share my taste in art.

Once the whole bishopric had been rounded up, the settings-apart began. Alex went first. The men put their hands on her head, and the bishop pronounced a whole cartload of blessings on her.

Alex was promised a new spirituality. She was blessed with the love and respect of everyone who knew her. She was also promised Ethan would look at her with renewed appreciation if she had faith in him. Alex liked that part. Anything that promised something good about Ethan, Alex wanted to hear.

Bess was next. Pete Swarthmore, the first counselor, said the words. He mentioned a lot of things, but the one that stood out was when he gave Bess the "strength to do the things she had to do in life."

I looked up, puzzled, and was even more surprised to see the same puzzlement on Pete's face. Even Pete didn't know why he'd said that. The words made Bess's life sound like a chore, instead of the uninterrupted bliss everyone knew it to be. I wondered if she had a physical ailment I didn't know about and needed strength for that. She didn't look sick, but it sure couldn't be anything else.

Bess knew what Pete was talking about, though. She wiped tears from both eyelids. That was interesting. I didn't have her pegged as a weeper.

I came next. It was Howard Carston's turn to say the words, and he got right to the point. My blessing said three things. It told me to be ready for change. That was easy. Just being put in the Relief Society presidency was a big one. It also gave me a "new compassion," and said that new compassion would lead me to friends in unexpected places. At the time I didn't understand it, but I liked that. It sounded intriguing.

Finally, Howard blessed me with patience. I opened my eyes then and looked across the room at Emma, the person who would try my patience the most. Emma was glaring at her watch, scowling, so she didn't see me looking at her. Too bad, I thought, seeing her preoccupation. If she's not listening, she won't suspect she's the one Howard's talking about. Then I realized Emma wouldn't have recognized herself if she *had* been listening.

Emma's blessing was short, and when it was over I didn't think she was happy with it. The bishop told her in the prayer that she had been called as secretary for a purpose. That's right, I thought. Remember you're not the president.

He also told Emma she'd been made secretary to learn lessons she needed to learn. I uncharitably made a mental list of them — humility, empathy, charity. Looking back on it now, I realize those were all things *I* needed to learn. But at the time, I was delighted to read a subtle chastisement in Emma's blessing.

When the words ended and the hands were taken off Emma's head, Emma smiled just as sweetly as you please. "Gee, thanks for such a *won*derful blessing," she said. Even as she smiled, I could almost hear her thinking: "There's nothing wrong with *me*, and there's nothing *I* can learn from Alex or those other two." Emma's big smile didn't fool me, and I couldn't understand why it fooled everyone else.

I went home and wrote the whole thing down in my journal, delighted that the Lord was speaking to me through priesthood blessings again. As Alex said over the phone the next day, the priesthood sure beats a palm reader.

# 3
# First Visits

Tuesday, before any human being had a right to be awake, somebody walked in my bedroom. I opened one eye, hoping it was Alex dropping by, instead of a hardened criminal. She sat down so hard on the edge of my waterbed that she almost bounced me out the other side. The mattress sloshed mercilessly.

"If you're not going to lock your front door, at least you should close it," she said. "One of these days you're going to get raped and pillaged, and I'm going to have to go to Don Antonio's alone."

"What time is it?" I groaned, pulling the covers over my eyes. It couldn't be a minute after 6 A.M.

"Nine after ten." Alex's Rolex never lied. "You promised we could go visiting in time for me to get back for my soaps. I've been waiting an hour."

I washed my face and got dressed while Alex inspected my work in progress, a giant oil I was going to call "Rhinoceros." It was a big cityscape with white clouds above the horizon. Bordered by the clouds and the skyscrapers, the blue sky was shaped like a rhinoceros in profile — hence the name. I'd been working on it for weeks, and it was finished except for the pigeon that, strategically placed, would form the rhino's eye. This was a painting I was going to keep, and I waited for Alex to tell me how pretty it was. She didn't.

"Who are we visiting?" I asked. Alex nodded and smiled. That was a bad sign. If Alex wasn't telling, we weren't going anywhere I wanted to be.

When we got in Alex's car, three fresh loaves of bread were lined up in the back seat. Alex was a worse cook than I was. Last time she baked me a cake, she'd forgotten to wash the Ajax out of the cakepan before she cooked in it. I hoped today's lucky recipients would remember the thought behind the bread instead of the bread itself. I picked up a loaf and sniffed it. It was still warm, and it smelled pretty good. "Zucchini?"

"No, pumpkin. And now that we're in the car, we're going to visit LaRue Ford and Maria Gomez." She smiled so wide I could see the gold crowns on her back teeth. I heard a click as she simultaneously locked all four doors of the Jag.

Alex was right to lock the doors. It was frightening enough to visit any of the ladies, especially as a spiritual leader. I felt like a humbug. But it would be especially hard to visit the two Alex had chosen. Maria Gomez didn't speak English, and LaRue Ford was something else again. I thought of my priesthood blessing and asked myself, How in the world can *I* help *her?*

"I don't know who the third one'll be," Alex said, parking in LaRue Ford's driveway. "After the first two, let's try someone easy. In fact," she added, "if you're good I'll treat you to lunch."

"I was counting on that anyway," I said. "Why do you think I'm working with you?"

I walked up LaRue Ford's steps with leaden feet. She opened her front door with a pained smile. The smell of sickroom billowed outside like a toxic cloud. I walked in behind Alex, dreading my first Relief Society hug. I'd never hugged women easily, and thousands of awkward embraces stretched before me. I watched the way Alex did it, realizing only when I was paying attention that Alex didn't hug the way everyone else did. She put one arm around LaRue in the usual manner, but she clasped her other hand around the old lady's biceps as she hugged her. It was an odd gesture. When my turn came, I clumsily offered a more traditional hug.

LaRue Ford had been dying as long as I knew her. Alex had known her ten years longer than I had, and she'd been dying all that time, too. Delta Mae Eliason told me once that she'd known LaRue for thirty-five years, and she'd been dying at least that long. If there was a quick and easy way to die, LaRue didn't know about it.

The old lady hobbled to her easy chair, moving in her walker as if she hadn't had it for twenty years. The walker was just a prop, as everyone in the ward well knew. I myself had gone to visit her one day and found the door ajar. When she didn't answer my calls, I walked in. I thought LaRue was finally dead, and I felt a prickle of excitement thinking maybe I'd be the one to find her. But there she was, hauling a big hamper of clothes up from the basement. I finished carrying it to the top of the stairs, and it must have weighed forty pounds. When nobody was watching her, LaRue could do whatever she wanted.

Once she was settled, she turned beady eyes on me. "Get the Relief Society president some orange juice. And there's cookies in the teddy bear jar." Alex said no thanks, but LaRue said, "Oh, go on. It's no trouble at all." She was right. I was the one doing the work.

I walked out to the kitchen, obeying LaRue's orders. I'd never been in her kitchen, and I looked around curiously to get my bearings. Her floor was covered in vintage linoleum, and the appliances were at least that old. Pictures of grandchildren littered the wall like flyspecks. But true to her word, there was fresh-squeezed orange juice in the refrigerator. One thing about LaRue — she was always ready for company.

I served refreshments in three trips. When I came out with the first tray, LaRue waved her hand and said, "No, no, dear. Those are my dinner glasses. Orange juice goes in the small tumblers." I scurried back into the kitchen, poured the juice into the proper glasses, washed the first glasses, and put them away.

Next LaRue saw I'd used paper towels for napkins. She gave me a cross look and said, "No, Amy. I always use the red scalloped napkins for company." She shook her head at Alex as I retreated to the kitchen.

I didn't mind a bit. Maybe making LaRue happy would teach me that "new compassion" I'd been promised in my blessing. Besides, it gave me an excuse to be out of the room. I heard enough snatches of conversation going to and from the kitchen that I knew LaRue was talking about her son Darren, known to the ward as my-son-the-bishop. Since the day he'd been sustained as bishop of a ward out in Holladay, Darren had been LaRue's favorite topic of conversation other than illness. I'd heard all the my-son-the-bishop stories. LaRue talked about Darren at every testimony meeting.

When I finally settled down, LaRue stared at the plate I'd given her. "Crumbs," she said accusingly, as if I'd shed them instead of the cookies. "You left crumbs on my plate." I tried to take the plate away, but she snatched it back from me. Then she picked them off, one by one, stabbing them with a sharp and spindly finger.

"When *I* was the Relief Society president," she said, speaking only to Alex, "young girls knew how to serve food properly. We had classes on housework and crochet. We made quilts. I still have the grapes we made in Relief Society for a centerpiece." She was right. There they sat on her dining room table, glistening like mackerel eyes at a fish counter.

"Amy's the new homemaking counselor," Alex said.

"I know all that. I may be old, but I'm not stupid." She was still talking to Alex. Once I'd served the juice and cookies, I was out of the picture. She took a dainty sip of orange juice and belched loudly.

Alex changed the subject. "How are you feeling today? You look terrific. Your complexion is beautiful."

"Well, I always did have beautiful skin," LaRue confided, "but it doesn't mean I'm healthy. I just ache all over. My eyes are acting up again, too. I haven't been able to read." I looked at the open book on the table next to her. It had obviously been put down when we rang the doorbell. It was a self-help book, *Stay Alive All Your Life.*

"Have you been having a lot of visitors? I know you have lots of friends."

"Nope. Nobody comes to see me anymore. I've lived my life like a saint, always doing for others. Now nobody wants to do for me. No one ever stops in. No one ever calls. No one takes me to the DUP meetings. No one remembers all the good things I did for other people. But God remembers. When He takes me home, I'll be rewarded the way I should be."

"I'm sure you will be," I said, with perhaps too much enthusiasm.

LaRue had had enough of us. She reached for a remote control switch and turned on her television. A church choir was singing "Love at Home" at eighty decibels. "It's time for you to go," she said. "The BYU devotional is on. I never miss my BYU devotional. You can put the plates away, Amy. You won't break them, will you?" I didn't break a thing, but I was sorely tempted.

LaRue pulled up her walker and raised herself up to lead us out. She tottered to the big calendar beside the door. Every day was penciled in with the names of people who had visited her. Who said she was all alone? We wrote our names in the right square and submitted to a final Relief Society hug. This time, Alex did it the traditional way. I followed suit, and we escaped into clean air.

"What a sad old woman," Alex said.

I wasn't feeling too charitable about the visit. "She's sad because she wants to be. LaRue has made up her mind to be miserable, and nothing's going to get in her way. And did you see all the visitors she has? Last week, Delta Mae Eliason was there four times. Her visiting teachers were there three times, her kids were there every day, and the bishop was there once." I had a real head for figures when I was proving a point.

"I can't argue with that," Alex said. "LaRue Ford is the original squeaking wheel. But there wasn't one person who was on the list because he wanted to be."

"Who would come if it wasn't a duty?"

"Exactly my point. By the way, did you notice whose name was absent?"

I'd thought the whole Salt Lake telephone book had signed that calendar. "Who missed it?"

"Darren."

Alex was right. LaRue Ford's son-the-bishop, the only person who mattered, hadn't signed the guest list. Everyone signed that calendar — even the physical therapist and the delivery boy from Emigration Market. If Darren's name wasn't on the list, he hadn't been inside the house. In LaRue's eyes, if Darren hadn't visited, nobody had. She really was alone.

Even so, I thought, LaRue was no fun to spend time with. When I'd thought of visiting the women in the ward, it was people like Lillian Jackson and Letha Cannon I had in mind. LaRue Ford wasn't on my list.

"Can we visit Lillian later? Or Letha? You can choose. Just make it one of the fun ones."

"Sure," Alex said. "But first let's go to Nicaragua, *sí*? *¿Se habla español?*" She was such a comedienne. I didn't *habla* anything but English, and Alex didn't either.

Hector and Maria Gomez had escaped Nicaragua before I was born. I don't even know what they were escaping in those days. Politics eludes me.

At any rate, he was a doctor of some kind in Nicaragua. He'd brought enough money out with him that he could afford to do carpentry work in Utah and still live comfortably. He'd made a little effort to learn English and could speak the language brokenly. She never learned to speak English — not a word of it. A lot of people in the ward prayed he'd never leave her a widow.

Maria greeted us with open arms, literally. She enfolded us both, in one huge embrace. Looking toward Alex's side, I saw her grasp the old lady's upper arm, just as she had the first time at La-Rue's. Maybe it was a way to keep her distance. I decided to ask her about it later.

Alex was seated in the place of honor, a worn recliner. I took one end of the flowered couch. Maria left the room and came back, laden with big glasses of lemonade. I took a big gulp and almost choked on it. It was so syrupy a spoon could stand up in it. Then I realized she'd thawed a can of concentrate, unable to read the English instructions for diluting it with water. "Good stuff," I said, and coughed. I put the lemonade down and fiddled with a contact lens, hoping Maria would think the tears came from a speck of dust.

Maria patted her lower stomach. *"Me duele cuando orino,"* she told Alex.

Alex smiled happily and patted her own stomach. "Yes, it's delicious lemonade," she said. "It sure hits the spot."

*"Hector dice que debería ir al doctor."*

Hearing Hector's name, I jumped into the fray. "So Hector's at work," I said conversationally. "You must miss him when he's gone."

*"Piensa que tal vez tengo piedras en los riñones."* She shook her head ruefully and pinched a leaf off a philodendron. I decided Alex was right. It was easy to converse with Maria. All I had to do was follow her lead.

"You do take beautiful care of your plants," I said. The Gomez living room was packed to the ceiling with ferns and ficus and all sorts of other plants I recognized but couldn't name. She'd added color to the greenery by sticking plastic flowers among the leaves. "I can't keep my plants alive. Do you use plant food?"

"Food!" she said, pouncing on a familiar word. She scurried into the kitchen, returning a minute later with a platter of vanilla wafers. Alex poured some lemonade in a fern while she was gone. I thought it was a great idea and watered a rubber tree. Sugar never hurt a plant.

Maria seemed surprised I ate only one cookie. She put the rest aside and I chewed my vanilla wafer, grateful she hadn't fed me some of Alex's pumpkin bread. She turned to Alex and asked her, *"¿Piensas que debería escuchar a Hector y ir al doctor?"*

"Yes, Hector has made this house beautiful," Alex said. "He carved your mantel, didn't he?"

*"Entonces, haré una cita hoy,"* she said, nodding. *"Estoy agradecida por haberme ayudado. No sabía que hacer."* And then,

*"Todas están contentas porque fuiste elegida para dirigir a las hermanas. Todas las mujeres te aman."*

"Yes, I know," Alex said. "You must be so proud of his work." We hugged Maria again and left, each carrying a handful of vanilla wafers she pressed on us as we walked out the door. I was glad we'd visited her. She was such a nice lady that language wasn't a barrier at all.


True to her promise, Alex drove straight to Lillian Jackson's house. We knocked optimistically and then stood there for at least five minutes before we realized Lillian wasn't home. I was a little miffed she was gone; after LaRue's house, I deserved a treat. You just don't expect a 93-year-old to be gone in the middle of the day, but Lillian was always doing something.

Letha Cannon wasn't home, either. We stayed on her doorstep even longer than Lillian's, standing there like two dorks with a loaf of pumpkin bread. It wasn't fair. All the great ones weren't home.

Suddenly, the pyracantha hedge left of Letha's house called, "Hell-o, sisters." Marilyn Miller stepped around the hedge, clippers in air, with a fat smile illuminating her face. Alex brandished her pumpkin bread like a weapon. Of course, it could be argued that Alex's pumpkin bread *was* a weapon. Then Alex said "Hah!" and put on her Relief Society smile. Our third visit had been picked out for us.

Marilyn was roughly our age, I think. Her hair had gone prematurely slate-gray, so it was hard to tell. But the oldest of her five hell-raisers was only eleven, and her youngest hellion was four. Unless she'd married late, she was still in her thirties.

Other than the gray hair, which Marilyn wore like a badge of honor, Marilyn's distinguishing characteristic was chewing gum. There was always — I mean always — gum bouncing around her mouth. I'd never seen anyone so old with an oral fixation. Even worse, she was a popper. Sitting next to Marilyn in church was like living next door to a firecracker test plant. Just when you hoped she'd chewed her wad of Dentyne to bits, her mouth would explode like a bowl of nuclear Rice Krispies. Whenever Marilyn sat next to me in Relief Society, I found a discreet reason to move across the room.

Alex moved from Letha's house to Marilyn's reluctantly, but smiling broadly. One thing about Alex — the broader she smiled, the less she meant it. Walking in Marilyn's front door, Alex was a Cheshire cat.

"I'm so glad you ladies stopped by," Marilyn said, accepting her loaf of pumpkin bread without comment. "I've been meaning to call you and congratulate you on your high honor." Marilyn's goal in life was to be Relief Society president, and she didn't care who knew it. It was only two days after we'd been sustained, and already there were snippets of rumors that Marilyn wasn't happy about the calling. But right now she was buttering Alex up for something, so we murmured our thankyous and waited for the pitch.

She prefaced her request with a volley of gum-pops. "I know you're awfully busy right now, but it's never too early to be thinking about your spiritual living teachers for next year." In our Relief Society it was the custom to change teachers every year or so. "You're well aware what a good teacher I am. I've been teaching social relations for four years, and I'm sure you know I'm everyone's favorite. Of course, spiritual living teachers are the most important ones." The gum popped noisily. "You need people who are, well, more spiritually *attuned* to teach spiritual living. I've looked at the Relief Society roster and talked to my friends, and everybody agrees I'm the best one for the job.

"Of course," she added, "I want to teach the spiritual living lesson that's taught on Fast Sunday. That's the *real* spiritual living lesson, don't you think?"

Marilyn gave us a big smile and chewed her Doublemint cud, waiting for Alex to give her the plum teaching assignment. I waited, too, wanting to see what Alex would do.

Alex wasn't about to be intimidated. "I appreciate your suggestion, Marilyn," she said diplomatically. "I haven't made any decisions yet. Someone who is as spiritually attuned as you are, of course, knows I'll be choosing all our teachers by prayer. How are Bob and the kids?"

She looked so sincere, grinning that big Cheshire grin, that Marilyn didn't even know she'd been put in her place. When we left, Marilyn thought she was right in the running for spiritual living teacher.

Alex's car headed for Don Antonio's with a mind of its own. But Alex gunned her engine at the traffic lights, a sure indication she was annoyed. "You wouldn't believe it, Amy, but that was the sixth demand I've had in two days for that job. They aren't even requests. People who think they can demand a job teaching spirituality to other women are missing the whole point. If they don't believe in inspiration, how can they teach it?"

I agreed, of course. But I was also curious. "Well, who's asked you? And who are you going to get?"

Alex was noncommittal. "I'm so angry about it, I don't think I'm going to tell you who the rest are. You'd get just as mad, and with both of us angry I'd never calm down. I've chosen one spiritual living teacher, and whoever the other one is, I expect it won't be anybody who asked for it." A kid in a red Volkswagen cut her off, and she honked and shook her fist. "The one I've picked is Elsie Hunsaker."

"That's a nice choice," I said. Elsie Hunsaker was the most spiritual woman in the ward, bar none. Even better, she wasn't sanctimonious about it. Of course, as a teacher she was a little tedious. No, I've got to be honest. She was chloroform on wheels.

"I know what you're thinking," Alex said. "'Chloroform on wheels.' You're the loudest thinker I know. What could I do? She was an answer to prayer. By the way, I'm eating fajitas today. And I've just remembered it's your turn to treat."

Don Antonio's isn't a dark restaurant, but it was bright outside. Even after we'd trooped through the kitchen and found our table, our eyes hadn't adjusted to the change. We blinked in tandem for a minute or two.

When I could finally focus, I wished I hadn't. There was Ethan Roundy, sitting at the booth behind ours. Alex had her back to her husband, and it was just as well. He was sitting on the same side of the booth with a tiny redhead who was wearing a mini-skirt slit up to here. Dirty dishes littered the table. If we'd arrived ten minutes later, we would have missed them.

I watched the woman for a minute as I chewed on a taco chip. She was maybe twenty-two years old, the same age as his older daughter. She and Ethan were so absorbed in each other that he didn't notice we'd come in.

For years, Alex had told me Ethan had to be seeing other women. I'd always laughed off. Now, for the first time, I wasn't so sure. I wished we'd never come to Don Antonio's.

Alex noticed my discomfort. "Hot sauce too much for you?" she asked. One of Alex's hobbies was calling me a wimp. "Should we get you a malted milk instead?"

"No thanks." Then, offhandedly, "You don't have any redheaded relatives, do you?"

"Why? We're all blondes. Even under this blonde rinse I'm a blonde."

"I'm looking at a redhead — short, small, lots of makeup, kind of cheap-looking. Looks like she buys her clothes at Frederick's of Hollywood. Do you know anybody like that?"

"Only Ethan's secretary." And then the light dawned. She drank a big gulp of water. "Is he with her?"

"Yep," I said. Just about then, Ethan spotted us. He reacted worse than I had. His eyes darted around furtively, looking for an escape route. As soon as I saw his reaction, I knew Alex had been right all along. I felt sickened and sad.

Ethan must have realized there was no way he'd get past Alex unnoticed, so he brazened it out. He threw his napkin on the table, strode over and boomed hello. I *hi*-ed back. Alex's "Hah!" sounded a little more militant than usual, and she grinned that Cheshire grin. She hid her face behind her glass of water. Ethan introduced me to the secretary, Becky something-or-other.

"I thought your name was Trixie," I said, and Alex spewed a sip of water across the table. Oops, I thought. I've screwed up again. "My mistake. That was somebody else."
I may have fooled Trixie, but I certainly didn't fool Alex and I probably didn't fool Ethan. Alex's name for Ethan's secretary was "Trixie the Bimbo." I'd assumed the Trixie part was her real name. Ethan looked at his Rolex, told Alex he'd see her at home, said goodbye to me, and off he went. Trixie trotted after him like a fox terrier. Her sandals flapped furiously as she trotted.

"Boogers!" Alex said, as they disappeared through the kitchen. Boogers was Alex's new swear word. She had reformed. I knew I wouldn't hear a damn or a hell out of her the whole time she was Relief Society president. "I bet that little sleazebag is seeing Ethan on the side."

Alex had a fertile imagination (at least, before that day I thought it was imagination), and all her imaginings centered on one person. In her defense, though, I would have been worried about Ethan — and I'm not the jealous type. Ethan was pushing fifty, but he could have passed for thirty-five. He was tall and blond and had a year-round tan, thanks to the tanning bed in Alex's basement.

Ethan had had bad luck with the church, and he didn't show up much anymore. The way he told it, he was simply one of those men who didn't have the right look to be a stake president or a bishop or even a bishop's counselor, so nobody ever thought of him for a major calling. He was doomed to spend his life doing low-level church jobs while others got the glory. Sometimes the ones who got the fancy positions weren't as capable as Ethan, and Ethan couldn't accept that. "An ounce of image is worth a pound of performance," he'd always say.

He might have been right. Maybe lots of men get overlooked because they don't look good in a suit. They spend their church careers in the clerk's office, counting tithing or updating membership records. They're still serving, and the Church can't run smoothly without them, but that wasn't good enough for Ethan. The last time the bishopric got changed and he wasn't in it, he got fed up and decided to spend his Sundays on a golf course.

Alex was devastated, but things got worse. Next Ethan started spending Saturdays on the golf course. When Ethan started staying out after dark and saying he was playing golf *then*, Alex got suspicious.

As a result, we'd done quite a bit of detective work on Ethan in the past year or so. Some Saturdays, we'd drive to all the golf courses in the area, scouting the parking lots for Ethan's silver-gray Porsche. We never found it. Ethan would arrive home at night, unload his clubs, and tell Alex what a great day he'd had playing golf. Alex never said a word. Whenever she'd get upset, she'd go in the basement and make another clock. A lot of clocks had been made in the Roundy basement.

So as soon as Alex said boogers, I knew exactly what she had in mind. Alex was on the Ethan Roundy case again. I was only thankful Alex hadn't noticed one detail I had in the restaurant: Trixie the Bimbo's toenails were brightly painted with purple nail polish.

Seeing Ethan ruined Alex's mood for the rest of the day, and it didn't help my disposition either. After lunch we went shopping at Trolley Square, but I don't think Alex saw a thing in the stores. She was just pacing in a picturesque setting. I kept up with her as well as I could, but Alex was a fast walker. She was so preoccupied she walked halfway up a down escalator before she realized it *was* a down escalator. Then she rode sheepishly down with it, stubbornly facing the wrong way.

When she dropped me off, it was dinnertime. I put a Lean Cuisine in the microwave and then cooked it too long, steaming every last bit of nutrition out of it. The food sat limply in its plastic tray when I uncovered it, looking so unappetizing it was almost as if the Lean Cuisine were daring me to eat it. I didn't take the challenge. I left the dinner on the counter for Samson to discover later. I abandoned the idea of eating and got ready for bed.

No sooner had I started reading than the phone rang. I dreaded the thought that it was Alex, because I didn't know what to say to make her feel better. But when I heard her voice, it was animated and businesslike. She was being the Relief Society president again. "You won't believe this," she said without even saying *hah.* "Bishop Nebeker just called. Maria Gomez is in the hospital. I'm coming to pick you up."

I pulled a pair of jeans over the surgical scrub suit I always wore around the house and was just tying my tennis shoes when Alex arrived. We drove to LDS Hospital together, stopping en route for a bouquet of cut flowers at Smith's Food King. Then we got lost in the maze of corridors at the hospital, looking for Maria's room. Alex said that as a Relief Society presidency we'd soon have the floor plan memorized, but that night the hospital was still alien and forbidding.

"I just don't understand this," Alex said, as we crossed the same stretch of hallway for the third or fourth time. "We just saw her less than ten hours ago."

I knew what she was thinking. "A lot of people don't like to tell their problems to strangers, Alex. Maybe Maria's one of them."

Alex checked a directional sign and turned left, following an arrow. "She didn't act reserved to me. She hugged us like her best friends."

"Then she must not have known she was sick," I said. "Do you think she had a heart attack?"

"Don't people look gray or pasty or something before they have heart attacks? Maria looked fine to me. Maybe she had an accident."

"If she'd been sick she would have told us something," I agreed. "It must have been an accident. I hope it wasn't anything serious."

Alex checked a number on a door against the room number written on the skin of her hand and reached for the handle. I stopped her for a minute — just long enough to hike up my scrub suit so it didn't hang below the hems of my jeans. They were longer than the jeans, and the green fabric kept peeking out at the bottom.

When we went inside, Maria lay asleep on a bed that was so large it made even her round body look small. Hector, a little man, was darting nervously around the room like a bird. He hurried over to us when he saw us and took both Alex's hands — flowers and all

— in his. He spoke a rush of words quickly, in Spanish. Then, remembering, he talked so we could understand him.

"I will be grateful always to you," he said in his broken English. "I have been trying to get Maria for weeks to the doctor. She did not listen to me, her husband. But when you told her to go to the doctor, she listened. I thank you."

He released Alex's hands and stepped behind her to take mine. "Thank you for giving my family help," he said. Maria stirred in her sleep, and he turned back to her. Looking up, I could see Alex's face, and mine behind her, in the medicine cabinet mirror. Her expression was no more surprised than mine.

When had we told Maria to visit the doctor? I tried to remember what we'd said during our visit, and all I could remember was something about carpentry and plants.

If Maria had said a word about being sick, we would have been glad to take the credit for sending her to the doctor. But I thought then that as soon as Maria felt a little better, she'd remember somebody else had given her the advice.

Alex filled a hospital drinking glass with water and arranged the flowers in them. She put them on the windowsill, and the two of us quietly left the room.   As I eased the door shut behind us, the bishop hurried up the hall.  He had his suit coat flung over his shoulder, and his tie was loosened. He looked as if he hadn't been home yet from his law office. He gave Alex, then me, a hearty handshake.

"Hector told me what you did. Already you're giving help where it's needed. You'll be a good Relief Society presidency," he said.  "I knew you would be."  And while Alex and I stood there dumbfounded, he put on his coat and slipped quietly into the hospital room.

# 4

# Scavengers
# and Diet Coke

Paradise Vue Ward buried a lot of strangers. The stained glass front of the chapel made the building a status symbol of sorts, and for years people would choose the ward for funerals, just the way non-Mormons find a picturesque church for a wedding. Finally it got out of hand, and by the time Alex was sustained, people who lived in the area had to be buried from their own wards. But people who'd lived outside Salt Lake and were returning to Zion to be planted could get buried from any ward they pleased. A bunch of them pleased to be buried from Paradise Vue. The Relief Society wasn't crazy about the idea, but we lived with it. There was even a contingent of old ladies who attended every funeral to show their support.

So it wasn't surprising when Alex opened our first official Relief Society meeting by asking the sisters, "Does anybody here know a Mabel Ledbetter?" Blank stares met the question. I'd never heard of her: that's a name I would have remembered. Alex looked at the upturned faces and continued, "Well, she croaked. She's having her funeral here on Tuesday, and we're passing around a sign-up sheet."

Hubbub ensued. The old ladies loved it when Alex acted irreverent about something as frightening as death. "Isn't she cute?"

Thirza Finlayson cackled to the blue-hair next to her. The blue-hair nodded, bobbing her head up and down like a chicken after corn. She must have been a visitor — she wasn't anyone I knew. Once I know someone, I can't think of her as a blue-hair.

Alex had purposely not used "croaked" until she knew nobody was a friend to the departed Mabel, but the word was a good one. It put everyone in a merry, conspiratorial frame of mind — just the mood we needed to get names on the sign-up sheet and contributions for the ham. Even strangers expected to be fed when a relative died. Whoever thinks there's no such thing as a free lunch has never been to a Mormon funeral.

Sure enough, when the sign-up sheet came back it was full of volunteers for Jell-O salads and sheet-cakes. Alice Barnes had made her own category and signed up for homemade French bread, which was something she always did. Nobody had signed up for green salads, but nobody ever signed up for green salads. I put my name in a green salad slot, assuming I'd be doing that in addition to the potatoes au gratin the Paradise Vue Relief Society presidency furnished for every funeral. I'd never signed up for funeral duty before, but now it was my church job.

We also got enough money for two big Corn King hams, which were on sale down the hill at Smith's. Delta Mae Eliason, veteran of many funerals during her hundred-year tenure as Relief Society president, told us Corn King was the brand we *always* served. She also gave us the exact recipe for the Paradise Vue funeral potatoes. In our ward, you don't turn up your nose at tradition.

Tuesday was a sweltering July day. On this kind of day I liked to turn the swamp cooler on high and paint watercolors in my bathing suit. But instead I got dressed in something that I could wear in public, dreading the funeral but determined to do my duty in the church kitchen. In a surge of respectability I even found Samson's cat brush and ran it through my hair. On the way out, I grabbed my salad from the refrigerator. It was already starting to wilt. I didn't know lettuce wouldn't keep overnight once it was torn up.

As homemaking counselor, I guess I was supposed to be the one who put the funeral dinner together. But when we got to church, Alex and Bess had already taken over. Alex had gone over to church the night before to get ready for it. She stocked the refrigerator with Pepsi and Diet Coke, adding two lonely 7-Ups in case anyone didn't like cola drinks. Now she was unwrapping the hams, ready to put them in the oven without oil or glaze or anything.

Bess, who wore a frilly apron over her church clothes, elbowed Alex and me out of the way and started organizing the buffet. She made an inventory of all the food, separating the contributions into categories as she made the count. Then she opened the refrigerator to put it all inside.

Bess stopped cold for a moment, and I didn't know why. I moved in behind her and saw her staring at the soft drinks. She looked uncomfortable, as if she hadn't known the drinks were there and didn't think they should be. I reached around her and grabbed a Pepsi. Then I passed Alex a Diet Coke.

Bess moved the drinks to the door compartments. Then she organized the refrigerator, putting Jell-O salads on the middle shelf, cakes with Cool-Whip on the bottom shelf, and green salads and condiments on the top. "Nice salad," she said, inspecting the one I'd brought in a Tupperware bowl. "Is there anything here besides lettuce?" I rooted through my purse, producing a box of croutons and some Wishbone dressing. She took them without comment. A few minutes later, I caught her pirating radishes and carrots from other salads, adding them to mine. It did make the salad look a little more festive. I would have done it myself if I'd thought of it.

More food arrived. Bess commented on the items after they were dropped off. "Lime Jell-O goes last. At funerals, people want it red." "People like chocolate cake the best, but everybody brings chocolate. Then the other flavors go first because they're a welcome change." "People eat like vultures at funerals. After three or four days of grieving, they'll eat like there's no tomorrow."

Alex went to her car and brought back the standard-issue potatoes, covered in foil and ready to bake. She hadn't even asked me to help put them together, and that hurt my feelings a little. I wasn't *that* bad a cook. At least, I was no worse than Alex.

With nothing else to do, I stood around, braiding the fringe on my jacket and watching Alex and Bess look busy. The only bright spot was that Emma wasn't here. The only thing worse than a funeral would be a funeral with Emma at it.


The Larkin Mortuary cars pulled up outside, and Mabel Ledbetter's casket was wheeled into the Relief Society room. The driver and the funeral director opened the lid and put the body on display, surrounding it with flowers — your basic funeral chrysanthemums. Somebody should have told the grieving Ledbetters our whole meetinghouse is done in royal purple and shades of mauve. The bright red and orange and blue-dyed flowers looked tacky in the setting.

I wandered over to take a peek at Mabel Ledbetter in her casket. I was always curious about dead people, wondering what they knew that I didn't. But Mabel didn't look serene or wise. She just looked old and dead.

The Larkin man smiled at me from the corner, a short and balding fellow with big dimples. I walked over and introduced myself to him. Unless they're talking to mourners, morticians are the happiest people I know. The ones from the big companies, Larkin's and McDougal's and the Russon Brothers, are the happiest. During my stint with the Relief Society they would give me all sorts of presents — smelling salts and nail files and other stuff, all with the mortuary name printed somewhere. Maybe they thought I might steer business their way.

Today I got my first funeral souvenir, a pocket mirror in a pink vinyl pouch. "Hold it to your mouth," the funeral director said helpfully. "If it clouds up, you're still alive." I tested the mirror. Sure enough, it worked.

I was polishing my breath off the glass when a door opened behind me. "A turquoise cowboy jacket? You're wearing a turquoise cowboy jacket to a *funeral?*" It was Delta Mae Eliason, here to offer funeral advice to the new Relief Society presidency. I turned around to say hi, but Delta Mae didn't hi me back. She was staring down at my feet, looking like a wide-mouthed bass. She'd discovered my matching boots.

"Good grief, Delta," I said. "I'm not going to the funeral. I'll be in the kitchen. Nobody's going to see me." Delta Mae stalked off to the kitchen. I put my funeral mirror in a pocket and followed her.

This was the first funeral in donkey's years that Delta Mae hadn't directed, and she must have thought the whole ward would fall apart if she didn't talk us through it. It's hard to let go of being a Relief Society president once you're released.

With just a murmured hello to Alex and Bess, Delta Mae grabbed a sponge from Alex's hand. She circumnavigated the kitchen, cleaning up imaginary bits of dirt with energetic swipes. Her high heels clicked rhythmically on the kitchen tile, so even her feet sounded efficient. It was an impressive performance.

Delta Mae studiously ignored Alex and Bess and me as she inspected her former domain. We could have been pillars rooted in the floor, the way she walked around us. All her concentration was centered on the sponge in her hand, the counter in front her, and the imaginary bits of grime she had to eradicate. For just a moment, Delta Mae was Relief Society president again.

Suddenly she stopped dead. There, sweating water droplets on the metal counter, was Alex's can of Diet Coke. Delta Mae was one of those people who thought the caffeine in *chocolate* was a sin. Her carob cakes were lethal. And there, right in *her* church kitchen, was a Diet Coke.

With her thumb and forefinger, Delta Mae picked up the soft drink. She carried it over to the garbage can, as gingerly as she would have a Gila monster. Then she dropped the Diet Coke straight down to the bottom of the can.

Alex said not a word. She walked over to the garbage can, reached inside, and pulled out the Diet Coke. She took a messy swig of it and wiped her mouth with the back of her hand. Then she put the can back on the counter where it had been just a minute before.

*

The mood was broken. Suddenly, Delta Mae realized she wasn't the Relief Society president anymore. And when Delta Mae realized it, I did, too.

Humbled, Delta Mae stayed a few minutes to offer her advice. For the most part, we could have managed without her. I think we could have figured out all by ourselves to sit eight people at the octagonal tables, or to put the plates at the front end of the buffet. I had to admit, though, I never would have figured out the industrial dishwasher without her help.

She also had a bit of grim news for us: the Relief Society presidency was expected to attend the funerals, not just cook for them. Even for people like Mabel Ledbetter that we'd never even met and didn't recognize lying on satin in the Relief Society room.

Worst of all, the place we *traditionally* sat was the front row on the right side of the chapel — the row that was absolutely the farthest from Paradise Vue's only restroom. I'd just had one whole bottle of Pepsi and had started my second one, and there was no way I'd make it through a Mormon funeral without a trip down the hall. Delta Mae thought my cowboy suit was a tragedy, but my clothes didn't bother me a bit compared with my bladder.


Mourners started arriving, filing past Mabel after hugging her family. "Don't she look natural?" they asked, shaking their heads as they peered into the casket.

When the time came we trooped into the chapel as somberly as we could, considering none of us had ever met the departed Mabel Ledbetter. A few professional funeral-goers from our Relief Society were already there, giving relief to the stranger being buried from our ward. Eve Parker pointed to my cowboy suit and gave me a thumbs-up sign, which made me feel conspicuous as Alex and Bess and I settled into our pew.

The Relief Society members arranged themselves behind us until we were clustered up like LaRue Ford's chartreuse Relief

Society grapes. Then the sun came out from behind a cloud, and all the locals put their sunglasses on. Even at funerals, you couldn't be too formal at the Paradise Vue meetinghouse after noon.

The processional music started, and the former Mabel Ledbetter's relatives marched to the center seats. Mabel herself glided in from the rear on a Larkin's casket mover, just as smooth as you please. A handful of gangly pallbearers followed, looking a little subdued. Grandsons, probably. Or great-grandsons. There's nothing like a funeral to take the stuffing out of your sails.

As soon as the family faced forward, we knew they were strangers to Paradise Vue. The few women who'd brought purses riffled through them frantically, looking for dark glasses. Some of them were successful, but more of them weren't. Eventually Alex would take a collection of used sunglasses from the Relief Society members, keeping them in a box to be passed out at funerals. But today Mabel's kin were on their own. One young mother whooped and then shushed herself when she found three dirty pairs of 3-D movie glasses at the bottom of her purse. She kept the best ones for herself and her husband and passed the third pair forward to one of Mabel Ledbetter's daughters, who peeled a squashed M&M off one lens and wore the glasses for the duration of the funeral.

Mabel Ledbetter herself, with the coffin lid firmly bolted down on top of her, was pretty well in the shade.


By the time the funeral began, I was already squirming. If I'd known I had to sit through the service, I wouldn't have drunk anything all day. Mormon funerals aren't like funerals anywhere else in Christendom. In most churches, when somebody dies you plant 'em two days later in a five-minute ceremony. It seems downright civilized, compared to the way we're buried.

When a Mormon dies, the funeral usually isn't until four days later. Until then, all the friends and family members put their lives on hold, afraid to start healing until the service is over. When the funeral finally arrives, it's guaranteed to wring every bit of emotion out of you. I didn't cry at my own parents' Protestant funerals. But

I've never been to a Mormon funeral where I didn't end up crying —
even when I'd never met the dead person or had actively disliked
him. If Attila the Hun had been buried in a Mormon funeral, people
would've cried.

Mabel Ledbetter, being a good Mormon lady and not Attila the
Hun, got more than her share of sniffles. She'd been pushing ninety
when she died, and for the last few years she'd been stuck in a rest
home. She couldn't bathe herself, she couldn't feed herself, she
couldn't relieve herself, and she'd forgotten all the people who loved
her. She ended her life in an Alzheimer's haze. At least, that's what
the Larkin man told me before the service. Surely death was a relief.

But the way the family carried on about the "tragic loss," you'd
think Mabel had been a thirty-year-old mother of six, who was five
months pregnant with twins. The truth was that Mabel Ledbetter
was probably rejoicing from wherever she was, kicking up her
spiritual heels in the sheer joy of being free of her aged body.

I made it through most of the service, squirming a little as my
bladder processed the Pepsi. But when one of the sons, a doddering
old geezer himself, stood up to list Mabel's achievements, I got
noticeably more uncomfortable.

Mabel Ledbetter, who'd looked like a normal dead person to
me, had lived her days as the wife of a celebrity. Her husband had
been a chief architect of the local sewage treatment plant. The son
gave us that information in sonorous tones befitting the woman
who'd lived with a hero. He went on to tell us how many gallons of
raw sewage had been processed since the plant had been built near
Rose Park. The figures were very impressive. Mabel would have
been proud.

But the real theatrics began during the first chorus of *God Be
With You Till We Meet Again*, when a woman in the audience started
wailing. "Cut down in the prime of her life!" she shrieked through
her sobs. My head whipped around to see who'd said it, and it was
the daughter in the 3-D movie glasses. The red and green lenses
wiggled on the tip of her nose as she mopped up tears with a hanky.
I couldn't help it — I started giggling. My bladder, which was al-

ready struggling, rebelled when I giggled. Shooting pains doubled me over. I crossed my legs and put myself in a holding pattern.

"She had so much *left to give!*" It was another mourner, an angular chicken of a woman with a big adam's apple. My shoulders heaved, and I rocked the bench trying to keep my laughter down. Eve Parker, sitting behind us, patted my shoulder to calm me. I only laughed the harder. It was so humiliating. Stranger or not, Mabel Ledbetter deserved better than that.

When I laughed, it was like putting my bladder on a rowboat. In a wave of nausea, I rocketed out of my seat and fled to the bathroom, escaping the service. All eyes were on me as I left. My only consolation was the tears rolling down my face, which made me look overcome with grief.

Altogether, it was a typical Paradise Vue funeral.


We worked hard while the mourners planted Mabel in the Salt Lake City Cemetery. We had just a half hour or so to set up all the octagonal tables, warm Alice Barnes's french bread, heat the potatoes, slice the ham, and get ready for the vultures. Bess warned us again and again that the mourners would indeed eat like buzzards, but I knew she was exaggerating. Altogether I'd counted twenty-seven adults in the family, and that little group couldn't possibly eat all the food we had on hand.

Bess was wrong. Those people didn't eat like vultures. Vultures go for the soft parts and leave the rest of the carcass behind. Mabel's grieving relatives were locusts who descended on the Relief Society room in a cloud. When the cloud lifted, every thing in the room that could be chewed or swallowed had disappeared. Only the lime Jell-O was left, and even that had been nibbled on.

We huddled in the kitchen during the feeding, watching the carnage incredulously through the peephole. The mourners increased in number to thirty-three between the funeral and the cemetery, and there were eleven or twelve little kids. But together they put away two ten-pound hams, three industrial-sized trays of potatoes au gratin, nine pans of Jell-O, seven green salads, a dozen loaves of french bread, and fourteen sheet-cakes. Toward the end, strangers started popping in the kitchen. "We need some more potatoes," they'd call helpfully, long after all the potatoes had been consumed. Or, "We're out of raspberry preserves. All that's left is strawberry." And, "Is there another oatmeal cake hidden back here? Aunt Jessie didn't get any on the first trip, and now it's disappeared. It's just not a funeral without oatmeal cake."

At one point, a distinguished-looking man walked into the kitchen like he owned the place, opened the refrigerator, and left with a Diet Coke. Didn't say a word to us. We watched him leave, wide-mouthed. Two minutes later, a whole handful of people stormed the kitchen looking for soft drinks. Alex barred the refrigerator door with her body, and they left disgustedly.

These people didn't want a Relief Society. They wanted a McDonald's.


Even after the food was gone, Mabel's family hung around to visit. Mourning was officially over, and it was family reunion time. If we'd put on a record, they would have square-danced. If nothing's as sad as a Mormon funeral, nothing's as happy as the dinner afterwards. Especially if the deceased is someone whose time has long since come and gone.

Of course we couldn't leave until we'd washed all the dishes and cleaned up the place. We couldn't even start cleaning until everyone else had left. There we sat, trapped in the kitchen, picking on ham scraps we'd kept hidden from the locusts. Since all we could do was talk, that's what we did. And since the three of us collectively had no common interests but Relief Society and men, we talked about men.

"Why don't you date?" It was Bess, asking about my life of celibacy. The answer was obvious, but I gave it anyway.

"I got married in the temple. I'm married forever. Marrying somebody else seems like adultery."

"Polyandry," Bess said. "*I* think the idea sounds intriguing." That was a surprising comment, coming from Bess. I would have bet Bess had never had a sexual thought in her life. "You know what I mean." I dipped a finger in a bowl of mustard and licked it off. "What man's going to marry you when as soon as you die, you belong to somebody else?" Alex gave a humph. "Lots of people would. Live for today. Let the next life take care of itself. I agree with Bess. I don't know how you can live alone after being married after all these years. I couldn't live without sex."

"Yes, you could," I said. "It's not all that bad. Besides, what percentage of your marriage do you spend in bed, anyway?"

"Not nearly enough," Alex said. "Marriage is a funny thing. Nobody tells you about marriage before you do it. You think it's going to be sex every night and flowers on the table. How many times do you get flowers after you're married? And how much time do you spend in the sack? Not near as much time as you do washing dishes. But nobody says, 'Oh boy! I'm going to get married and spend the rest of my life scraping plates and filling the dishwasher!' If they did, nobody'd get married."

"I would," said Bess. "I would." She was silent for a minute and then, as if to change the subject, said, "I'd think funerals would be awfully hard on you, Amy. Don't they all remind you of Tim's funeral?"

I got up and went out to the hallway for a drink of water.

After nearly two hours of visiting, the last of Mabel's relatives finally left. It was probably time for them to eat again, and they'd reconnoiter at the nearest Wendy's. When the door slammed, Alex and Bess and I went outside to survey the damage.

I was wrong: the people hadn't eaten all the food. Quite a bit had been ground into the carpet. We cleaned up as much as we could, leaving the rest for old Jericho Thompson, the janitor. Delta Mae Eliason had told us to look out for Brother Jericho. She said he was a nasty old man who never did any work. But Alex had a way with people. She surprised the janitor by fixing him a plate of ham and Jell-O even before the mourners ate. That one plate of food made her a friend for life.

We learned quickly that all he needed was a little appreciation. He'd work overtime for a compliment, and he'd move the world for you if he were properly bribed. Jericho Thompson sold himself cheap. Usually, a big bottle of Dr. Pepper would do the trick. For major concessions, Alex would slip him an extra bonus — a fiver, or sometimes a ten spot.

But for this first funeral, we were on our own. Alex and Bess, who'd done the cooking, let me do most of the dishes. I soon learned that Delta Mae Eliason's dishwasher instructions were woefully inadequate. By the time I'd done eleven loads of plates and glasses — most of them twice — water was everywhere. Turquoise dye leeched off my jacket onto my yellow blouse, putting me in a foul mood. I mopped up with a vengeance.

"Boogers!" said Alex, as we put the last of the silverware away. "And this was a *small* funeral. I can't wait till we do a big one."

# 5
# The Dangling
# Goldfish Affair

**A**lex didn't want to show favoritism in the Relief Society presidency. Even though we'd been best friends for years, she wanted Bess and Emma to get just as much official attention from her as I did. So she went out to visit the Relief Society members two nights a week as well as in the daytime — once with Bess and once with Emma.

She also wanted Bess and Emma and me to go visiting without her. She said it would help us get to know one another so we could work together better. I didn't want to know Emma any better than I already knew her, but I didn't mind going out to visit with Bess. So when Alex went on a business trip to Kenya with Ethan, I called Bess and asked her to go visiting with me.

Bess was so beautiful she outshone any movie star you could name. Her long hair was so thick she actually had to thin it. I used to swear three or four hairs grew from every follicle on her head. She had big, luxuriant eyebrows and lashes that made her face stand out so you had to stare at her. I'm not very observant about looks, but Bess was beautiful enough that even I noticed her. And coveted. I could fairly say there wasn't a thing about Bess that wasn't covetable — especially if you didn't mind having the brain of a pencil sharpener.

Bess had an odd habit I'm sure she didn't even notice. When she felt strongly about something, often she'd say it twice in a row. "It's awfully hot today. It's awfully hot today," she'd say, just like a broken record. It reminded me how the Cajuns emphasize things with double adjectives ("That's *black* black"), but Bess hadn't even heard of Cajuns. She did it on her own.

There was one other thing about Bess, and it was something that could put a crimp in our Relief Society presidency. She had a positive fetish about the mail. Although Bess swore there was nothing in her mail to get excited about ("just catalogues and bills — what else would an old married woman get?"), she had to be home when the mailman arrived.

Bess's mail couldn't sit in the box for fifteen seconds without being swooped up. In fact, it didn't sit in her box at all because she was always at the front door waiting for the mailman. Bess didn't leave her house until the mailman showed up. Sometimes she'd forget it was a holiday and stay home all day waiting.

Women on Brigham Circle used to tease Bess about the mailman, and whenever a new baby arrived there was always some ribbing if the child didn't look just like a Monson from the day she was born. But Bess and I were on the same route, and we didn't have a regular mailman. It was a different carrier nearly every week, and sometimes it was even a woman. It wasn't the mailman Bess waited for; it was the mail. I thought then that catalogues were awfully important to Bess.

I made an appointment with Bess to go out on Tuesday at eleven, but when I got to Bess's house she wasn't ready to go. She was sitting on the front step in a ruffled apron, looking nervously up and down the street. The mail hadn't arrived yet, she said, and she wasn't going to budge until it had been delivered.

There was no use arguing, so I sat on the front step with Bess, watching for the blue mail Jeep. We didn't know each other well enough yet to feel comfortable with one another, so I entertained myself by watching a big black ant carry a corn chip the length of

Bess's front walk. Its destination was a wide crack in the sidewalk, just to the left of my foot.

When the ant finally reached the crack, it couldn't get the corn chip down through the opening. Several other ants arrived to help, and all of them raced around furiously for a few minutes. Suddenly Bess squashed the whole committee, corn chip and all, flat under her tennis shoe. Bess obviously didn't like bugs.

At long last, the mail arrived. Bess met the mailman before he even reached the house, snatching her mail with a hurried thankyou and glancing at it quickly. She lost interest in it as soon as she looked at it, and she stuffed it all in an oversized apron pocket. Then, apron and all, she trotted down her front walk to my car. Finally she was ready to go.

Our first visit was to one of the young women in the ward. (*Young*, in Paradise Vue, referred to anyone under age fifty.) DeAnn Wilkerson was in her late thirties, a mother of three little girls and a boy. I'd seen her and Bess shopping together at ZCMI, so the two of them were friends. It made me feel like an outsider.

DeAnn opened her front door just as we walked up the steps. She was carrying something between her thumb and forefinger. I couldn't make out what it was at first, but as we got closer I saw it was a goldfish. It swung in the air like a pendulum, swaying back and forth every time DeAnn took a pace.

Bess, standing at the foot of the steps, looked mildly sick at the sight of a goldfish carcass flapping in the breeze. As many diapers as she'd changed in her day, a dead fish should have been nothing in comparison.

DeAnn stalked to the edge of her top step and dropped the goldfish headfirst into the ground cover. Instead of falling discreetly inside the foliage, it landed squarely atop a leaf. "Damned goldfish," she said, hopping off the porch and into the groundcover. She moved the leaves aside so the fish dropped to the earth below. Then she climbed back up on the step and marched to the kitchen to scrub her hands.

I was only glad DeAnn's kids hadn't been around to see the disposal. Then I realized I hadn't seen Bess's children either. It was the dead of summer. They should have been everywhere. "Where are all the children in the ward?" I asked.

"Day camp," Bess said with a broad smile.

"Blessed day camp" DeAnn added. "If they'd been here, we would've had to bury the damned fish. Then we would have had to go downtown and buy another one."

DeAnn was the most pet-impaired person I'd ever met. Every animal that entered her home met with an untimely fate. She ran a horned toad through the washing machine in her son's jeans pocket. She sucked up a turtle with a vacuum cleaner. She banished the Angora cat in disgrace after it had kittens in her sweater drawer. (The irony would have been rich if they'd been Angora sweaters, but they were only cardigans.)

She even bought a talking parrot once. The pet store owner swore the bird sang *Love at Home*, a perennial Mormon favorite. But whoever taught the bird had substituted *lust* for *love* all the way through, and DeAnn donated the parrot to Hogle Zoo.

Despite all her failures, DeAnn never learned. Children needed pets, and her children were going to *have* pets. She was great at buying pets. She just wasn't so good at keeping them.

"These damned fish are impossible," she said in exasperation. She dried her hands and put them on her hips for emphasis. "How in the *hell* are you supposed to clean the bowls?"

"With soap and water, DeAnn," I said.

"I *tried* soap and water. I squirted some dishwashing soap in the bowl last week and scrubbed the sides with a sponge. Damned fish floated right to the top."

"You left the fish in the bowl while you cleaned it?" Bess sounded horrified. "You're supposed to take the fish *out* first."

"Well, that's what I did today. I took the damned thing out and put it on the counter while I washed the bowl. When I turned around to get it, it was lying dead on the floor. You don't think it flopped off the ledge and broke its neck, do you?"

"I think it drowned in the air," Bess said. "That's why they live in the water."

"Well, how are you supposed to get the damned bowl clean? No, don't tell me. This is my third fish in two weeks. I don't think I want another one."

I had to ask. "What happened to the third one?"

"Remember that hot spell we had two weeks ago? It was so humid that the swamp cooler didn't help. I was hot and miserable, and the kids were hot and miserable, and even the damned *fish* looked hot and miserable. So I put a tray of ice cubes in the fish bowl."

I looked at DeAnn, aghast, and she snapped back, "Well, it's just *water*. I was going to give him lemonade, but I didn't know if fish eat sugar. *Do* fish eat sugar? *Now* what kind of pet am I going to get?"

I'd been looking for a home for my remaining gerbil, Socrates, and I almost said something then. But Socrates and I had had good times together. I didn't want him sacrificed as DeAnn's pet of the week.

Our second visit was with Letha Cannon, one of the nicest women Paradise Vue had ever seen. The old lady was never home, and we only found her there because Bess had used a tactic that never would have occurred to Alex or me. She'd made an appointment.

Thanks to the late mailman, we arrived at Letha's nearly an hour behind schedule. When we got there, it was clear that Letha'd given us up for lost. No Mormon woman would be outside with a can of beer in her hand if she were expecting the Relief Society presidency.

"Murder and devastation!" Letha said when she spotted us. "You're just in time for the harvest." She led us around back without another word. I navigated the cobblestone walkway, but Bess missed one and put her foot in a puddle. She couldn't take her eyes off that can of beer.

Letha reached her destination before us and knelt right down in the mulch and the mud. There was a white plastic pool, about the size of a TV dinner tray, buried in her garden. A veteran of many TV dinners myself, I realized when I got closer that it *was* a TV dinner tray. I'd eaten that brand lots of times.

Lying in that pool, belly-up, were garden snails — big, black ones. It looked as if a whole college fraternity of snails had tried to see how many of them could crowd into one plastic dinner tray. Bess took one look at the mess of snails, cringed, and turned her back on the scene. She'd found one thing that could take her mind off the can of beer.

"Look at the little beggars!" Letha said triumphantly. "Dead as doornails!"

"What killed 'em, Letha?" I asked, peering at the slimy mess. Snails had defoliated my zinnia patch. Whatever chemical had done that to snails, I was going right downtown to buy.

"Beer. Does it every time. Bet I got two hundred of them in that tray."

I knelt down beside Letha, fascinated. She pulled a plastic bag from a pocket and scooped up the snails by the handful. Once she'd crammed them all in the bag, she poured fresh beer into the plastic tray. Then she went to a different spot in the yard and scooped a big batch of dead snails from another pool of beer.

"You've got to do this right," she said. "Get the dark stuff. Snails don't drink light beer. They go for the flavor. They don't drink Coors." Letha Cannon fed her snails Budweiser.

"Where do you *buy* it?" I couldn't imagine a sweet old Mormon granny buying a six-pack.

"That's the hard part, I'll admit. I used to buy it down the hill at Smith's, until I ran into Delta Mae Eliason in the check-out line. Now I have to drive to Granger. Pain in the neck. I buy it by the case."

She refilled the second snail pool with beer and stood up. "Looks like we lost Bess," she said. I hadn't noticed until then, but Bess was nowhere to be seen. We found her sitting on Letha's front porch. She smiled wanly.

"Sun too hot for you?" Letha asked. "I have some punch and cookies inside." We followed her in. When we got to the kitchen, she started to upend the bag of snails into the garbage disposal. Then she saw Bess's face and thought better of it. She hid the bag under the sink and washed her hands.

Once we were sitting in the living room, drinking punch and eating cookies, Bess was on familiar ground. "And how are you *do*ing?" she asked Letha, intently.

"Better than you are, I think." Bess still looked a little green around the gills. "Haven't been sleeping too well, though. Oscar's been snoring like a buzz-saw."

I remembered snoring. Tim's snores had driven me crazy. He used to sleep with his mouth so wide open that I wanted to put an apple in it, just like you put an apple in the mouth of a roasted piglet. Now that Tim wasn't around anymore, I missed the snoring. But I hadn't liked it then, so I commiserated with Letha.

"That's the most annoying habit," I said. "I don't know why wives put up with it."

Bess gave me a round-eyed look. "It depends how much you love the person who snores," she said. "If you love him enough, it doesn't bother you at all." As far as she was concerned, that ended the discussion.

Bess just drove me crazy sometimes. She was always comparing Tim and me with Rick and herself, and Tim and I were always coming up short.

After a few more amenities, Bess and I left Letha's for our next appointment. Letha offered me a can of beer for my own snails, but I said I'd buy my own. I didn't want any of the neighbors seeing the homemaking counselor wandering around the ward with a can of Bud.

Letha hugged us both and waved us off. When I turned around for one last goodbye, she'd disappeared. I heard Letha's garbage disposal grinding away as we walked down the front walk to the car.

Our final visit was to Scarlett Donahee, a new woman in the ward. She was right out of college — so young that I felt as if I had more in common with the grandmas than I did with her. She'd married her husband about fifteen minutes after he got home from his mission, and they lived in a basement apartment on Benson Drive. I didn't know Scarlett at all: as soon as she'd moved into the ward she'd been put in the Primary, and none of the Relief Society people ever saw her.

Scarlett was hugely pregnant. She compensated by walking sway-backed, and she looked as if she were going to fall over backwards any minute. Pregnancy had been hard on her, cruelly transforming her from a little slip of a girl into a dark moose of a woman. She used to smile all the time, but now she looked miserably unhappy.

Bess, who'd been surrounded all day by dead things, perked right up with the promise of life sitting across the room. "Isn't pregnancy wonderful?" she asked, blissfully. Scarlett didn't look as if she agreed.

"How are you doing, Scarlett?" Since Bess didn't ask her, I thought I should. Scarlett burst into tears, and Bess and I exchanged worried glances. Clearly, Bess hadn't been expecting it. I, who *had* been expecting it, didn't know what to do when it happened.

I moved over on the couch next to Scarlett and put my arm around her. Then I didn't know what to say to make it better. "What's the matter? Tell us all about it."

"I'm so ugly. Aaron doesn't love me anymore."

"Of *course* Aaron loves you," Bess said. At the same time, I said, "What makes you think so?" Our words drowned each other out, and Scarlett didn't know who to answer. So we sat for a few difficult moments in silence. Finally she spoke.

"All he thinks about is sports. He waits for the *Sports Illustrated,* and when it comes he won't speak to me till he's finished it. During baseball season, he watches baseball. During football season, he watches football. On weekends he'll watch racing or tennis or bowling or *fish*ing, for heaven's sake.

"He eats every meal in front of the television. He never talks to me at all. And," her voice lowered in embarrassment, "he hasn't touched me in three months."

I could well understand why Aaron hadn't touched her. She looked so ungainly and bloated. But even so, it was depressing. The uglier a woman looks, the more she needs to be told she's loved.

"What are you doing about it?" Bess asked.

"Everything. I make him three meals every day. I bake him cookies. I give him massages. I put love notes in his lunchbox. I buy him presents all the time. I call him at work every morning and every afternoon. I spend every minute he's home in the room with him, doing whatever he's doing. I even watch *sports*. And I tell him I love him at least ten times a day."

Aaron sounded like a Boston fern that had been over-watered, but I didn't know how to tell Scarlett that. Bess didn't stop to think, however. She just jumped right in.

"I think, Scarlett, you love him too much."

"That's crazy. You can't love somebody too much." She looked at me as if she wanted confirmation, but I couldn't give it to her.

"How many girlfriends did Aaron have before he met you?" Bess asked.

"Oh, lots. He was a football player in high school."

"How many boyfriends did you have before Aaron?" Bess looked intent, but I couldn't see where the conversation was going.

"He's the only one," Scarlett said. "Aaron's the only person I ever loved."

"That's the problem," said Bess. She nodded sagely. "You're smothering him."

"*I'd* want to be smothered like that," Scarlett said.

Bess shook her head. "Trust me. He doesn't. Some people fall in and out of love all their lives. Other people fall in love just once. The people who do it just once focus all that love on one person the way light through a magnifying glass shines on a leaf."

I caught the drift of what Bess was saying. "What happens when a magnifying glass shines on a leaf?" I asked Scarlett.

"Well, it smokes for a minute and then it burns up."

"Maybe Aaron feels like a leaf. Maybe being loved so much is too much for him."

Scarlett looked at me, then at Bess. "I can't help how much I love him. I don't know how to stop."

"We're not asking you to stop," Bess said. "You can't stop loving just because you want to, anyway. We're just asking you to step back. Let Aaron come to you because he wants to — not because he feels sorry for you."

"Do you have any hobbies?" I asked.

"Just Aaron. He's all I care about. When the baby comes, I'll care about that, too."

"That's not enough," Bess said. "You won't be interesting to Aaron unless you're interested in other things. What was your major in college?"

"Child development and family relations." She smiled hopefully. Mentally I rolled my eyes.

"That won't do it. What does Aaron do for a living?"

"He's a stockbroker."

"That's a start," Bess said. Start reading *The Wall Street Journal*. Subscribe to *Business Week*. When he gets home from work, ask what he did that day. Then be able to talk about it."

Scarlett said "Oh," in a small voice. I could tell *The Wall Street Journal* didn't sound appealing to her.

"And find an interest of your own."

"The baby will be a good one." Scarlett smiled brightly, for the first time since we'd said hello.

"*Besides* the baby. Aaron will love the baby, but he isn't going to want to talk about it all the time. The more interests you have apart from him, the more interesting you'll be to him."

Scarlett promised she'd find some new interests. I hoped she realized how important it was. I'd seen too many marriages fall apart when the kids grew up and the parents didn't have anything to talk about anymore.

"That visit was depressing," Bess said as we got in the car. I agreed. Letha's snails had more hope of surviving than Scarlett had of patching up her marriage — unless she changed her ways.

Bess twirled a lock of hair around a finger. "That kind of love is dangerous. It doesn't make you happy. It only makes you sick and miserable. It ruins your life, but once you feel it there's a part of you that can't let it go."

I wondered then how Bess was such an authority on life and love. Surely she'd gotten married the same way Scarlett had — right out of high school, with no interests to speak of. She'd been one of the lucky ones. Most people who got married that young changed sooner or later and found themselves miserable.

"It's almost unfair, the way life works," Bess said. "When a man loves a woman, it's part of his life. When a woman loves a man, it *is* her life. It's as if we're different species."

"Humph," I said. I used Alex's favorite expression, even as I made the same protest she would have done. "That's not a very enlightened attitude."

Bess looked surprised. "I wasn't saying women are dumber than men — or less competent. It's just that we have a different orientation. The things that are peripheral to us are, well, peripheral. Most women are too practical to think our careers, or our hobbies, or sports, are the most important things about us."

"I'll bite," I said. "What *is* the most important thing about us?"

"Nothing's more important than who we are. We define ourselves by who we are in relation to the people we love."

I thought then that Bess's views were a little extreme. Bess might think of herself that way, but I certainly didn't define myself by a husband who'd been dead for six years.

Nevertheless, the conversation had taught me one thing: Alex was right about Bess. There was more to her than I'd thought. I wasn't going to be able to rule her out.

# 6
# Cooking with Hemoglobin

**I** dreaded the end of summer, when the ward got back to its regular schedule and monthly homemaking meetings resumed. Even though Carol Ann Little, as homemaking leader of the Relief Society, was officially in charge of the meetings, I was now the homemaking counselor. I was the final authority for the cooking classes and the craft projects, and all the other things I'd assiduously avoided for so many years. If the meetings succeeded, Carol Ann Little would get the credit. If they failed, I'd take the blame.

Inadequacy loomed so large that by August first, I was a twitching case of nerves. Alex took me aside one afternoon to put her arm around me and give me some motherly advice.

"Amy, you're taking this far too seriously," she said. We were standing in Smith's, where we did our grocery shopping every week. "Look at this stuff in your basket. Where are the TV dinners? Where is the Kraft Macaroni 'n' Cheese? There's no chocolate in here, and we're almost finished shopping. You've got a whole cart full of vegetables. You don't even know what half of them are."

"That's not fair," I said. "I know what they all are. I just don't know how to *cook* them."

She picked up an oblong fruit from my cart and held it up to me. "What's this?"

"A mango. I'm not culturally deficient."

"It's a persimmon. It's a *green* persimmon. Just do me a favor and don't eat it till it's ripe."

I put the persimmon in a refrigerator shelf next to the sour cream, where it wouldn't rot. "Are you happy? Now I'll never taste one. I'm just trying to do my ward job."

Alex took a carton of sour cream. Then she retrieved the persimmon and took it back to the produce section. She put it back on the pile with a shake of her head.

"Amy, I didn't choose you because you're a good homemaker. I don't expect you to turn into a good homemaker. Let Carol Ann do her job and run the homemaking meeting. All you have to do is walk around from class to class, visiting everyone and making them feel loved."

With a big sigh, Alex motioned for me to wheel her cart for her. She took my cart and unloaded the okra and the snow peas and the bib lettuce. Then, with me following her like a short-legged puppy, she toured the supermarket and loaded my basket with Lean Cuisines and ice cream and the other things I usually bought.

"You didn't have to do that," I said as we rounded the deli and headed for the check-out line. "I could have cooked all that food."

"Yes, I did have to do it," she said, throwing a *National Enquirer* in her own basket. "If you didn't get food you'd eat, you would have been eating at my house all week long."


Homemaking day was held on a Tuesday. All our ward meetings were held on Tuesdays, because we shared our building with a ward who held all *their* meetings on Wednesdays. The only exception was funerals, which were held whenever somebody keeled over.

Alex was right. All my worrying had been futile. Carol Ann Little orchestrated the homemaking meeting like she was leading the

Utah Symphony. Before the opening song was over, I knew I was as superfluous as the extra toes on Karma Stooble's pet cat.

When we separated for classes, I looked enviously at the group walking down the hall to the book review. Katie Segall was reviewing *Dandelion Wine*. The book was as old as I was, but it was a perennial favorite with church ladies who wouldn't read about sex and violence.

As the door closed on the book review, I turned my back on *Dandelion Wine* and went to the kitchen for the Oriental cooking class.

The teacher was a small, round-faced woman with the incongruous name of Doris — Doris Chan. She surveyed us all expectantly, looking up at us with a sunny countenance. The shortest of us towered over her. She gathered herself into as tall a package as she could present, adding a good three inches to her stature. Only when she was closer to our height did she begin to speak.

"Today we will cook *Hung Sao Hai Sun* — Red-Cooked Sea Cucumber. Sea cucumber is swimming creature from sea. No shell. No bones. Like sea anemone."

She rooted through her ingredients and produced a Tupperware bowl. She set it on the counter and opened it carefully. Inside was a grayish liquid that looked and smelled like bath water. Some long cylinders of congealed bath water floated lazily in the bowl.

"Sea cucumber," she said proudly, pulling one out and holding it aloft between two fingers. It hung limply at each end, like a giant, dead worm. "Great Chinese delicacy. Is soaking in salt water. Sea cucumber was dried. Now is reconstituted."

The little woman scrutinized each of us individually, as if measuring our worthiness for the task ahead. Finally she asked, "Does anyone know how to hold a knife?"

No hands went up, so I admitted some expertise. After all, I used to teach sculpture at Brigham Young. I thought that made me a professional.

Doris gave me a sage smile. She rooted through a paper sack and pulled out a meat cleaver — the kind of knife usually seen in butcher shops and horror movies. Its sharp blade glinted wickedly in the light.

As she stood over the tools of her trade, she became formal and Oriental. She bobbed her head in a traditional bow, and when she spoke her accent deepened.

"Demonstrate, prease," she said to me. "Cut sea cucumber for stir-fry."

I laid the sea cucumber out on a chopping board. It was about the size of a zucchini squash, but grey and gelatinous.

"Bite-sized pieces, prease."

I held the reconstituted sea animal immobile with my fingers. *Whack!* Almost before I knew what I was doing, I'd cleanly cut a nubbin off the end of the gelatin with the cleaver. A familiar tingle told me I'd gone through part of my finger, too.

"DON'T BREED ON SEA CUCUMBER!" Doris snatched up the sluglike creature, which was already covered with blood. Quickly, she rinsed it out in the same salt water where the other sea cucumbers were still soaking. Bess, who'd been standing in the corner, blanched and left the room.

"*I* show you how to hold a knife." Disdainfully, the teacher took the cleaver away from me. Holding it firmly in her right hand, she steadied the sea cucumber with her left. She pinned it down with fingers bent to the knuckles.

"I hold it this way so as not to srice my fingers," she said pointedly. Everyone ignored my injured finger, which bled enthusiastically on the metal kitchen counter. "This is what I mean by holding a knife. When Chinese say, *Can you hold a knife?* is the same as asking, *Can you cook Chinese food?* Today you will all hold a knife."

I discreetly took a paper towel and wrapped it tightly around my finger, trying to staunch the flow of blood. Then I took another towel and mopped up the blood from the kitchen counter.

Meanwhile, the Relief Society ladies practiced holding a knife. As she grew more familiar with the group, Doris developed a sense of camaraderie with them. She barked orders and encouragement to each woman individually.

"Grasp knife tightry!" Doris said to Sally Armstrong. "Imagine sea cucumber is husband." Sally, whose husband had left her for her younger sister, almost chopped the cutting board in half.

Doris gleefully took the cleaver and passed it on to the next student. "This time, sea creature is tax corrector. Bad man!" *Whack!*

Each woman in turn successfully chopped off a bite-sized piece of sea cucumber. When the pieces were all properly chopped and set aside, Doris beamed at her pupils. "Now ready for other ingredients," she said. She took them out of her paper sack, one by one. "Two ounce Virginia ham, shredded. Two chicken leg. (Can use pork shoulder.) Soy sauce. Oyster sauce. Green onions. Sugar. Salt. Sherry." She reached to the bottom of her sack to pull out the final ingredient.

Bess returned to the kitchen during this recitation. As soon as Doris's attention was diverted into the sack, Bess got my attention. She mouthed the words, "We can't drink sherry. It's *alcohol.*"

I looked down at the printed recipe. It showed a teaspoon and a half of sherry. Even if the alcohol didn't cook out, a teaspoon and a half divided among the nine people in the class wouldn't kill anybody. I tapped my uninjured index finger on the measurement. Bess read the words and nodded in acquiescence.

The last item Doris produced was a quivering thing I couldn't identify. It didn't look like seafood.

"What the *hell* is that?" DeAnn Wilkerson asked the question for all of us.

"Is pork stomach," Doris said. "Steam with other ingredients. Makes dericious Chinese meal. This recipe come from Beijing — Peking province of Chinese cooking."

To my surprise, only Bess looked disgusted with the pork stomach. Everyone else was in high spirits. If they could chop sea cucumber, I thought, pork stomach was a piece of cake.

I slipped out of the room as soon as Doris started showing the ladies how to slit a pork stomach. Class was running so smoothly that no one looked up when I left. I went to the rest room and took the paper towel off my wound. There was a deep cut in the pad of my finger, still bleeding heavily. I took a square of toilet paper and wadded it in the cut, hoping the fibers in the tissue would help the blood coagulate.

I peeked in on the book review. The older ladies always went to the book review, having no interest in cooking or crafts. I liked the book reviews, too. People sat in islands of one or two, listening to the teacher in their separate reveries. But now I was homemaking leader. Cooking and crafts were my responsibility. Nobody but the teacher saw me stand in the back of the room for a few moments and then walk out.

A hubbub from the Primary room told me where the action was. Today a group of at least twenty women were sitting at the child-sized Primary tables making chopping boards. Each held a square of clear acrylic. They'd taped patterns on one side and were tracing the patterns with black marking pen through the plastic. Next they were going to paint the designs, coloring all the way up to the black lines the way children color in coloring books. When the project was finished and the boards were turned over, they would look like ersatz pieces of stained glass.

Alex was sitting near the center of the room, worrying a cold sore on her lip with her tongue as she concentrated on her work. She'd chosen a stained glass pattern to decorate her cutting board, and was hard at work tracing the pattern with black marking pen. Alex, who'd always been craft-oriented, was going to have the prettiest chopping board in Paradise Vue.

I pulled up a chair near Alex, but not too near her. She needed to mingle with the women of Paradise Vue during homemaking meetings, just as I did. On homemaking days, the Relief Society presidency traditionally went from class to class, visiting in each one just long enough so every woman at the homemaking meeting could say she'd talked to the Relief Society president or her counselors. I watched Alex as people approached her one by one, offering compliments on her handiwork and telling her about their lives.

Molly Crandall walked over to inspect Alex's tracing job. Her own board was decorated with a scene from a Mickey Mouse coloring book. Most of the young mothers had gone the easy route and had borrowed their children's coloring books to use as patterns for their chopping boards. The idea of slicing eggplant over a picture of Wilma Flintstone didn't do much for me, but the room was buzzing with excitement. People enjoyed homemaking meeting.

"Guess what!" Molly told Alex in a voice that could be heard across the building. "I'm pregnant! Maybe this one will be a girl."

Women gathered around Molly like drones around a queen bee. Molly reveled in her status. Suddenly I remembered why I'd never liked homemaking meetings — or any gatherings of women, for that matter. Sooner or later, the talk always turned to pregnancy. Even if the women hadn't had children in twenty years, they remembered every excruciating detail of how many days they had morning sickness, how long the labor was, how many centimeters they'd been dilated, and all sorts of other stuff I didn't want to hear.

Bess drifted in from the kitchen, taking names for Emma's Relief Society roll. She pulled up a chair next to mine and watched me as I eavesdropped on the motherhood conversation. Finally she said, "Amy, you're bleeding all over your blue jeans. Let's go to the bathroom."

The bleeding showed no signs of stopping. Bess ministered to my wound, treating it with a mother's hands. There was no sign of queasiness in her face as she wiped off the blood and bound my finger. I hadn't been touched so gently in years.

"I saw you in the Primary room, Amy," she said. "That kind of talk makes you uncomfortable."

I'd been concentrating on Bess's medical treatment, and I didn't catch her words. "What kind of talk?"

"Pregnancy. Motherhood."

I had to admit that Bess was right. "Was it that obvious?" I asked.

"Only to someone who's looking for it."

"Why were you looking for it?"

"Because I feel the same way."

"You?" I was incredulous. "You're a professional mother. You were born to be a mother."

"Let me tell you a secret," she said. "I feel as uneasy about children as you do. I've never even wanted to hold a child, and I have four of them."

For a moment, I forgot my injured finger. "Well, why *did* you have them?"

"I had children because that's what you do. If I can't do what I want to do, I'll do what I have to do — and I'll do it so well nobody can tell the difference."

"I don't understand," I said. "What *do* you want to do?"

"We all have secret dreams, Amy. All of us look for our purpose in life." I had to agree with that. I daydreamed about being a famous artist. I wanted to change people's lives with my work.

As if changing the subject, Bess asked, "What bothers you so much about the pregnancy talk? Is it because you never had children of your own?"

"No," I said. "That's not it. At least, I don't think it is. It's just that these women are *people*. Before they know they're little girls, they're people. When they go to school, they're people. When they get married, they're *still* people. But when they become mothers, all of a sudden it's as if they aren't people anymore."

"Alex is still a person."

"Yes, she is — and some of the others are, too. But most of them forget they're people and define themselves, even in their own minds, as mothers."

"They *are* mothers," Bess said. "Is it so bad for them to think of themselves that way?"

"It is when they forget they're anything else."

"They don't do it on purpose," Bess said. "They're just too busy to think about anything else. Motherhood is important, you know."

"Of course I know. But can't mothers be people, too? So many of them are like Scarlett Donahee. Motherhood becomes everything. It's like a weed. If you let it go, one day you look around and see the weed has choked out everything else."

"What can we do about it?" Bess asked.

"Nothing. It's the way people are."

"People can be changed, Amy. Maybe that's our job as a Relief Society presidency. Maybe we should make life so interesting that people want to explore *all* its facets."

The rest room door opened with a creak, and Doris Chan walked in. "Still breeding?" she asked, peering at my finger. Blood had soaked the fresh bandage, and the bleeding showed no signs of stopping.

"You should see doctah," Doris advised. She disappeared inside a stall. "Sea cucumber all finished," she called out to us. Her voice echoed in the tile bathroom. "Dericious."

Bess looked at her watch. "We're late for the luncheon. Let me wrap this one more time for you. If it doesn't stop bleeding, maybe you *should* see a doctor."


When Bess and I arrived in the Relief Society room, the monthly luncheon was in full progress. The luncheon committee had removed the Relief Society chairs and set up the octagonal tables. It looked just like a funeral dinner, with two exceptions — there were no chrysanthemums, and we weren't eating ham.

Most of the chairs were taken. Bess found one at the same table with Alex, leaving me a seat at a table of blue-hairs. I got a bowl of soup and sank into my chair with a sense of relief. These were women who wouldn't talk about pregnancy. If only they stayed off the subject of widowhood, we could have a pleasant visit.

Germaine Duffey was in the middle of a monologue when I sat down, so the other ladies at the table only gave me pleasant nods as I sat down and reached for a hard roll.

Germaine was always exercised about something. Once you got to know her, you realized she wasn't angry as much as she was ascerbic. She lived by her own set of rules, and if she didn't win many converts, she did have a lot of friends. Today she was talking about Albert Neugent, our short and myopic and mean-looking stake president.

"When Albert got put in, back in the Dark Ages, it was the first time I didn't raise my hand to sustain a church leader," she admitted, munching a gherkin. "I didn't raise my hand to *not* sustain him, you understand. But when he was made stake president I didn't know if I could support him, and I didn't want to lie with my upraised arm."

She stopped to get another gherkin from the pickle dish. She had one picked out, but then she saw a pickled onion and swooped down on it instead. She ate it with a furious snap of her jaws, and then she licked mustard sauce from her skinny lips like a cat.

"Is there an option?" I asked. "I thought we voted *yes* for everybody, just as a courtesy."

"Maybe *you* do, Sweetpea. *I* think about it." She searched the dish of mustard pickles for another onion. "What do you do when you vote for someone and then find out you can't support 'em?"

I thought of Emma. "I guess you sit around and wait for them to be released."

"But meanwhile, do you help them do their job?"

"I don't know. I guess I don't. You can't do somebody else's job for them, can you?"

"Maybe you can't do it all, but you sure can make it easier." It was Rose Violett, a woman whose marriage had saddled her with the unfortunate name. "If it's a Sunday School teacher, you read the lesson before class. If it's a chorister, you sing the songs. If it's a pair of missionaries, you invite them in for dinner."

I hadn't thought about that before, but Rose had a point. I said, "Hmmm," through a mouthful of hard roll.

"People have different philosophies of churchwork," Germaine continued. "Do you put them into callings to help the church run better, or do you put them in to teach them how to lead or follow?"

I swallowed a spoonful of soup. "It depends on the situation. Sometimes you need a certain person to do the job right. Other times, a person needs to learn the job. When they're learning, you have to sit back and let them succeed or fail."

"But you can't sabotage them," Rose said. "Once you raise your hand to sustain them, you've promised to help them succeed in their job. Then if you don't sustain them, you're a liar."

I thought that was a little strong. Lots of times I voted *yes*, even though I didn't want to see a person take a particular job. I didn't want to hurt their feelings.

"When I'm not sure about someone, I just don't vote," Germaine said. "If I haven't sustained them, I'm not lying afterwards when I don't support them."

"Does that happen often?"

"No. Even with President Neugent, I voted *yes* the second time around. He's an old sourpuss, and he was a terrible bishop. Being a bishop takes compassion, and he doesn't have a speck of it. But you can be a sourpuss and be a good stake president. That's an administrative job."

Germaine pushed aside every lump in the pickle dish, looking for another onion. She'd eaten them all, and she settled on a piece of cauliflower. She chewed it open-mouthed. "I've got to admit it," she concluded. "President Neugent is still nobody's favorite. As Ezra Thorpe told me the day President Neugent was sustained, 'some are sent to lead us and some sent to try us.'"

The ladies around the table nodded their heads in unison. Again I thought of Emma. Emma was a shadow over the whole Relief Society presidency. The frustrating thing was, nobody knew it but me.

Germaine's speech left one question unanswered in my mind. I shouldn't have asked it, but I did anyway. "Did you vote for me when I was sustained?"

"I sure didn't," Germaine said with a laugh. My heart sank. "You're the worst excuse for a homemaker in Paradise Vue. But next time they ask me to raise my hand for you, I'll raise it high. You're working out fine in this job. You're learning what you need to learn."

I gave her a relieved smile, but I didn't have any time to ponder her words. "By the way," she added, "do you know you're bleeding all over the tablecloth? What in the world did you do to that finger?"

I went back to the bathroom for more first aid, but I never could staunch the flow of blood. After Relief Society ended, I had four stitches taken in my finger at Holy Cross Hospital.

# 7
# Limerick Sunday and the Yellow Geranium Incident

"**L**ook at that," Alex hissed, as we settled into a pew for church one Sunday. She crooked a finger toward a man walking into the chapel. Six little kids, lined up like stair-steps, followed him obediently. Well, five followed obediently. The sixth was in open rebellion.

She raised her eyebrows at me. "Well, what do you think?"

"Well," I said, "that little redheaded girl could be trouble. I'd hate to be her Primary teacher."

"Not *her*. The *father*." I took a second glance. The father looked okay. Actually, he looked better than okay. Tall. Thin. The Clark Kent type. I'd always been a sucker for Clark Kent types, but this one had already found Lois Lane. Or Lana Lang. Lana Lang was the redhead.

"Not bad," I said. "I bet his wife thinks so, too."

"He hasn't got a wife. Brain tumor. I found out about him in correlation meeting this morning. They've just moved into the Johnson house."

We had to shut up then, because the man had circumnavigated the chapel and was standing opposite our row. He needed seats for seven, and our row was empty except for Alex and me. Children

69

scooted down the bench toward us, and I found myself next to the feisty redhead. She looked at me maliciously, but I stared her down. No kid, not even a redheaded kid, could intimidate a person who lived with Samson.

Sacrament Meeting started, and I forgot Clark Kent. It was one of those Sacrament Meetings that became ward folklore almost before the meeting was over.

We had a whole nest of brothers and sisters in Paradise Vue who comprised the Byrd family. There were nine of them then. Later there'd be more. They were tall and good looking, and well-behaved considering the number of them. They were also spiritual enough that you could tell even then that none of them would ever stray away from the church. They were just the kind of kids you'd want your own son or daughter to marry.

They were also afflicted — every last one of them — with reading disabilities. Some of them could barely read. Others could read to themselves but not orally. Some of them knew the words individually but couldn't understand them when they were all put together. A few of the crueler children in the ward called the kids Byrd brains, but it wasn't a fair assessment. The Byrds weren't stupid, but whatever synapse it takes to process words in the mind was lacking in every one of them. They had genes for basketball, not literature.

Last week, Dell Byrd had turned sixteen and was made a priest. This week was his first turn to bless the Sacrament. I didn't think anything of it until it happened, but Dell must have been white-knuckled all week. Other than baptismal prayers, Sacrament prayers are the only ones Mormons say that have to be said correctly, word for word.

After the Sacrament hymn, Dell knelt down to bless the bread. From the moment he opened his mouth, the whole ward knew he was in trouble. He couldn't recognize the word *O*.

Everybody in the chapel shared Dell's agony. He started over and over again, massacring a prayer that's only ninety-two words long. Those ninety-two words went on for eternity. Nobody seemed to want to breathe until that prayer was over.

About two-thirds of the way through the prayer, the pressure was too much for Dell. After repeating the same phrase four times in a row, messing up something different every time he said it, Dell stopped cold and muttered, "Dammit to hell!" The words, though whispered, bounced off the walls of the chapel: Dell had said *dammit to hell* over a microphone.

The sheer gravity of what he'd done galvanized him, and in a burst of adrenalin he finished the prayer. The bishop, knowing he'd never get anything better from Dell and wanting the scene to be over, nodded that the prayer was okay. Everything else went smoothly after that, but it was if the whole ward were waiting for the Sacrament service to be over. As soon as the water was put down and all the priests and deacons took their seats, the room exploded in a cacophony of whispers and embarrassed titters.

Dell's humiliation was complete. He never said a Sacrament prayer in our ward again.

Sacrament Meeting never settled down after that. A high councilman was the speaker, and it was with good reason that Alex called them *dry* councilmen. Today the poor man didn't have a chance. Everyone was too revved up from *dammit to hell* to pay much attention to a bad speaker.

I pulled out a small sketchpad and started drawing. Brother Limerick was glaring at Dell furiously, even fifteen minutes after the event. He was a goodhearted man, but kindness never showed in his face. His mouth pursed and his brows knitted as he stared down at the priest.

I drew Brother Limerick as an avenging angel, swooping down to mete punishment on a fleeing Dell. I drew a thought balloon coming from his head and handed the sketchpad to Alex to fill in. She thought a few minutes and wrote,

*There was a poor priest, name of Dell,*
*Who got scared and said, "Dammit to Hell!"*
*Now here is a fact:*
*He got caught in the act.*
*Now he's running from justice, pell-mell.*

I laughed louder than I should have when Alex finished writing the words, and a few people turned around and looked. One of them was Clark Kent, who caught my eye quizzically. I looked away, but Alex saw the exchange and poked me. I didn't poke her back.

Alex returned the sketchpad to me, but the little redheaded girl snatched it right out of my hands. Her father took it from her, and instead of returning it discreetly he inspected the artwork and read the limerick. He smiled. A lone dimple creased the right side of his mouth. There's something appealing about a lone dimple, but I wasn't interested. There were six reasons, in addition to Tim.

Instead of returning the pad, Clark Kent pulled out a pen and scribbled something on the paper. He passed the sketchpad back to me, and I read:

> *A handsome young priest, filled with hope,*
> *Said he'd pray when he should have said "nope."*
> *In a fit of insanity,*
> *He uttered profanity.*
> *Now they're washing his mouth out with soap.*

It was a nice try — even better than Alex's. The best part was that he did it without saying anything nasty about Dell. I couldn't have forgiven a stranger if he'd walked into the ward and made fun of a boy with a learning disability. I nodded approval and put the drawing away. He smiled again. He did have a nice smile.

A few minutes later, I saw the stranger looking at me surreptitiously. Enough was enough. Alex, who never missed anything, wrote on her program, "He's checking you out." Sure enough, he was angling for a peek at my ring finger. I hid my left hand. I didn't want him getting ideas.

Tim had given me an engagement ring, and a wedding ring too. It was one of those big, gaudy sets, with four million little stones and a few big ones. I wore them for exactly two weeks after the wedding, but I couldn't help feeling that they looked like they came out of a gum machine. Jewelry like that just wasn't me.

Finally I told Tim that as much as I loved him, I couldn't wear the rings. I gave the excuse that it was too much trouble to scrub out the pthalo blue from all those crannies and nooks every afternoon when I put my paints away. He accepted the explanation. Tim knew I didn't have to wear a ring to prove I loved him. Besides, I was halfway telling the truth. Those rings were murder to clean.

As much as I hated my wedding ring, I wished fervently that Sunday I were wearing it. I resolved to make a trip to the bank on Monday and retrieve it from the safe deposit box.

I studiously paid attention to the rest of Sacrament Meeting. Alex had a meeting with the bishop during Sunday School, so I took out my scriptures and attended that meeting alone. We met again when it was time to set up the room for Relief Society.

"His name's Reynolds," Alex said, as we moved the padded Relief Society chairs into orderly rows. I hadn't asked, and I didn't want to know.

"As in Wrap?"

"As in Reynolds Cleese, the attorney."

I'd heard the name, but I wasn't impressed. Everybody I knew was either a lawyer or married to one, or had one for a next door neighbor. In Paradise Vue, it was a status symbol *not* to be a lawyer.

"Not interested, Alex," I said. "Every time you see a new man, you try to set me up. Do you really want to see me married to a man with six kids?"

I didn't hear Alex's reply. The door opened as she spoke, and a group of ladies waved hello and found their seats. We put on our Relief Society smiles. Our Sunday duties had begun.


Alex called me on a Thursday morning, sounding disgusted. "Tragedy," she said. "We have to go visiting. There's been an emergency in the ward."

Alex usually wasn't so cryptic, so it meant I was supposed to ask her what was going on. I did. "Brother Thygerson piddled in the geraniums again," she said. "Iona's livid. You know how she feels about those flowers."

Iona Thygerson had never had children, except for petunias and impatiens and geraniums. She talked to her plants the way I talked to Samson, but at least Samson talked back. She gave the indoor plants names: George Ficus, Harry Dieffenbachia, Sally Philodendron — things like that. When poor old Morton piddled on the geraniums, it was a serious problem in the Thygerson household.

I had a great idea for a watercolor, and I was just getting ready to put in the background wash when Alex called. But the idea would keep. I put a lid on the palette and got dressed. Maybe Alex would treat me to lunch.

Iona was pacing on the front sidewalk when we drove up. There was no sign of Morton, but I knew where he'd be. For ten years, ever since he started getting senile, the poor old man had been mesmerized by cartoons. Iona, trying desperately to keep him out of her hair, was the first person on her block to get cable TV. People criticized Iona behind her back, but I had to respect her. Most people would have stuck Morton in a home if they could have afforded it, and the Thygersons were rolling in money. But Iona took no easy ways out: Morton stayed with her. If cartoons were what it took to keep him there, it was fine with me.

Morton may have been happy, but today Iona was hopping mad. She led us to the geranium bed in front of the house and pointed accusingly. Sure enough, the fuzzy leaves were turning yellow. Things looked bad for Morton Thygerson.

"How do you know it wasn't a stray dog?" Alex had a point: People in Salt Lake City have never heard of leash laws.

"The mailman caught him. There he was, piddling in the flowers for all the world to see. Sometimes I just want to whack it off."

Whacking it off wasn't an original idea. Ralph Moody, who'd tended the Paradise Vue flower beds for years, caught Brother Thygerson in the act one day and told the bishop the same thing. But Morton remained intact. As long as he was in one piece, no flower bed was safe.

Iona ruthlessly pinched off a few yellowed geranium leaves and then led us inside. She poured us some red punch and set out a plate of brownies. There wasn't a woman in the ward who would let the Relief Society president cross her threshold without being fed, and we ate whatever was offered. I hadn't had breakfast yet and the idea of sugar was unappetizing, but I drank my punch and ate my brownie with gusto.

While Alex and I ate, Morton wandered downstairs to the kitchen. His shirt was inside-out, and there was a gap in the front where he'd put a wrong button in a button-hole. He walked through the room with a wave, but it was plain he didn't recognize us. Morton had known us for years.

"I don't see much you can do about this," Alex said after he got out of earshot. "You can't just pick out a particular geranium and tell him to piddle on that one. If he could remember to do that, he'd remember to use the toilet."

"What about diapers for adults?" I asked.

"I'm afraid to try 'em," Iona admitted. "He still remembers enough to unzip before he goes. If he's wearing diapers, he may take off his clothes altogether to get free of them."

Iona had a point. Piddling on the geraniums was one thing; wandering starkers around the front yard was quite another. At times like this, I felt helpless in my ward job. As much as I wanted to help people, sometimes there wasn't anything I could do.

We hugged Iona and told her we'd visit her again. Then we drove up and down the streets of the ward, looking for someone else to see. As long as we were out, Alex reasoned, we might as well say hello to some other people.

The day was sweltering. Most people were indoors, which was certainly where I wanted to be. Don Antonio's beckoned me like a siren. We'd almost given up when Alex spotted Eve Parker, appearing from around the corner of her house with a trowel in hand.

Eve was in her early seventies. She was maybe six feet tall, which meant she must have been significantly taller than average in her heyday. For all that height, I'm sure she weighed less than I did.

She was a praying mantis of a woman — all arms and legs, with a long thorax of a body.

Eve would have been one of a kind in anyone's book, if there hadn't been two of her. Sure enough, right behind her was Eden, carrying an identical trowel and walking in step with an identical gait.

If I ever saw professional twins, they were Eve and Eden Parker. Eden was a widow who took her maiden name back the day she buried her husband. The two of them lived in Eden's marital house, dressing in identical clothes, doing identical things, and — as far as I knew — thinking identical thoughts.

The only way anyone could tell them apart was that Eve always wore a flower at the nape of her neck. Otherwise, they were so much alike that people who knew one of them probably wouldn't have realized there were two.

The Parker Twins had an interesting trait that made them fun to watch — what Eve Parker would start, Eden Parker would finish. If Eve made cookie dough, Eden baked the cookies. If Eve started a sentence, Eden broke in and ended it. They were a binary person, each woman seemingly incomplete without the other. They even spoke of themselves as *we*. You seldom heard an *I* out of either one of them.

Eve and Eden saw Alex and me at the same time. They broke into identical broad smiles and gave us duplicate waves. Then Eve took Alex's arm and Eden took mine, and they ushered us inside their communal home.

For a good fifteen minutes, the Parker Twins told us what was new in their lives. A daughter had opened a Hallmark shop. A grandbaby was cutting a tooth. One grandchild broke her arm falling off a garbage can. Although the progeny were Eden's, both sisters seemed to have an equal interest in them. How lucky, I thought, for the children to have three grandmothers.

As we were getting ready to leave, Eve's face clouded, then Eden's. "We suppose you've heard the rumor —"

"— Betty Jo Jennings has been spreading it. She says we were Siamese twins, joined at the hip and separated at birth."

"It's terrible," Eve said, with a mournful shake of her head. "Just terrible," Eden echoed, following the motion with her own cranium. "We don't know why Betty Jo says things like that." "I don't think Betty Jo can help it," Alex said. "Nobody believes anything like that anyway. Don't worry about it." We said our goodbyes and left, giving each of the Parker Twins a hug on the way out. Breaking the pattern, Alex hugged Eden first. Eve stood puzzled with outstretched arms.

"We'll have to have a little talk with Betty Jo," Alex said as we got in the car. "It won't do any good, of course. I don't know where that woman gets her stories."

Betty Jo Jennings was the scourge of the ward. She was a compulsive liar. She couldn't even tell the truth about what she had for dinner last night or when she went to bed. In Betty Jo's memory, casserole became pheasant under glass.

If Betty Jo lied on purpose, she would have subscribed to the Adolf Hitler philosophy of lies: the bigger the lie, the more likely it is to be believed. Betty Jo told whoppers, and if people had believed them she could have done some real damage.

But she tripped herself up on two accounts. First, her lies were so frequent that they punctuated her conversation like commas. People who first met Betty Jo might fall for a lie or two, but soon they realized she was lying randomly, without thinking about it, the way teenagers end every sentence with *you know*.

Second, Betty Jo was so far gone that she'd lie about a person while the person was in the room, pulling them into the story like an accomplice. I could never forget the time Betty Jo told Alex, right in front of me, that she'd seen Bishop Nebeker and me through an open window, kissing passionately in the Primary room. Never having even *been* in the Primary room with the bishop, I just sat there at the time and drank my Pepsi. But it did hurt her credibility. Once you'd heard Betty Jo tell a story about you in your own presence, you couldn't believe a word she said about anyone else. Since nobody believed Betty Jo, her lies were only a nuisance. She struck blows at many a reputation but, like the children's taunt, they all bounced back and stuck on her.

Amazingly enough, she was a popular person. She was almost always out shopping or going to movies with somebody or other. If anyone had a problem, Betty Jo was the first to help them out. She was good company. And even her lies weren't malicious. She would have been crushed to think her stories hurt people's feelings.

Today, Betty Jo was home when we knocked. She greeted us warmly. "Oh, the Re*lief* Society presidency!" she exclaimed. "This is a red-letter day for me. The bishop just left five minutes ago."

Alex didn't point out that Bishop Nebeker was camping in Kanab. It wouldn't have done any good. Betty Jo believed every word she said. Once something left her mouth, it was as true to Betty Jo as scripture.

"Let me get you some refreshment," she said, leaving Alex and me to entertain ourselves while she worked in the kitchen. I heard water running and then what sounded like a paper envelope ripping open. Then there was a sound of furious stirring. The spoon clinked as it hit the sides of the pitcher.

Out she came with three tall glasses of cherry red drink on a tray. "It's passion fruit juice," she said proudly. "Passion fruit's on sale this week at Smith's, and I squeezed the juice this morning."

Alex and I took the juice gratefully. It looked like Kool-Aid; it smelled like Kool-Aid; it tasted like Kool-Aid, and I saw it stain Alex's upper lip like Kool-Aid. But it was cold drink on a hot day, and that was all that mattered.

After Alex drained her glass, she asked Betty Jo what was new in her life.

"Well, I've been rather busy lately. A reporter from *People* magazine came here last week to write a story about that new strain of rose I developed. He couldn't get any pictures, because it rained the night before and knocked all the petals off. He'll have to come back after I get some more blossoms."

"What a pity," Alex murmured. "I do enjoy *People* magazine."

"I've been in it before, of course. Back when I saw the UFO over in Tooele. They gave me a two-page spread. It was very impressive."

I could almost see Betty Jo's nose growing. Without thinking I asked, "Do you have a copy to show us? I'd love to see your picture." Alex threw me a dirty look. *It does no good to confront Betty Jo,* the look said. *That was a cheap shot.*

I retracted my request quickly. "Don't go to the bother of getting it. We'd rather just visit you anyway — wouldn't we, Alex?"

Betty Jo settled back in her chair, looking relieved. Alex gave me a radiant smile. I'd been forgiven.

"Tell us about the UFO incident," Alex said. "I don't think I've ever heard it." Happily, Betty Jo launched into a tale of little yellow men with suction-tipped fingers and three eyes. They'd abducted her into their saucer when she was on her way home from Wendover. They'd taken a blood sample and given her a pregnancy test, and then they'd let her go.

"And of course the Tooele sheriff saw the whole thing," she finished. "He got a color picture of the ship and two pictures of the little yellow men with three eyes each. That's how I got my spread in *People.*"

"That's fascinating," I said. Betty Jo did have a way with a story. "It must have been exciting for you."

"*I'll* say. It was even more exciting than eating dinner with Richard Nixon."

"And eating dinner with Richard Nixon would be pretty exciting itself," Alex said. "You'll have to tell us about it sometime. You have such an interesting life." She put her punch glass on a coaster and felt around on the floor for her purse. "This has been terrific, but I guess we'd better go. We're visiting lots of the ladies today. We just left Eve and Eden Parker. Aren't they cute?"

"Yes," Betty Jo said, "and so much alike! That's what happens when you're a Siamese twin. Separated at birth. Imagine!"

"Yes," I said. "Imagine!"

Alex said, "By the way, I don't think Eve and Eden like people to think of them as Siamese twins. Let's just keep that our secret, shall we?"

We hugged Betty Jo, and off we went. Alex had handled her masterfully. Betty Jo may have been a horrible liar, but she knew how to keep a secret.

Alex drove me to Don Antonio's. After establishing that it was her treat, I ordered the most expensive thing on the menu. Alex and I played that game all the time. The person who paid would order something cheap, like a taco or a bean burrito. The person being treated ordered carne asada or fajitas. I got the carne asada today, washing it down with two Cokes and a sarsaparilla. Alex picked distractedly at her cheese enchilada.

"Bess and I went visiting last night."

"Of course you did. You and Emma go visiting on Thursday nights. You and Bess go visiting on Wednesday nights. You and I go visiting in the daytime. Who'd you see?"

"Undine Halliday. She just took first prize in a garden show. Maureen Hollberg — her sprinkler's acting up again." She paused for a moment and chased some melted cheddar around her plate with a taco chip. "Oh — and Reynolds Cleese."

"When did *he* join the Relief Society?"

Alex finally caught the cheese with her taco chip and scooped it up. "Since when do you have to be a member of the Relief Society to get relief from it?" she asked. "Those kids are driving him crazy. He does his laundry after midnight because that's the only time he has to himself. He had a pile of dirty dishes in the sink, halfway up to the ceiling. Bess washed them for him, and he wouldn't have been happier if she'd given him a million dollars."

"Sounds like Reynolds Cleese needs a maid."

"Reynolds Cleese needs a wife," she said. "He asked about you. He thinks you're a fox."

"He *is* desperate, isn't he? I hope you told him I'm unavailable."

Alex took a sip of Diet Coke. "I did, but I shouldn't have. You need to get on with your life."

"It's my life, Alex. Let me decide when to get on with it."

Despite her hints about Reynolds Cleese, Alex was preoccupied all during lunch. She didn't say a word all the way to my house afterwards. I wondered what was wrong, but I didn't ask. Alex had a way of telling me things in her own time.

As she pulled in my driveway to let me out, she let out a long breath and said, "Iona Thygerson's going to die soon."

"*Iona* Thygerson? You mean Morton, don't you?" Alex shook her head. "Come on! She's as healthy as a horse. Where did you come up with that one?" And then, remembering Alex's calling, "Did you get that from inspiration?"

"Nope. Simple biology. Have you ever noticed anything odd about the way I hug people?" I nodded, remembering the way she put one arm around them and squeezed their biceps with the other hand. I'd been meaning to ask her about it.

"Years ago, I noticed that old people, before they die, lose something in their upper arms. Maybe it's muscle tone — maybe it's just fat. Whatever it is, something that you feel in most people isn't there anymore when they're about to die."

"Where in the world did you come up with that? It sounds like folklore to me."

"It isn't folklore. Folklore is something you hear from somebody else. This is something I figured out on my own. It always seems to work."

"Well, I hope it doesn't work this time. I'd hate to think of poor Morton in a home. No hospital staff would tolerate Morton's piddling in a corner."

"They wouldn't put up with the cartoons, either," Alex said. "I hate to think of that, too, but it's going to happen. I've never known the arm test to fail. I wish I'd never discovered it."

I went inside and wrote the conversation in my journal, planning to show it to her and Iona a year or two up the road and laugh about the prophecy together. But I never did get a chance to do it. Three weeks later, Iona Thygerson died in her sleep.

# 8
# Emma

Alex called me on a Thursday night, sevenish. I could barely make out her voice, and at first I thought she was an obscene phone caller. No such luck. Alex had just returned from Insta-Care. At the age of 43, she had the mumps.

I got a chuckle out of that, but the chuckle died fast when Alex asked me to go visiting with Emma. I'd only been visiting with Emma once before. That was the night we visited two cancer patients, one after the other.

The first one we saw that night was Helen Richardson, who'd had her leg amputated for bone cancer before the doctors learned it had already spread. Emma told Helen she knew *just* what she was going through, because she'd sprained her ankle once and had been wadded up in bandages for *months on end*.

Then we'd stopped to see Susan Fox, who'd just had a double mastectomy. Emma told Susan she couldn't imagine anything worse than being scarred for life the way Susan was — "I'd feel like *half* a woman." Susan was crying when we left, and Alex had to call her three times before she'd let anybody from the Relief Society presidency in to see her again.

I was so upset with Emma that night at the hospital that I cancelled our third appointment and told Alex I didn't want to go visiting with Emma again. Instead of being sympathetic, Alex thought I was exaggerating because I didn't like Emma. She even wrote off the Susan Fox episode as post-op hysteria on Susan's part. When the subject was Emma, everything I said to Alex fell on deaf ears.

So this time when Alex asked me to visit with Emma, I didn't bother arguing with her. Instead, I dragged myself to Emma's house with a martyr's countenance. Emma greeted me like a long-lost friend. I gritted my teeth and feigned cheerfulness.

"Come on *in*, Amy," she said through all those perfect teeth. "It's just *won*derful to see you. Of course I'm not ready yet. I have to put on a little makeup. I feel just *na*ked without makeup, don't you?"

I smiled weakly and settled down on the living room sofa, thumbing through an *Ensign* magazine and glancing surreptitiously at my watch while Emma primped. In exactly seventeen minutes, she reappeared. "How do I look?" She waited for the compliment.

I didn't give her one. Seventeen minutes earlier, she'd been beautiful. Now she looked like a blonde raccoon. "You look like Emma to me," was all I could manage.

But in Emma's opinion, that was the best compliment I could give her. She gave me a friendly smile. "You know, Amy, you could be pretty, too. I could help you." She reached up and smoothed my hair. I shook my head, and the hair fluffed out again. Emma ignored the gesture.

"Look at those clothes! Layers everywhere. How many scarves are you wearing? You look like Isadora Duncan." Emma walked around me, inspecting every miserable inch. "You don't look all that good in green, you know. What color *is* that lipstick, anyway? And why is a splotch of it on your nose?"

I rubbed the lipstick off my nose, hoping to distract Emma's attention from my pink high-tops. It didn't work. She looked at my shoes and shook her head. "Amy, I could be a great help to you in the fashion department. Do what I do. Dress like me."

I looked Emma up and down. She was dressed in her attorney clothes — the requisite beige skirt, a white blouse, a navy jacket, a muted paisley scarf. It looked good on Emma, but I wasn't Emma. It annoyed me that Emma never could see that. "I want to look like Amy," I said. "It was good enough for Tim. Why isn't it good enough for you?"

Emma sighed heavily. "You always ruin everything," she said. Now she was pouting, giving me a petulant look that had probably been practiced in front of a mirror. "I was in a perfectly good mood, and you had to mention *him*. All I wanted to do was help you."

"We haven't got time for that, Emma. We have to go visiting. Let's do it and get it over with."

Emma and I walked outside, passing her car in the garage as she made a beeline for mine. There was never any question who would drive when Emma went on an excursion. Years ago, before I'd even met Emma, she'd broken her arm. She found it was so easy to get rides wherever she wanted that when the cast came off, the car stayed in the garage. Now Emma would let someone drive her somewhere in it every month or so, just to keep it running. But Emma was never seen behind the wheel, and she never paid a penny for gasoline for the people who drove her around in their own automobiles. Just having Emma's company in the car, she no doubt reasoned, was reward enough for her chauffeurs.

On the night Alex had the mumps, Emma had scheduled three appointments. Three seemed to be a magic number for Relief Society visits. We never went to two homes or to four. Emma had chosen three young people. True to her word, she was staying as far from the blue-hairs as she could get.

Our first visit was to Nelda Budge, a divorced mother of two children. I didn't know her well because she worked during the day and had to be visited at night. She lived in a basement apartment and commuted down the hill to a local elementary school, where she taught kindergarten.

Nelda welcomed us into her apartment with a broad smile. She ushered us inside, past the children who were coloring at the kitchen table. Even with two children living there, her apartment was spotless.

"It is such an honor to have you here," she said as she settled us down in the living room. "The children and I are always happy to have representatives of the Church in our home. Peter, Andrea — say hello to the Relief Society sisters." Peter and Andrea looked up and said hello in unison.

Sitting in Nelda's living room, I felt as if I'd been plunked down in the middle of a 1950s television show. The scene was in color, and there weren't any commercials, but the rest of the situation seemed rehearsed and unreal. Even Nelda's words were strange, in a way I couldn't immediately place. As she and Emma exchanged pleasantries, I listened to the words themselves, instead of their content. Then I had it: Nelda's conversation sounded stilted because every syllable was pronounced with a dictionary precision. She didn't use contractions when she spoke. She didn't emphasize any syllable of a word more than another. She didn't even drop her *g*'s or slur her words in any normal pattern. Her voice sounded almost computerized.

"...and Peter has begun to take vi-o-lin lessons," she said pleasantly. "Peter, will you please perform for the ladies?" Peter obediently placed his crayon on the table and fetched his violin. Fixing a performer's look on Emma and then me, the child played a version of *Twinkle, Twinkle Little Star* that was as technically correct as his mother's speech. It had never occurred to me before listening to Peter Budge play *Twinkle, Twinkle Little Star* that the child's tune could be played with passion, but Peter played the song with such a lack of emotion that it sounded as if it had been performed by a robot. It gave me the creeps.

When Peter had returned to his coloring — using the correct colors and coloring inside the lines — I waited for a break in the conversation and asked Nelda how she was getting along. "Fine, as always," she said perkily, but I got the feeling that something was wrong. She reminded me of a violin string wound a little too tightly, and the perkiness seemed edged with hysteria. I chewed a homemade cookie and let Emma do the talking for both of us, observing Nelda in action until it was time to go.

"Isn't Nelda in*spir*ing?" Emma asked as we drove off, with the mother and two children still waving goodbye behind us. "How that *brute* of a husband could leave her with those two little children is be*yond* comprehension. And those children are so perfect. Wouldn't you love to have children like that?"

"I don't know," I said. "Don't you think the children were a little *too* perfect?"

"Amy, there's no such thing as being too perfect. You need to change your attitude. Every silver lining has a cloud for you. Please *try* to be a little more cheerful at Janna Lee's house. She has problems enough without you sitting there, making things worse."

Obediently, I tried to cheer up for Janna Lee. Emma was right about one thing: Janna Lee Simonsen didn't need any aggravation from me. So when we crossed her threshold, I tried to be as relentlessly cheerful as Emma was. Emma noticed the effort and gave me a satisfied look.

Janna Lee Simonsen was fearful of things. She always looked as if she were afraid life was going to sneak up behind her and bite her on the tail, and she didn't want that to happen. She was so eager to please, you could talk her into anything. You could tell her the moon was made of steamed cabbage, and she'd smile and nod hopefully. She wasn't stupid, just scared. And if I sometimes got annoyed because she never, never gave her own opinion, there were other people who liked her just the way she was.

Janna Lee was a sucker for any nasty assignment, because she was so insecure she didn't know how to say no. Did your kids have the flu but you wanted to go to ZCMI's Christmas toy sale anyway? Janna Lee would tend them, and her own kids would have the flu on Christmas morning. Was there a Primary class so full of juvenile delinquents that nobody would teach it? Ask Janna Lee. She'd be scared to take the kids — and she sure as heck couldn't do anything with them — but she'd never turn you down. Even bishops used Janna shamelessly. She was so *willing* to be used.

Janna Lee was so desperate for friends that any overture was gratefully accepted. Emma exploited that desperation ruthlessly. Emma would never have to drive a car again as long as Janna Lee Simonsen lived in the ward.

Often Emma wouldn't even accompany Janna Lee on her own errands. Instead she'd give her a grocery list and a smile. Janna Lee fueled herself with the smile and went to the supermarket by herself to save Emma's precious time. No job was so odious that Emma felt guilty about dumping it in Janna Lee's lap.

The way Emma tried to turn everybody into copies of herself, it was no surprise she succeeded with Janna Lee. Emma cut and tinted Janna Lee's hair to look like hers. She made Janna Lee up to look like a perfect copy, complete with those raccoon eyes Emma thought were so becoming. She even chose Janna Lee's wardrobe to look just like her own, but after bearing three children Janna Lee didn't have the figure for those tailored, expensive outfits Emma wore in court.

For all Emma's efforts, Janna Lee looked like a mouse. Her beady eyes, outlined with Emma's makeup, reminded me of rodent eyes. She quivered when she talked, the way a mouse does when it's afraid. She even held her hands up in front of her face like a mouse does when it stands on its hind legs and sniffs the air.

If Janna Lee was a mouse, Emma was her prize piece of cheese. As she greeted us at the door, all Janna Lee's attention focused on Emma. "You look lovely tonight, Emma. You always look lovely."

"Why, *thank* you," Emma said, beaming at Janna Lee. She walked past Janna Lee and settled herself in Stan Simonsen's easy chair, the place of honor in the living room. Emma perched in Stan's chair like a queen on her throne. I found a seat at the end of the sofa.

"Where are the children?" I couldn't help noticing that all three of them were gone, which was a little strange so late at night. Janna Lee, remembering I was in the house, blinked several times in my direction. "Oh, I had Stan take them to the movies. I didn't want anything to ruin our little visit. You just relax, and I'll bring you some pound-cake and peach nectar. It's your favorite recipe, Emma — the one you gave me."

Emma and I didn't have anything to say to each other, so we sat in an uncomfortable silence while Janna Lee was gone. When Janna Lee returned, Emma lit up like a light bulb. I settled back and ate my piece of cake as I watched Emma perform.

"Turn around, Janna Lee. Let me *see* you." Janna Lee stood up and obligingly submitted herself to Emma's inspection. Janna Lee wore a beige skirt and a white blouse. Her scarf wasn't paisley, but another muted pattern. I looked around the room for a navy jacket, but I didn't see one anywhere. The more I looked at Janna Lee, the more depressed I got.

"Looks like you and Emma are twins tonight," I said.

"Yes." Janna Lee was delighted I'd noticed. "Emma's teaching me how to buy new clothes."

Emma took a dainty sip of nectar. "Have you finished that book I told you to read?"

"I'm on the last chapter. It's been a big help."

I changed positions on the sofa. The Simonsen sofa was old and lumpy, and it was hard to sit in one position for more than a minute or two. Emma knew what she was doing when she appropriated the easy chair. "What book is that, Janna Lee?"

"*Dress for Success.* Emma was right — it's changing my whole life."

"How's it doing that?" It had been years since I'd read the book, but I couldn't remember any chapters telling mothers who didn't have careers how to dress while they cleaned up after their children.

"Oh, it's given me so much more confidence. You know," Janna Lee confided, "I didn't know how to dress. I wasn't wearing the right fabrics, or the right colors, or the right makeup. My hair wasn't cut right, either. I don't know what I'd do without Emma."

"I hear that from a lot of people, Janna Lee," I said. Emma chose to take that as a compliment, and she gave me a regal smile from the comfort of her throne. But despite Janna Lee's delight and Emma's satisfaction, I felt increasingly uncomfortable. In a desperate effort to change the subject, I fell into the oldest rut in the world. "Well, Janna Lee, what do you think of the weather?"

From the frightened look on Janna Lee's face, I knew I'd made a mistake: I'd trapped Janna Lee into giving an opinion without first telling her how I felt. So without giving her a chance to commit herself, I added, "I'm crazy about the rain. I love the way it smells and the way it sounds."

"I like the rain, too. It's my favorite weather. It does smell nice, doesn't it?"

"Well, I *hate* the rain," Emma thundered from across the room. "I think it's smelly, and it sounds like static. I wish it would *never* rain. *I* like the sunshine."

Janna Lee looked from Emma to me and then back to Emma in a panic. "Oh. Yes. I'd forgotten about sunshine. *Sun*shine is my favorite weather. Rain does smell like mildew, and I can't hear the television when it's raining hard outside. Emma has a point there."

I sank back on the sofa, pretending to be engrossed in the ice that had chilled my peach nectar. It was cruel to put Janna Lee in a group with differing opinions. I let Emma and Janna Lee visit until it was time to go, keeping just close enough tabs on the conversation to insert an occasional "Yes" or "Um-hmm" at appropriate spots. Free of any more conflicting ideas, Janna Lee was able to agree with everything Emma said.

Emma rewarded her protegee by combing her hair and trimming her bangs for her before we left. When we walked out the door, Janna Lee looked radiant from all the attention.

"Isn't Janna Lee coming out of her shell?" Emma asked as we drove away. "She's turning into another person."

"I noticed that. She's starting to remind me of you." Again, Emma took the words as a compliment. It was almost impossible to insult Emma Austen.


Jason and Molly Peeples were newlyweds in the ward. They'd lived in Paradise Vue for about six months, and Molly was our Relief Society social relations teacher. She had a good sense of humor, and everyone looked forward to her lessons. Other than that, I didn't know much about her.

When we got to Molly's house and saw it was dark, Emma's good mood evaporated quickly. "I *made* an appointment. How *rude*."

"Maybe they're home, Emma. Maybe they've got a light on in the back somewhere. Let's at least knock."

"And stand there in the *rain?* You do it."

Leaving Emma in the car, I walked to the Peeples door and rang the bell. Almost immediately, I heard noise from inside. It sounded like giggling. Then Jason Peeples called from somewhere, "I'm *com*ing!" That inspired more giggles and some loud scurrying around. Lights went on inside.

When Jason got to the door, he was in his bathrobe. "Oh, hi," he said. He recognized me from the ward, but I don't think he had any idea who I was.

"I'm Amy Hardisty," I said, holding out my hand to be shaken. "From the Relief Society. We had an appointment with Molly, but if this is a bad time we'll come back another night."

"Oh, nonsense," Emma said from behind me. She'd obviously gotten out of the car when she saw the lights turn on, and now she was ready for a visit. She gave the man an ingratiating smile. "Wouldn't you like us to visit you *now?*"

"You bet!" Jason Peeples took one look at Emma and only barely remembered he had a wife inside the house. He invited us in and excused himself, calling Molly to tell her we were here.

When Molly arrived, her normally pale Irish face was as red as a radish. She was dressed, but it looked as if she'd recently been undressed. The big tip-off was her feet, which were shod in two different pairs of loafers. One was a penny loafer, and the other shoe had a tassel. As I looked at them, I thought they might both be left shoes.

We sat down together and started talking Relief Society talk, but we didn't exchange more than a few sentences before a fully dressed Jason Peeples reappeared and took a seat. He was wearing about a handful of expensive cologne — Paco Rabanne, maybe. I didn't know if he'd put on the cologne in lieu of a bath, or if he'd done it to impress Emma. For Molly's sake, I hoped it wasn't the latter.

As soon as Jason sat down, Emma shifted position to face him. "We're already friends with Molly," she said. "Why don't you tell us about *you?*" She batted her eyes and gave him her most captivating smile. I looked quickly over at Molly to see how she was taking it, but Molly had all the confidence of a newlywed. She didn't even know Emma was flirting.

Jason Peeples knew Emma was flirting, and he loved it. Forgetting Molly and I were in the room, he told Emma all about himself, from his mission in Brazil to his basketball career at Utah State. Molly, smitten with her husband, looked as proud as if *she'd* been the center at Utah State. Meanwhile, sexual energy was flying between Emma and Jason like sparks from a Roman candle.

When Jason finished talking, he leaned forward toward Emma. "Now, tell us about *you.*" Emma was all too ready to talk about herself, although she edited her biography to omit any mention of all the men who loved her. When she was talking about herself, Emma was her most captivating. Molly was so engrossed with Emma that I caught her practicing the way Emma cocked her head when she was making a point. First it was Janna Lee — now, Molly. The way things were going, eventually I'd be the only woman in Paradise Vue who didn't act like Emma Austen.

When Jason and Emma had exchanged their life stories, they sat back and smiled at each other. Nobody asked for my biography, and I didn't volunteer it. When, after an hour, I told Emma it was time for us to go, the other three looked annoyed with me for making the suggestion.

We walked to the door in groups of two, with Molly and me leading the way and Emma following behind with Jason. As we got to the door, Molly turned to me and said, "You're so lucky to be visiting with Emma. She's so cheerful all the time. Don't you wish you could be just like her?" Standing beyond Molly's vision, Jason Peeples ogled Emma appreciatively. Emma, always aware of the man in the room, gave him a coy wink.

*

I didn't expect anything to develop between Emma and Jason Peeples, and nothing ever did. But the situation with Nelda Budge and her family made me nervous. When Alex got well, she paid a few private visits to Nelda. She also had Nelda's visiting teachers keep an eye on her.

Nelda moved out of the ward a few months later, and I never heard of her again. But occasionally, whenever a violin soloist at church has his strings wound a little too tightly, I wonder what happened to her and her two perfect little children.

# 9
# A Vengeful Dishwasher

**H**aving an industrial dishwasher in the ward kitchen was a dubious blessing. People purposely didn't learn how to work it, because once they knew how they'd be expected to wash dishes at every ward function. So when the annual Harvest Dinner rolled around in mid-October, I knew where the Relief Society presidency would be.

The dinner fell on a beautiful October evening. The walnut leaves were knee-deep behind my house, and all I wanted to do was stay home, harvest walnuts, and rake the leaves in the twilight. Samson liked to help, although helping consisted of looking for field mice in the rotting leaves next to the ground. He also liked to eat the concord grapes Tim and I had planted years ago along the fence. Heaven knows *I* never ate them.

But at the stroke of five, I put my rake away and got dressed for church. Samson followed me around the house forlornly as I pulled on my clothes. Finally I cooked him a Lean Cuisine, and he abandoned me immediately to dine in the kitchen. Samson had a weakness for salisbury steak.

Paradise Vue had two ward dinners in the course of a year. The winter one was a catered affair for adults only, where everyone sat around in Sunday clothes, ate stuffed cornish hen, and pretended to

94

have fun. The Harvest Dinner was a lot more interesting. The children were invited, which increased the noise level by about twenty decibels. Some of the older people didn't like the racket, but I thought it made the evening much more festive and uninhibited.

The food at the Harvest Dinner was also an adventure. A telephone committee assigned each family to contribute a casserole or salad or sheetcake to the potluck meal. Some of the food was excellent, with women taking pride in their contributions in case people wondered who'd made the halibut au gratin.

Of course, some of the food wasn't so good. Some of us couldn't cook. A few people didn't have enough money in the household budget to afford anything but macaroni. Everyone who attended the dinner was judge and jury, picking over the filled casserole dishes to fill their paper plates. By the end of the evening it was easy to see which dishes were popular — and which ones weren't.

That year, I was on sheetcake detail. With a lot of assistance from Duncan Hines, I made a chocolate cake that looked almost normal, except for a few bumps and dips and a big crack along the surface of the cake. I hid the blemishes with extra frosting and crushed peppermint candy, and I was pretty excited with the finished product. I carried it carefully into the church kitchen, where Alex immediately ruined it by dipping a finger in the frosting to taste.

"This looks pretty good for you, Amy. Did you buy it at Smith's?"

"I made it myself. Duncan Hines. And it *looked* pretty good until you put your finger in it."

Alex sucked the remnants of chocolate frosting off her finger. "You're lucky you only had to bring cake. I got to bring a casserole. It's chicken." She held it up for my inspection. It contained chicken, peas, sliced egg, some mystery ingredients, and some brown chunks that could only be the chopped mushrooms from condensed cream of mushroom soup. Most of the casseroles at any given Paradise Vue potluck dinner would contain condensed soup of some kind — usually either mushroom or cream of chicken.

The back door opened with a clatter. Emma walked in, carrying a sheetcake of her own. Hers was a masterpiece, covered with pink frosting rosettes and little green frosting leaves. Alex didn't stick her finger in Emma's frosting, which said something to me: Emma's cake was so pretty that Alex didn't want to ruin it.

"*Hi*, Alex! Hello, Amy!" she said, lowering her cake to the counter with a flourish. When it sat next to mine, I could easily see how smooth hers was on top — and just where the crack was across the top of mine. "I'm all ready for the cake contest. I took the day off work to bake this cake, and it's going to win."

"*What* cake contest? Nobody told me this was a contest."

Emma scrutinized my cake. "It was *in* the ward newspaper. Don't you read the ward newspaper? Well, I don't think you'll have to worry. That's obviously a mix cake. *Mix* cakes don't count." She gave me a sunny smile and left the kitchen. I stabbed her in the back with an evil look.

It seemed as if everyone knew about the cake contest but me. Delta Mae Eliason produced a lemon angel-food that was about three miles high. Loabelle Hickey made a checkerboard cake in three colors. (I later heard it tasted horrible, but it did look pretty.) Georgina Staples made a three-layer chocolate torte that looked like a winner to me. Emma was in for some stiff competition.

Alex and I spent a half hour setting up the kitchen and turning on switches so the dishwasher would have hot water when we needed it. Women dropped in to say hello and leave their contributions for the dinner before moving on to the cultural hall, which is the Mormon euphemism for *gym*. We looked over each salad and cake and casserole appreciatively, offering a compliment about each.

The most interesting offering of the night, however, was not donated by a Relief Society member. Omer Smoot brought it in, and Alex and I inspected it in wonder.

"My! That looks professional. What *is* it?" Alex asked. "I didn't know your wife could cook like that."

"Hawley didn't cook it. I did." He puffed his chest out with pride. "It's a chilled garbanzo bean salad. The green flecks are cilantro."

We took one look at that salad — fit for a gourmet meal — and knew that no matter how hungry the Paradise Vue members were, they were never going to eat it. People in our neighborhood didn't *recognize* a salad unless it was propped up by lettuce or held together with Jell-O.

"That's beautiful, Omer," I said. "I hope I get to taste some. We'll try to squeeze to the front of the line and get some before it's gone." Omer beamed. With a little wave at Alex and me, he disappeared.

A few minutes before the dinner was due to start, we went to the cultural hall to get our places in line. The cavernous room had been magically transformed by the decorating committee into a cultural hall with balloons in it. Halloween decorations were taped to the walls. A scarecrow was woefully propped against a lone bale of hay at center court, bolstered by a few fat pumpkins. Children ran everywhere, trying to pull down balloons for themselves. Most of them were successful. The noise level exceeded the worst nightmares of our older ward members.

To our dismay, there were already about three hundred people ahead of us in the buffet line. Alex surveyed the crowd ahead of us. "I hope you're not hungry," she said. "We won't have much of a selection. Last time I was this far back, everything was gone by the time I got to the buffet table. All I got to eat was three flavors of Jell-O."

"I hate Jell-O."

"That's because you don't know how to make it. I've got a better idea. Let's pour punch at the buffet table instead of eating. We can visit the Relief Society ladies that way. After we've washed all the dishes, I'll take us to Don Antonio's for dinner."

"*You'll* take us?"

"I'll drive. It's your turn to treat."

We put our plates back and stood at the foot of the buffet table, where we dipped out hundreds of cups of homemade root beer. Alex had trouble with the ladles, which were designed for right-handed pourers. She spilled some root beer from every cup she poured, but nobody seemed to mind. Everybody liked Alex.

As the procession of ward members passed us, we got to exchange snatches of conversation. Doris Belcher said her arthritis
was better, but Shelby Tucker confided that her pet schnauzer, Phi-
deaux, had died. The Ellstrotts were moving to St. George in November, tired of Salt Lake City winters. Everyone who passed
through the line had good news or bad to tell the Relief Society
presidency.

"Written any good limericks lately?" It was the widower,
Reynolds Cleese.

"Nope. Can't rhyme to save my life. You have me confused
with Alex. Have some root beer," I said. He held up a full cup.
"Well, have some more." I handed him another one. He grinned
and balanced the second one on his plate.

I reached down to fill a cup for Leona Drinkwater, but he didn't
move along. He cleared his throat and said, "I have tickets for the
ballet on Friday. Would you like to go with me?"

"No thanks," I said. "Ballet sounds deadly. You need to move
along now. You're blocking the line." I finished filling Leona's cup
of root beer and said hello to her. Next to me, I saw Alex and
Reynolds Cleese exchange shrugs.

I had barely recovered from Reynolds Cleese and passed out
root beer to the Byrd kids when Emma reached the punch bowl.
She nodded toward Dorothy Byrd and said, "*That* woman gets a lot
of mileage out of a dollar's worth of Jell-O."

I had no idea what Emma was talking about, and I said that.
"*Well,*" she explained, "she brought a Jell-O salad to the dinner. *All*
she brought was a Jell-O salad to the dinner. And look how high
she's loaded her own plate. *And* her husband's eating just as much.
*And* the kids are, too." She gave the whole family a look of disgust,
as if the Byrds had taken food out of her mouth.

"It all evens out in the end," I said. "I brought a whole cake,
and there's only one person in my family. You brought a whole
cake, and there's only one person in your family. Alex brought a
whole casserole, and she's not eating anything."

"You always have to disagree with me, don't you?" She didn't
take the root beer I offered, but instead stood silent until Alex was

free. Then, moving over to Alex, she acted as if the exchange between us had never taken place.

"*My!* Look at the kitchen help! Having fun, ladies?" Emma smiled innocently. She picked up an empty cup and held it out to be filled.

Alex laughed and poured Emma's drink. A few drops splashed, and Emma jumped back as if the liquid were battery acid. But Alex didn't see the gesture; she was already looking down the line for the next customer.

There were days I felt more charitable about Emma than others. The night of the Harvest Dinner, everything she said angered me. I was so attuned to her that night that everywhere I looked, there she was, flitting from single man to single man with the dedication of a worker bee. People watched her admiringly. I watched them watching her, and I was envious — not of what Emma was, but of how they looked at her.

After every plate was filled and the root beer was gone, Alex and Bess and I went to the kitchen to wash Paradise Vue's heavy china plates. We surveyed the buffet table as we walked past it, hoping there was something left to eat. Only one dish still had any food in it — poor Omer Smoot's garbanzo bean salad. Two scoops were gone, a big one and a smaller one. I could imagine Omer taking a big helping with gusto, and Hawley taking a smaller one out of loyalty.

Feeling sorry for Omer, I took the salad to the kitchen with me and scooped out servings of it for Alex and Bess and me. It was an amazing salad, with Italian plum tomatoes and Anaheim chilies and more than a hint of garlic. Before Omer claimed his bowl at the end of the evening, I dished up a big baggie of his salad to take home. I didn't want his feelings to be hurt, seeing how little of his salad was gone.

"Isn't it interesting, how this was the best stuff on the table and nobody even tasted it?" Alex talked through a mouthful of garbanzo beans. A bit of cilantro stuck to one of her front teeth.

Bess was less enthusiastic. "It looks so *different*. Are you sure this is okay?" She moved it around with her fork, but she didn't eat it.

"If you don't want it, Bess, I'll take it." After seeing three hundred plates of food pass under my nose, I was starving. Bess gratefully upended her bowl in mine, and I ate both helpings. I smelled like green onions and garlic for the rest of the night.

When we finished our salad, we started working on the dishes. I ran the dishwasher, scraping the plates and arranging them in the plastic baskets before running each load through the machine. Alex and Bess stood on the other end, drying the dishes as they came out. We desperately needed help, but Emma was nowhere to be found. Finally she arrived. Mentally, I breathed a sigh of relief: the dishes had to be stacked pretty high when I even welcomed Emma's help.

But instead of helping, Emma leaned against a counter, first checking to see that the counter was clean and dry. Alex and Bess and I were elbow deep in soapsuds, but Emma had come for a visit.

I waited for Alex to enlist Emma's help, but she didn't. She seemed glad for Emma's company. Bess didn't say anything, either. Then I realized they were both at the other end of the dishwasher, drying silverware. They had no idea how stacked up I was on my end.

"I'm so glad you're here, Emma," I said as sweetly as I could. "Do you want to load the dishwasher or scrape the dishes? Or dry? Here's a dishtowel." I threw her the towel. It was clean, but she let it fall to the floor without touching it, as if it were dripping with grease and infected with plague.

"Amy," she said patiently. "This is a silk blouse. I can't wash dishes in a *silk* blouse."

I looked at her incredulously. "You *came* here to wash dishes, Emma."

"Well, she can't do it in a silk blouse," Alex said. "What's gotten into you, Amy? We'll just have to do it for her." And then, to Emma, "Go out with everyone and mingle. You can be the Relief Society presence in the cultural hall."

Emma gave me a triumphant smile as she marched out the kitchen. I couldn't believe it. The whole world always sprang to Emma's assistance. Nobody ever did my job for me.

Eventually, we were saved by some members of the Elders Quorum. The Relief Society presidency always had to wash the dishes, and the Elders Quorum usually did the rest of the clean-up. Leo Byrd, Dell's older brother, joined me at the dishwasher. Men seemed to like the big, industrial machine.

Despite his reading handicap, Leo Byrd had attended BYU on a football scholarship. He came back to Paradise Vue six years later, after completing a mission, starting as quarterback on a winning team, and getting his college degree. Leo still couldn't read worth a darn, so after graduation he lent his name to a football theme restaurant in Bountiful. He wasn't married, and the single girls in the Relief Society considered him a prime catch. At age thirty-two, he still lived at home.

"How's the restaurant business, Leo?" I blew a lock of hair out of my eyes, but it flopped right back in.

He grabbed two plates and scraped them at once, with a massive stroke. "Not bad. How's the art business?"

"Not bad. Well, I still haven't sold anything." I tried again to blow the hair away. Again I was unsuccessful.

Leo scraped another handful of dishes. "Can I ask you something? Friend to friend?"

"Sure, Leo." I was always glad to help him out. Tim had been Young Men's president when Leo was in high school. Leo had been around so much he was almost part of the family. "You can ask me anything."

He smiled broadly and reached for another handful of plates. "I knew I could. It's about Emma Austen. I'm crazy about her, Amy. You work with her, don't you?"

*You can ask me anything but this,* I thought. Even my own friends liked Emma more than they liked me. I wiped off my hands and stuck the lock of hair behind my ear, where it wouldn't come unstuck anytime soon. Then I sighed. "Sure do, Leo. What do you want to know?"

"Well, is she as perfect as I think she is? I've never seen a more beautiful woman."

"She is beautiful, Leo," I admitted. "I don't know about perfect."

I almost told Leo the truth, but he looked so smitten that I didn't have the heart to do it. Instead I wiped a glob of soapsuds from my cheek. "Almost everyone seems to think Emma's perfect, so I guess she is."

"I *knew* it! Do you think you could fix me up with her? I'd be eternally grapeful."

*Grapeful?* I thought, but I didn't say anything. Leo had probably read the word somewhere, or thought he had. I didn't want to embarrass him.

I also didn't want him going out with Emma, but it was none of my business. I pushed the button to reset the dishwasher for another load. "I'll talk to her, Leo, but I don't have much influence with Emma. You'd have better luck if you went through Alex."

We took a break from our dishwashing at the end of the evening, when a flurry of taped trumpet music signalled that the judges had the results of the cake-baking contest. Bess and Alex and I wiped our hands on our aprons and hurried out to the cultural hall to see the awards.

Emma stood near the front of the crowd, smiling graciously as she waited to claim her honor. The prizes themselves were pretty good, but it was more the celebrity that people wanted. People liked to see their names in the Paradise *Vuepoint*, the monthly ward newspaper that chronicled the achievements of every man, woman, and child in the ward. Shirley Pederson, the editor, once told me she'd write about Karma Stooble's parakeets if it would fill space, but people still thought a mention in the *Vuepoint* was a major achievement.

A replay of the taped trumpet heralded the awards, and the bishop stepped up to the microphone. "Testing!" he barked, tapping the microphone as if it hadn't been used all evening. "Testing!" He tapped the microphone two or three more times, and the sound of each tap ricocheted painfully around the cultural hall. The audience covered its ears in unison. Bishop Nebeker had a lot of charisma, but he didn't have much faith in microphones.

"First off, I'd like to tell you on behalf of the bishopric that no cake-baking contest in the history of Paradise Vue has attracted more — uh, delicious — entries." Light applause greeted the announcement. Emma smiled graciously. The microphone groaned with an ear-piercing wail, and we all covered our ears again while the bishop tapped the mouthpiece for silence.

"Well, the microphone seems to be acting up, so without further ado I'd like to present the awards. Third prize goes to the Parker Twins, for their orange and lemon marble cake." The Parker Twins stepped forward as one person, looking identically humble and pleased. I could visualize Eve and Eden making the cake together, with one of them swirling in orange batter and the other swirling in lemon until the two flavors were intertwined.

"We only have one prize for them," the bishop continued, "— *The Joy of Cooking* cookbook. Eve, you're in charge of the recipes in the first half of the book. Eden, the second half of the book belongs to you."

Everyone laughed appreciatively — no one more so than the Parkers. With twin waves, they shyly acknowledged the applause and carried the book together back to their spot in the audience.

"Second prize this year is a well-deserved dinner for two at Finn's." There was a murmur of approval at that: the Activities Committee had outdone themselves finding prizes for this contest. "And the winner, for her cherry chocolate pudding cake, is Hawley Smoot!" Hawley broke into a broad grin and hurried up to the microphone, waggling her round fanny as she strode to the front.

The Smoot kitchen had been an active one for this dinner, and I was glad to see that at least one contribution was a success. Omer puffed out his chest when Hawley accepted her prize, as if he'd made the cake himself. Weeks later, Hawley told me that Omer *had* made the cake himself. It was only after the Harvest Dinner that Hawley let on Omer did all the cooking in the Smoot household.

After Hawley claimed her prize and rejoined Omer, the bishop tapped the microphone to get everyone's attention. Eric Watters played the trumpet call one last time over his boom box, signaling the announcement of the first-prize winner. Emma edged closer to the front of the crowd, ready to accept her award. She moved her lips silently as she waited, as if she were practicing an acceptance speech. I realized then that Emma put great store in that cake-baking contest.

"Before I announce the name of the winner," the bishop said, "I want to announce the prize. The Activities Committee has garnered a weekend for two at Sweetwater of *Bear Lake*." Everyone broke into applause, and Horace Ainsworth, the chairman of the Activities Committee, took a little bow. Horace made his living selling time-shares at Sweetwater.

When the hubbub died down, the bishop continued. "The winner is *Geneva P. Applegate,* for her authentic *New York cheese-cake.*"

The crowd parted like the red sea, leaving a path for Geneva Applegate as she claimed her weekend for two at Bear Lake. Only one person didn't move: Emma stood there stupefied. Geneva walked around her and turned graciously to the audience, as pleased as she was every time she won a ward cake-baking contest. She blew the ward a collective kiss, just like Dinah Shore used to do at the end of her television show.

Emma looked so crestfallen that I almost felt sorry for her, but I'd never seen anyone who deserved it more. I was still upset over how she'd wormed out of kitchen duty by wearing a silk blouse, and angry because nobody could see through Emma but me. I clapped hard for Geneva P. Applegate, wondering if she'd give me her recipe. I thought how much I'd like to cook that cheesecake when Emma was coming to visit.

Alex and Bess and I returned to the mounds of dishes in the kitchen. We'd barely loaded the dishwasher when Emma slammed into the room. Her face was red, but I couldn't tell if it was from crying or anger or embarrassment, or simply from the heat of the kitchen.

"It's not fair!" she said, stamping her foot. "I worked *all day* on my cake, and Geneva Applegate *stole* the prize. They shouldn't even let her *enter* the contests. She *always* wins. And she only uses the finest of ingredients." With that, she picked up her purse and stalked outside, leaving her cake platter behind.

"Poor Emma!" Bess shook her head mournfully as Emma slammed the door behind her. "She's right, you know. Geneva *does* use the finest of ingredients."

"That's not cheating," I said abruptly. Bess and Alex gave me startled looks.

"Of *course* it's not cheating." Bess patted my hand, but I drew it away. I hated it when she acted conciliatory. "I just feel a little sorry for Emma, is all. She wanted so much to win."

"We all have our little disappointments," I said, "but Emma gets more sympathy for hers than the rest of us do." I reached down to reset the dishwasher, and was knocked on my backside when a jolt of electricity crackled in a blue arc across the room. Alex and Bess ran to my aid, shutting off the electricity and pulling me to my feet.

There was a short in the dishwasher, and I was lucky the electrical current hadn't killed me. But I didn't think about it that way at the time. As we washed the rest of the dishes by hand, with Alex and Bess acting solicitous on my behalf, I felt as if even the dishwasher had punished me for disliking Emma.

After all the agony I'd suffered all evening, Don Antonio's was closed by the time we got there. Alex dropped me off at home, and I ate a big bowlful of Omer Smoot's garbanzo bean salad in bed by myself.

My arm tingled painfully for the rest of the night.

# 10
# Pal Joey

The mothers of Paradise Vue were like mothers anywhere. They carried their children inside their bodies for nine months, and they loved them fiercely. Some of the wildest battles Paradise Vue ever saw occurred when some adult treated a child with less respect than that child's mother saw fit.

I once saw Jeena Pigg hop a four-foot fence in pursuit of Caralee Jones after Caralee swatted a little Pigg for using the f-word. A Sunday School teacher was released from his job the day he disciplined the bishop's daughter by making her stand in the hall. And the Parker twins hadn't spoken to LaRue Ford since the day LaRue implied that Nora Parker might be a little *too* popular with the boys. Nora Parker herself was now close to being a grandma, but the feud continued.

Despite all this love and affection, the mothers of Paradise Vue turned into human spiders where Relief Society homemaking day was concerned. They abandoned their children at the door of the nursery and went their way as if their offspring didn't exist. No woman in the ward would take a calling as nursery leader for homemaking days. Even worse, they wouldn't even take turns in the nursery, watching all the little children one Tuesday morning every two or three years so the ward would have a babysitter.

As DeAnn Wilkerson told Alex when a co-op Relief Society nursery was suggested to the young mothers, "I *had* the damned kids, and I'm not about to go over to church and take care of them."

That left Paradise Vue with one option: hire a babysitter. Alex found a sitter — a college student with a high tolerance for screaming children, coupled with a dire need for money. Alex paid the girl twenty-five dollars every homemaking day, funding the babysitter out of her own pocket. If it occurred to any of the Paradise Vue mothers that sitters weren't free, they didn't say boo about it. Nobody ever volunteered to help pay for child care.

The plan worked well until the morning of November's homemaking day, when Alex called in a panic. "How would you like to babysit forty-six screaming children during homemaking meeting?" she asked.

I laughed.

"I'm not kidding," she said. "The sitter just called. She has a chemistry exam this afternoon. She didn't make the connection that today was homemaking day until she looked at her calendar this morning."

"Are you going to be in there with me?"

"Nope. I'm teaching the craft class — remember?" I remembered. Alex was teaching the ladies how to make Christmas reindeer out of cherrywood logs and twigs.

"What about Bess?" Bess was so good with children.

"You're the homemaking leader, Amy. I hate to say it, but this falls in your lap."

I sighed, but Alex was right. "Is *anyone* going to be in there with me?"

"Actually, yes. Marilyn Miller did say she'd help out."

The idea of spending three hours trapped in a closed room with Marilyn Miller and her chewing gum was even worse than spending the time trapped in a room with three dozen screaming children. Alex knew that. When I sighed again but didn't protest, she said, "Amy, I know how hard this will be. I owe you for this one. Don't dress in any clothes you care about. We'll bring lunch in to you, and I'll check on you whenever I have a chance."

I ate breakfast that morning as if it were my last meal. The scrambled eggs tasted gritty, and I realized there were dozens of little pieces of shell in them. I threw them down the garbage disposer and drank my Pepsi à la carte. Even Samson kept his distance from me that Tuesday morning.

As soon as I walked outside, I stepped in a fresh dog pattie. It got all over my shoe and foot, and I had to go back inside and bathe from the knee down. I threw the tennis shoes in the washer and arrived at Paradise Vue nursery room ten minutes late.

"You're late," Marilyn Miller said accusingly, with a loud gum-pop of condemnation. "I've been here seven minutes already, *by myself.*"

She didn't look alone to me. At first count, there were twenty-one children in the room with her — all under school age. Then a twenty-second crawled out from under a desk. That left eleven kids apiece for us to tend. It was a low number for a Paradise Vue home-making day, but that was small consolation. Marilyn Miller didn't look any happier about the situation than I was.

Alex arrived, dragging the ward video player behind her. "I've saved you!" she said, with a great show of cheer. "I've rented three videos. *That* should keep 'em entertained."

She handed me the movies, and I read the titles. "Indiana Jones? *Star* Trek? These kids are two and three years old."

"They'll watch anything," Marilyn said, grabbing the tapes from me with a loud crack of gum. Marilyn Miller looked like the kind of woman who'd sit her kids in front of the televised test pattern if it would keep them quiet. "Besides — the third movie is Care Bears."

"Gee, thanks, Alex," I said. I pinched her cheek and gave her an ironic grimace. Alex look wounded, and I felt guilty. "Don't worry about it. We'll have a great time. What can happen in three hours?"

Alex gave me a relieved smile. She thanked us, and off she went.

Once she was gone, I surveyed the nursery. In all my years at Paradise Vue, I'd never crossed the threshold of the room. It looked like a kindergarten classroom, with low windows and little tables and chairs. One end of the room was covered by a giant chalkboard that was both high enough for adults and low enough for little arms to reach.

There were two doors, each with big panes of one-way glass. Ostensibly, the mothers could watch their children to make sure they weren't causing any trouble in the nursery. In Paradise Vue, however, once the kiddies were dropped off, the mothers forgot all about them. It never occurred to them to see if their children were behaving. It was just as well: the one-way panes weren't very effective. Only the most obtuse of children couldn't see someone standing on the other side of the door.

The floor of the room was carpeted with building blocks, Noah's ark animals, Legos, dolls, stuffed toys, miniature trains, crayons, paper, and blunt-tipped scissors. If the children had only been in the nursery for seven minutes before I arrived, then seven minutes was time enough to pillage a room. The big toy chest in the corner was stripped of toys. Only Nathan Byrd was inside, lying on a narrow shelf with his hands crossed over his chest. He looked like Dracula in a mausoleum. The Sunday nursery leader had been telling people that Nathan always spent his time in the nursery that way. Now I believed it.

As I scanned the room, a fight erupted in the corner. Sally Stephensen had been holding a Raggedy Ann and Raggedy Andy together, making the dolls smooch as if they were parking after the prom. One of the Webster kids — I could never tell them apart — rescued the Andy doll from the clinch and flew it like a dive-bomber across the room. Sally hauled off and punched the Webster kid solidly in the stomach. The Webster kid fell on the floor and started bawling.

I looked at Marilyn Miller, who returned my glance with a challenging stare. Her expression said, *Well, what are you going to do about it?* and she punctuated the look with another pop of gum.

Then she turned her back on the whole scene and sat in front of the video machine, trying to figure how to work it.

I felt helpless. I'd never had a child. I didn't know how to handle them. I didn't even know how to change a diaper. But Marilyn had seceded from the roomful of pre-schoolers to play with the video machine. Until she got it working, I was all the children had.

I did the only thing that came to mind: I fell to all fours and crawled toward the crying children, mooing. The whole congregation fell silent. Some looked fascinated. Some looked as if they were wondering if I'd gone off my rocker. But two or three of them fell to the ground behind me and mooed in chorus. The children who'd been crying, stopped. In less than a minute, I had a herd of cows on the floor. Marilyn Miller, the only one of us with a cud, was the only person in the room who was still on two feet.

After just a minute or two, I realized I'd chosen the wrong animal. Cows don't do anything but moo and chew, with an occasional stop to lie in the shade. So I gave everyone farm assignments. Some children became chickens. Others were turkeys. We had horses and dogs and cats and ducks. Nathan Byrd, still lying in the toy chest, became a side of beef in the farm freezer.

I resisted the urge to make Danny Pigg a piglet, and he became the farmer. Sally Stephensen was the farmer's wife, to the disgust of her husband. The two of them immediately embarked on a marriage of convenience, with Sally tending the babies — Raggedy Ann and Andy, plus a stuffed giraffe — in one corner of the room, and Danny supervising the farm animals in the middle of the floor. Once they had something to do, the children played without me.

Feeling proud of myself, I got to my feet again and took a step backward to survey what I'd accomplished. It was a fatal move. Somebody was sitting on the floor behind me, and I fell backwards over the small body. As soon as I was off-balance, the child scurried out of the way. I fell full-length on a sea of small rubber toys.

I lay flat out for a moment with my eyes shut, regaining my strength. I half hoped that Marilyn Miller would fly to my attention, worrying if I was still breathing. But in true Marilyn fashion, she ignored me. Only a loud pop of gum indicated she was still in the room.

Slowly I opened my eyes. When I did, I found myself eyeball to eyeball with Reynolds Cleese's redheaded terror-child. The little girl's name was Joey, an appropriate name for a kid who bounced all over the place like a human kangaroo. In a little more than two months in the ward, she'd gone through three Primary teachers.

The little girl's face was less than three inches from mine, as she peered at me to see if I was still alive. "You tripped over me," she said, matter-of-factly. "I knocked you right down."

I said the only thing I could think of: "What are *you* doing here?" Nursery was for little kids. Joey Cleese was at least six or seven years old.

"I've got chicken pops," she confided. Sure enough, a few of the spots on her skin were scabs, not freckles. "I can't go back to school until Thursday. But Sister Roundy said I could come here with you. I'm the biggest one here."

"No. I am," I said. It was just like Alex to offer the Relief Society nursery as a refuge for a chicken pox patient. Slowly I raised myself to a sitting position. Around me, I heard the gentle clucks and moos of Danny Pigg's farmyard.

When I sat up, I was on eye level with the kneeling little girl. She put her hand out tentatively and touched my hair. "Our hairs are alike," she said in wonder.

With mild dismay, I realized she was right. *Hairs* was the right term to describe the mop of strands that grew in wild profusion from her head, each one going its own way and leading its own life. Hers were red and mine were brown, but none of them submitted to a hairbrush without protest, and no comb could discipline them for very long. In her eyes, the similarity made us kindred spirits. From the moment she touched my hair, she adopted me.

I rejoined the barnyard group, with Joey Cleese following me like a shadow. When I became a peacock, Joey was a peacock behind me. When I tired of spreading my arms and became a crowing rooster, Joey crowed at my side. She always stayed a step behind me, as if she were afraid I'd tell her to go away if she got too close.

Once she'd discovered me, Joey Cleese demanded my full attention. She watched pensively while I cleaned a booger off Sherry Marsh's face. Then, when I straightened up, she place-kicked the little girl in the bottom. Sherry sat down in a *whump,* bleating in surprise. Joey Cleese looked me straight in the eye. I got the message: I was to pay attention to no child in the room but her.

After a half hour or so, the barnyard game started wearing thin. Some of the animals sat down in open rebellion against Danny Pigg and played with toys on the floor instead of obediently lining up to be milked. Danny barked orders to a few of them, and a shouting-match began.

At that point, Marilyn Miller finally learned how to work the video machine. The strains of a *Star Trek* movie soundtrack filled the nursery, and the children filed over to the television as if they'd been called by the Pied Piper. They sat on the floor in a circle, looking open-mouthed in fascination at the television. It made me a little nervous to see their personalities evaporate as they stared at the television screen.

Marilyn Miller was wrong about one thing. To my relief, children weren't always interested in anything that moved. After a few minutes of "Star Trek," the children got distracted by all the dialogue. After all, some of the kids could barely talk.

Trinity Seebok had an accident in her diaper. She tottered over to me and smiled angelically, waiting for me to change it. I looked at Marilyn Miller hopefully, but she was mesmerized by the screen. So I found the diaper kit marked "Seebok" and changed my first diaper, with an audience of twenty-two toddlers in addition to Trinity. Only Marilyn Miller stayed immersed in "Star Trek."

"Wow! That's a lot of poop!" Danny Pigg said admiringly, as I folded the used diaper to throw away. The other children nodded solemnly in agreement. *"I'll* take the diaper to the garbage can."

I opened the door obligingly for Danny, who strode importantly to the rest room. I fervently hoped nobody else would need a diaper changed.

We returned to the television and sat in a circle around it, but the reverent mood was broken. "Do we have to watch all those old men?" the Wilkerson boy asked plaintively. "All they do is talk." I nudged Marilyn Miller, who reluctantly put the Indiana Jones tape on the machine. It was just what the children needed. From the opening scene, everyone was as hooked on the movie as Marilyn was.

After nearly an hour, Bess showed up with lunch. The milk and the sandwiches and apples and cookies took her several trips. She took me aside when she brought in her first tray. Opening her purse, she pulled out a can of Pepsi.

"This is from Alex," she said. "She said to share it with Marilyn."

"I don't think Marilyn will even notice I'm drinking it." I nodded in the direction of Marilyn, who was transfixed with Indiana Jones. She hadn't seen that Bess was in the room.

"Are you doing okay?" Bess asked that with concern, knowing how ill at ease I felt around children.

"So far, so good." Then I whispered, "That Cleese kid isn't contagious, is she?"

Bess inspected Joey Cleese from afar. "No. She's even past the itching stage. She should be back in school in a day or two. How *is* she?"

"Piece of cake." Bess didn't know whether to think I was kidding or to be impressed.

When the door closed behind Bess, I passed out lunch. The sandwiches were peanut butter and jelly. Each was wrapped in waxed paper, accompanied by a limp carrot and celery stick. I thought longingly of the day's Relief Society luncheon, which featured clam chowder in hollowed-out bread bowls. At least I had a Pepsi to drink. Marilyn Miller took her sandwich and milk without comment.

I'd never noticed children eating sandwiches until that day in the Paradise Vue nursery. Sally Stephensen took the halves of hers apart and stuck one half to each breast, like a whole wheat bikini top. Annie Morton broke off little pieces of crust and pushed them up her nose. Sandwiches were stepped on and sat on. Occasionally a child would surprise me by swallowing a bite.

The messier children gravitated to me instinctively, taking turns climbing on my lap to share bits of sandwich with me. Alex had been right on the money when she told me to wear old clothes. I wondered if grape jelly made stains.

Throughout the meal, Joey Cleese stood a few paces apart from the others. She didn't touch her food. Instead, she watched me unblinkingly, with an accusing look on her face. It was as if she were resigned to sharing me during the meal, as long as I understood she wouldn't share me afterwards.

Marilyn Miller put the movie on hold while the children ate. She seemed to do so reluctantly, because she kept returning her gaze to the blank television screen. She parked her gum in her upper cheek while she ate, retrieving it occasionally between bites of food for a quick chew.

She never spoke a word to me during the meal. Then I realized she hadn't said a word to anybody since Alex had dropped off the videotapes. I wondered if she was punishing me for my seven minutes of tardiness. Then I realized that I'd never seen Marilyn Miller interact with any children but her own. Nobody was sitting on Marilyn's lap, although I was covered with toddlers. Maybe she felt awkward around children, just as I did. Maybe she dealt with that awkwardness by watching movies and chewing gum.

I passed out Oreos to everyone. All the children pulled the cookies apart and licked the frosting from the center. Marilyn and I did it, too. I was amused to see we had at least one thing in common.

When everyone had finished eating, Marilyn turned on the video player and returned to Indiana Jones. With the exception of Joey Cleese, all the children watched the movie.

With everybody else watching *Raiders of the Lost Ark*, the little redheaded girl had me all to herself. She gave me a tentative smile that said, "Entertain me."

Never having had much exposure to children, I didn't know what to do. But then I saw some crayons in the corner, and I remembered the sketchpad I kept in my purse. I may not know children, I thought, but I could give anybody a drawing lesson. I took out my sketchpad and a soft pencil. Then I decided to do it right. Rooting around in the bottom of my purse, I found a chamois, a kneaded eraser, a piece of charcoal, and a paper stump. Michelangelo wouldn't have needed any more. Joey and I sat at one of the child-sized tables. She imitated me even to the way I sat, crossing my right ankle over the left to get comfortable for drawing. As she peered over my hands, I showed her how to put charcoal on paper, using the chamois as a brush.

Then I took an apple from the refreshment tray and pointed out shadow edge and reflected light and all the other components of artwork. I showed her how to illustrate each part of the apple on her piece of paper, using the eraser and the chamois and the paper stump.

After a few minutes, Joey impatiently took the chamois away from me and started drawing on her own. She stuck the tip of her tongue through her teeth as she worked, just the way people told me I did. She concentrated on her drawing the way a surgeon would concentrate on his work. She wasn't playing; she was creating.

Joey Cleese was a natural artist. I hadn't had my first drawing lesson until college, but her first apple was better than mine had been. By the end of Relief Society, she'd drawn two beautiful apples. She signed each picture with a kindergartner's penmanship.

A woman I didn't know picked Joey up after Relief Society. She didn't want to leave me, and she clung to the leg of my jeans. I didn't know what to do.

Finally, I opened my purse and got out all my drawing equipment — the chamois and the charcoal and the eraser and the paper stump, all in a zippered bag. I gave them to Joey Cleese with the sketchpad. She wrinkled her nose and grinned.

"I think," she said, "I'll let you be my new best friend."

"That's a big responsibility," I said. "Besides, what if I already have a best friend?"

"That's okay. You can have lots of them. My daddy is my best friend in my family, and Bishop Nebeker is my best friend that's a bishop. You can be my best friend that draws."

She was right. People do have best friends for different situations. "Okay, Joey," I said. "You can be my best friend who has hairs like mine."

# 11
# The Genuine
# Article

The days grew shorter and colder, and the holidays approached. First came Thanksgiving, a grim day spent with Tim's parents. I was always glad to see that day end.

Tim had died on a Thanksgiving eve, flying home from Denver on a snowy night in his Cessna. I never felt very thankful on Thanksgiving after that, especially sitting at the small, quiet table with Tim's parents.

He'd had a sister, but she died of whooping cough as a baby, so Tim grew up as an only child. Now I was all his parents had left, and I wasn't enough. It was a big responsibility, and I never knew what to say to make them feel better. I realized this year they looked much sadder and greyer than I remembered. They were getting old.

On December 6th, the first day of the Christmas month, I decorated the house in purple and green for the holidays. Tim had always hated red. I put a tree by the fireplace and hung our stockings on the mantel, getting ready for the endless Christmas season.

As if she didn't have enough to do in December, Alex decided the Relief Society presidency should give a Christmas gift to every woman in the ward. She chose a figurine of Christ with the little

117

children — the scene out of Matthew where He said to "suffer the little children to come unto me." It was a beautiful work in porcelain, but it was more than four people should have taken on at the beginning of December. The Relief Society was a hundred eighty-six ladies strong at Christmastime, and that meant a hundred and eighty-six bisqueware figurines had to be cleaned and then taken down the hill to a ceramics shop to be fired.

Alex and I converted my studio into a workshop for the project, and she and Bess and Emma and I spent every spare moment in December working on those presents. Alex did them the fastest, but her best time was twelve minutes. Emma, who had to worry about grit under her fingernails, could only do two per hour.

One Wednesday night, all four of us cleaned bisqueware until after one, stopping only to order a pizza about halfway through. Emma, who was even more relentlessly cheerful at Christmas than she was the rest of the year, chattered ceaselessly about all the men who loved her, speculating who was going to give her what on Christmas morning. How I wished she'd shut up, but I didn't have anything to say to change the subject. So I cleaned the bisque with a cellulose sponge and a wet finger, smoothing out the tiny air bubbles and hairline cracks as she talked.

"You should get some red in your house, Amy. It's *red* and green are the Christmas colors. And I really do think you'd be better off if you didn't hang *his* stocking by the mantel. It can only make you feel bad. You mope around enough as it is."

I dusted myself off and left the room to pour eggnog. Alex followed me out to the kitchen. "She means well, Amy."

"Does she?"

"Some people have a knack for saying the wrong thing. Emma doesn't think before she speaks."

"No, Alex, you're wrong. She knows but doesn't care." I poured Cream O'Weber eggnog in four green glasses and sprinkled nutmeg on top. Then I remembered a single chipped, purple glass in back of the cupboard. I found it, dusted it out, and poured Emma's eggnog out of the green glass and into the purple one. Then I sprinkled more nutmeg on top of that. From the corner of my eye I thought I saw Alex shake her head, but she didn't try to stop me.

Alex and I walked back into the workshop, each carrying two full glasses. Bess smiled up at me. Emma looked studiously downward, inspecting a fingernail. Alex gave me an understanding look and gave both the green glasses of eggnog she was carrying to Bess and Emma. Then she took the purple one for herself.

"My fingers are getting wrinkled. Look at them!" Emma held her hands up for inspection. "And my fingernails are getting *soft.*" She bent one for emphasis.

"*All* our fingers are getting wrinkled," I said pointedly, holding my own in Emma's face. "*All* our fingernails are getting soft. They'll harden up again."

Alex changed the subject quickly. "I forgot to tell you all — I just found out Karen Sheffield is moving in March. We're going to need a new spiritual living teacher."

Karen Sheffield was the one who taught in tandem with Elsie Hunsaker, the chloroform teacher. Karen was a good instructor, and the ward would miss her. But when the news leaked out, there'd be a royal battle in the Relief Society over who would take her place.

Bess asked what we were all thinking. "Who's going to replace her?"

"I have no idea," Alex said, disgusted. "I don't know why it's such a status thing, but there are going to be hurt feelings over this."

Alex put one figurine in the finished pile and started another one, after resetting a stop-watch she used every time she did a project. "There's a definite hierarchy among women in the church — at least as far as women who haven't got anything better to do than think about status are concerned. The Relief Society president is always at the top of the heap. After her comes the bishop's wife, if she's assertive." She didn't need to say that bishops' wives in our ward, however, usually kept a low profile. "The Relief Society counselors are next in the pecking order, but the spiritual living teachers are right up there with them. Then comes the Primary president, followed by the Relief Society secretary, followed by the other Relief Society teachers, followed by the Young Women's president. Everybody else is at the bottom of the pile."

I took a sidelong glance at Emma, and I thought she looked a little disgruntled. It made me glad that I was a counselor and she was only the secretary. It was a nasty thought, and I almost felt guilty about it. But it was Christmastime, and Emma had no right to be so smug in her happiness.

"I've always thought the whole hierarchy idea is ridiculous," Alex continued. "People change church jobs every week, and they're the same people no matter what jobs they have. But to some people in Paradise Vue, status is pretty important. We're just going to have to choose a new teacher and ride this one out."

I learned something that year about being in a Relief Society presidency: lots of people remember you at Christmas. I realized it wasn't Amy they were remembering as much as *the homemaking counselor,* but I felt more loved that holiday season than I had in a long time. Four or five women called me on Christmas day to tell me they loved me, and at least a dozen of them brought me loaves of bread or popcorn balls or some other holiday food. When the doorbell rang two nights before Christmas, I thought it was another Relief Society member and gladly went to the door.

There on the doorstep stood Reynolds Cleese, the Clark Kent of limerick fame, surrounded by all six of his children. It was a cold night, and they were bundled so heavily they looked like a family of snowmen, uniformly round.

Joey Cleese tugged on her father's coat. When he looked down at her, she said in a stage whisper, "Look at her hairs."

Reynolds Cleese looked at me and smiled. Then he looked down at his daughter and said, "I see them. They *are* like yours. They're very nice. Now, why don't you tell Sister Hardisty why we're here?"

"I have a Christmas present for you," Joey Cleese said. She marched inside, unbidden, with the package. The rest of the family trooped in behind her.

I waited uncomfortably to receive my present, wondering what the little girl had for me and why she'd given me a gift. She'd obviously carried it herself: the ribbon was untied and the paper bedraggled from being carried in a child's hands. But instead of giving me the package, she walked to the mantel and stared at the painting above it in wonder.

"That's an animal," she said. "What kind of animal is it?"

Her father walked up behind her and put his arm around her shoulders. "That's a rhinoceros, Joey. You remember them. You've seen them at the zoo." Then, to me, he said, "That's an interesting oil you have there. Where'd you get it?"

"I painted it," I said casually. Actually, I was pretty impressed. The painting had been hanging over the mantel since September, and Joey Cleese and her father were the first people to see the hidden rhinoceros in the cityscape.

"I like surrealists, too. I have a Magritte. You'll have to come over and see it sometime."

All my good humor evaporated. "Oh yes. And you'll show me your etchings, I presume?"

He looked chastened. "Sorry. I didn't mean it the way it sounded. I would like to see you sometime, though."

"I don't date," I said shortly. "I'm married." I wanted to be rid of this man. His eyes wandered around the room uncomfortably, coming to rest on the Christmas stockings at the mantel. He surveyed Tim's stocking without comment.

"Give Sister Hardisty your present, Joey," he said. "Then we have to go."

The little girl was crouched in the corner with her brothers and sisters. It looked as if they were torturing Samson, but I didn't worry about the cat. Samson could take care of himself. Joey looked up when her father called her. Leaving Samson to her siblings, she retrieved the gift from where she'd thrown it on the floor.

"Here," she said, shoving the present in my hands. That duty accomplished, she returned to Samson in the corner. I looked at Reynolds Cleese. "Should I open it? What is it?"

"Joey wanted to thank you for the drawing lesson. I do, too. I didn't know she had a talent for that. She's been drawing ever since. With lessons, I think she could be pretty good." He looked at my hands, still holding the present. "Do you give lessons?"

"I never have, but Joey *does* have talent. Why don't you send her over once a week after school? We'll set up a time after Christmas."

Reynolds Cleese smiled, showing his dimple.

"Now, should I open the present?"

The man looked over at his children, who'd totally forgotten us to play with Samson. Samson, who usually didn't take to strangers, was playing right back with them. "I don't think that's necessary. Save it for Christmas. It's not on the level of that rhinoceros, but Joey wanted you to have it to remember her by."

I didn't think that anyone, having met Joey Cleese, could forget her — but tactfully, I didn't say that to her father. I put the present under the tree, and I opened it on Christmas morning. It was the little girl's first apple, drawn in the Relief Society nursery. It had been triple-matted in greys and black and framed in oak, and it looked terrific. I hung it in my workshop, and every time Joey Cleese came for an art lesson, she went over to the drawing and touched it with pride.

Christmas arrived with a skiff of snow. Those with vivid imaginations could say our Christmas was white — at least until 9:30 A.M. or so, when the snow melted.

Alone on Christmas morning, I opened my gifts. Joey Cleese's drawing wasn't the only handmade gift under the tree. Bess gave me a scarf she'd knitted herself. It was kelly green, my favorite color. She'd put a lot of time into it, and I appreciated it.

Emma gave me make-up — the brands and colors she wore. Now I could wear my face like Emma did, if I were so inclined.

Hector Gomez gave me a beautiful hand-carved wooden angel. Hector had made it himself, and it was a gift to treasure. I also kept the note that went with it, a printed note from Maria that thanked me for sending her to the doctor.

The gift I saved for last was a big package from Alex. I thought it might be another clock, and it was — a big Edwardian wall clock made of rosewood and beveled glass. I hadn't seen her make it, but I had seen her making clocks for Emma and Bess. I gloated for a brief, uncharitable moment that my clock was bigger than theirs. Then, feeling guilty, I realized that Alex didn't prioritize presents like that. The other clocks had taken her just as long to make as mine had.

I got out a hammer and some anchors and hung the new clock in my dining room. I set the clock to chime a moment later than the other clock Alex had given me the year before. Now it would take twice as long for the hours to toll by.

After feeding Samson a dinner of turkey gizzards, I got dressed and went to Alex's house for my own Christmas dinner. It was an annual tradition for the past six years, giving me someplace to go besides Tim's parents' house. Christmas was always festive at Alex's. It was the only time the whole family was together, and I was glad to share it with them.

I went to the front door and knocked. Jean answered, wearing a sweat suit and fuzzy slippers. At age nineteen, she was a model in New York, but all she modeled was her hands. Jean, who looked pretty average otherwise, had a magnificent set of hands. They were famous in television and magazine ads, but nobody ever saw her face. Her hands were her fortune: they were making Jean more money than two hands could ever spend.

"Hi, Jean. Caressed any good product lately?" It was an old line, and I got tired of saying it. But Jean never got tired of hearing it. She giggled and covered her mouth with million-dollar fingers.

"Grapes. And telephone books, and sable coats, and the usual assortment of soaps and shampoos. *You* know. Merry Christmas, Amy." She kissed me on the cheek.

Clementine looked up from a love seat. She was draped over the furniture artistically while she read a book. The book was something scientific. Clementine, who was as beautiful from top to toe as Jean was in her hands, got her looks from Ethan and her brain from neither Ethan nor Alex nor the mailman. She was doing research on fractals at MIT, where she radiated beauty among men who never looked up from their equations. "Hi, Amy," she said. "Oh. Merry Christmas."

I looked around the living room, where among the presents I saw a hand-carved angel that could only have been from Hector Gomez. Then I went in search of Alex. I found her in the kitchen, where she was pretending to cook a Christmas dinner.

Actually, she'd ordered the whole meal from Neiman-Marcus. I knew it, and Alex knew I knew it, and the whole Roundy family knew it, but everyone pretended every year that the Federal Express man hadn't made a big delivery on Christmas Eve, and that Alex had been up since six A.M., slaving over her microwave.

Alex was stirring the Neiman-Marcus gravy, standing over the stove in her pajamas and a mink jacket. She looked happier than I'd seen her in a long time. She dropped the spoon in the gravy when she saw me, where it sank in the oversized pot.

"Do I look beautiful?" she asked. "Ethan gave it to me for Christmas. I'm never going to take it off."

It was a beautiful jacket. Alex was so excited about it that I forgot until two days later that Alex didn't believe in wearing furs. "It's beautiful, Alex. Gorgeous. What did you give Ethan?"

Alex returned to the stove, where she fished the spoon out of the gravy with a pair of tongs. She wiped the spoon off and then tapped it on the back window. I looked outside, expecting to see a car or a motorcycle or two of whatever Neiman-Marcus's his-and-hers gifts of the year were that Christmas. Instead I saw Ethan, frolicking like a kid with two of the biggest dogs I'd ever seen. They looked like snow-white St. Bernards, only maybe a little bigger.

Alex saw my look of dismay. "I wish you could see your face, Amy. They aren't *that* bad. Ethan's always wanted a dog, and when Neiman's had great pyrenees this year as their his-and-her gifts, I ordered him a pair of them. They're pedigreed, of course. The male is Man o' War, and the smaller one is Chesapeake. Ethan named them this morning. He's going to breed them."

At dinnertime, Ethan finally came indoors. He gave me a big hug, and when I pulled away I was covered with dog hair. Nobody seemed to notice. I had a feeling I was going to be seeing a lot of dog hair on my body in the future.

"That's a beautiful portrait you did of Alex for Christmas," he said. "We're putting it over the mantel, where that mountain scene is now." I was impressed. *That mountain scene* was a John Myrup. His paintings went for $20,000 a pop.

Ethan found a piece of celery — one of the few things in the kitchen Alex had actually prepared herself. He ate a bite of it. "If I pay you, will you paint another one of Alex for my office? I want a portrait of her in her workshop, making clocks." I nodded yes, delighted to get a commission. Ethan was one of the nicest people I'd ever met.

Ethan helped Alex set the table, while I sat at the kitchen counter sketching ideas for a new portrait of Alex. Whenever they passed each other in the kitchen, they'd find some excuse to touch each other. When the two of them were together, no one else was in the room.

Then Ethan called everyone for dinner. He sat us around the table, making sure he put the four of us where he wanted us. At each plate was a party favor, the kind you pull apart at both ends with a pop to release the prize. Alex opened her favor first. It was a dinner ring, with at least a dozen tiny sapphires set in gold. It was a real beauty, and Alex took off another ring and set it aside so she could wear the new one. She and Ethan exchanged loving looks.

Ethan beamed, and then he did something I rarely saw a man do. He blushed. He took a quick sip of raspberry juice, hiding his face behind the goblet. Setting the glass back on the table, he said, "Nothing's too good for Alex. She's one of a kind."

Jean opened her favor next, with Clementine right behind her. They were diamond and emerald birthstone rings, equal in beauty. Jean's diamond was no prettier than the rest of her hand, and she put it on in delight. Clementine, who'd always been her father's favorite, raised her eyebrows at Ethan in thanks and put her ring on a hand that was no less beautiful than her sister's.

When all the other favors were open, I pulled mine apart. A gold watch with a blue face fell on the plate with a clank. I picked it up and stared at it. It was a Rolex.

I looked quickly at Alex, then at Ethan. Ethan looked pleased with himself. Alex laughed out loud. "Isn't it terrific?" she asked. "Ethan got it for you months ago in Reynosa. He's been saving it for Christmas."

"I hope it isn't real."

"Nope. It's a twenty-dollar copy. It sure looks real, though."

I put the watch on and held my wrist up next to Alex's. The two watches were almost indistinguishable. Only my sweep second hand, which moved in increments instead of going smoothly around the face of the watch, appeared to be different.

Clementine peered over her emerald ring. "Aren't those things illegal?"

Alex and I shrugged in tandem. I didn't know why they would be. Ethan winked at his daughter. "If they are," he said, "it's a law everybody breaks."

I never found out if my fake Rolex was illegal: I didn't want to know. It was my favorite piece of jewelry, and I wore it every day. It reminded me how much I liked Ethan, and how happy he and Alex were that Christmas.

Although Ethan hadn't intended it, the watch also reminded me of my friendship with his wife. I felt like a fake Rolex watch next to her. I was only a pale imitation of the things I admired about Alex.

After dinner, Alex and I were left alone to do the dishes. Ethan went outside to play with the dogs, where they woofed in foghorn voices. Clementine went upstairs to read. Jean, whose model's hands were not allowed to touch dishwater, retreated to her room to take a nap.

Alex took the rings off her fingers, putting them in her bra so she wouldn't forget where she'd put them. She washed the silverware as I dried, and both of us watched Ethan out the kitchen window.

"He can't possibly love anybody but you," I said to her. "Look at the way he treats you. You're the most important thing in his life."

"On days like this, I think you're right." She handed me a fork to dry and said, "I've made a decision."

I thought Alex would tell me she'd decided all her fears about Ethan were wrong, and I smiled in anticipation. But instead she said, "I've found a new spiritual living teacher to replace Karen Sheffield."

It was just that kind of *non sequitir* that made Alex so unpredictable. "Who?"

"You're not going to like this. I'm going to ask Emma to do it. It won't happen until Karen moves, and Emma doesn't even know it yet. We need a secretary who's here to help us during the day, and Emma can't do that. Besides, Emma's so smart — she'll do a great job."

I didn't say a word, but Alex could tell how I felt from the set of my jaw. "Don't be upset, Amy. Please. You can never tell. Maybe listening to Emma's lessons will help you appreciate her."

Appreciating Emma was the last thing on my mind. Even as I promised Alex I'd try to sustain Emma in the new job, all I could think was that the Lord was punishing me for being glad I had more status in the ward hierarchy than Emma did. Now the two of us were on an even keel.

# 12
# Revelation

If Ethan Roundy hadn't taken Alex to Australia, I might never have learned the truth about Bess. But for Alex's birthday in late January, Ethan surprised her with a trip to the Great Barrier Reef. The two of them left on short notice for a week of scuba diving, leaving the Relief Society in Bess's hands.

Bess took the charge as seriously as she accepted every responsibility. She knew Alex and I always went visiting on Tuesday mornings, so on Monday night she called to say the Tuesday visit was on.

"This won't be easy for me," she admitted. "Stephanie gets home from kindergarten at 12:45, so we have to go in the morning."

"What about the mailman?"

"That's the other problem. Could you do me a favor and go out with me at nine? I know you're not awake by then, but my ox is in the mire. Could you help me out?"

When she put it that way, I couldn't tell her no. So I got up at eight o'clock Tuesday morning and bundled up to go out in the Utah winter.

January and February in Salt Lake City are lethal, but the very thing that makes the air so dangerous also makes the city beautiful.

Sometimes a dense fog settles over the valley for weeks on end. Old people die then in record numbers; everyone else just coughs and stays indoors. But outside, the fog freezes around the bare limbs and tiny branches of the trees, making them look like they're made of ice. The Tuesday I visited with Bess was one of those days. The cold sneaked under my cap and scarf as soon as I walked outdoors, bringing tears to my eyes and causing my nose to run. I envied Alex her Australian summer as I readjusted my scarf. I even envied Samson, who was warm and happy in my bed.

I honked for Bess, who peeked out her front window and waved. She locked her front door behind her and tip-toed slowly toward my Blazer, navigating her front walk as carefully as any blue-hair. Rick kept every scrap of snow and ice off the Monson side-walks, but Utah's winter frost also freezes on the cement. It only takes one wrong step to break an arm or a leg.

Our first visit was to Edna Gompers, the grand old lady of Paradise Vue. She had served as the first Relief Society president in Paradise Vue when the ward was formed and had been Relief Society president in the old ward for fifteen years before that, so Edna held a position of stature above the rest of us. When a thorny question of Relief Society etiquette came up, she was always the final authority.

Edna was in a cheerful mood when she let us in. She was absolutely euphoric — a ray of sunshine on a winter day.

"Come *iii*-in." She didn't say it; she sang it. People always seemed happy to see the Relief Society presidency, but I couldn't recall ever having been greeted with this much enthusiasm. "Sashay right behind me to the kitchen, and I'll fix you up a little liquid refreshment."

Edna owned a catering service that she ran out of her home — secretly, to avoid zoning problems. Her kitchen had been remodeled to accommodate the business, and the ward rumor mill said the work had cost more than $30,000. Betty Crocker herself wouldn't have had a better kitchen. I had no idea what all the gadgets did, and I didn't even want to learn. But the food that came out of that

kitchen was finer than any I'd tasted in a restaurant. All Edna had
to say was "kitchen," and my salivary glands kicked right in.

"It's a cold, cold day out there," Edna said in that odd, sing-
song voice. "Here's a little goodie to warm you *right* up." She
opened a cabinet door to reveal a big jar with a screw-top lid. The
words "sun tea" were printed on the jar, but if Mormons stopped
buying things just because they had "coffee" or "tea" written on
them, there wouldn't have been a set of canisters in Paradise Vue.

Edna's tea jar didn't pretend to have tea in it. It looked like a
jar of fruit cocktail — unrefrigerated fruit cocktail. Bits of foam
clung to the pieces of pineapple floating on the top. I hoped whatever Edna was feeding us wasn't rotten. If it had been any kitchen
but Edna's, I wouldn't have trusted the stuff in the jar.

I watched, fascinated, as Edna scooped generous portions of
fruit mixture into bell-shaped glasses. She added lots of liquid,
pushing the foam aside as she dipped for clear juice. Then she
carefully set a sugar wafer atop each compote, wedging a corner of
each cookie into a maraschino cherry to keep it from falling in.
Finally she presented Bess and me with a sterling silver dessert
spoon and dainty linen napkins. Edna was always the professional.

She led us to the living room to eat and visit. There was a
spring in her step, and her hips swayed cheerfully as she walked. It
wasn't that she was gaining weight; it was almost as if she danced
across the carpet.

She settled into an overstuffed chair and kicked off her shoes.
The right one flew halfway across the room, and she giggled to see
it fly. Then she put her feet up on an ottoman and wiggled her toes.
I'd never seen Edna so informal. It gave the room a nice, cozy feeling.

I nibbled my cookie while Edna entertained us. She loved to
talk about her days as Relief Society president, and today she had a
few stories I hadn't heard before. I finished my cookie and took a big
spoonful of fruit compote. The taste startled me so much that juice
went down the wrong pipe. Then I had to set the glass aside and
cough until I got my breath.

"Now *here's* a woman who's never tasted Funny Fruit," Edna said to Bess. She nodded her head in my direction and smiled indulgently. "Doesn't it have a nice bite to it?"

*Bite* wasn't the word I would have used. *Jolt*, perhaps. "It's a little potent, isn't it?" I asked when I finally caught my breath. That was an understatement. Funny Fruit was as toxic as anything you could find in the Utah State Liquor Store. Edna wasn't glad to see us — she was potted.

"This is just wonderful stuff," Bess said. "Wonderful stuff." She was eating the fruit like there was no tomorrow. It figured. Bess had never even tasted Coca-Cola. She couldn't be expected to recognize liquor when she tried it. "Please, tell me the recipe."

"Dearie, I never give out my recipes," Edna said. "But this is no secret. It's in the Paradise Vue ward cookbook. Do you have a copy?"

The Paradise Vue cookbook had been compiled ten years ago, long before Bess moved into the ward. "Don't have one," she said mournfully.

"Well, it's easy enough. You take canned pineapple and canned peaches and maraschino cherries, and you add sugar and yeast. I'll write down the proportions for you before you leave." She took a big bite of fruit, slurping the juice from the spoon and then licking it to get every drop. "Then you leave it on the counter till it ferments. Don't screw the lid on tight, or the jar will explode. That makes a big mess, I guarantee you. *Great* stuff. I couldn't start the day without my Funny Fruit."

Bess finished her Funny Fruit, and the spoon clinked against the empty glass. Edna took that as a signal and sprang up to get Bess some more. She lost her balance for just a moment and steadied herself on the arm of the overstuffed chair.

As soon as she left the room, I hissed at Bess to get her attention. "This is *booze*," I whispered. "Don't have any more or you'll get drunk."

"Don't be silly," Bess said primly. "If this were liquor, the recipe never would have been printed in the Paradise Vue cookbook.

And don't leave yours untouched. We're supposed to eat whatever is offered us. Don't hurt Edna's feelings."

Edna glided back into the living room, and Bess took another full glass. Only when I saw Bess wrapping her fingers around the bowl of the goblet did I realize Edna had served the fruit in brandy snifters. Edna *had* to know what she was eating.

I picked out some pineapple chunks and maraschino cherries with my fingers, eating them with conspicuous gusto so Edna wouldn't see I was leaving most of the fruit and all of the juice behind. When Edna turned her head, I motioned to Bess to do the same. She gave me an annoyed look that shut me right up. As far as Bess was concerned, if the recipe had been published in the ward cookbook, that was the end of it.

The visit went on and on, but Edna and Bess weren't aware of the time. After awhile, Edna started repeating stories she'd told when we first sat down. When I saw that Bess didn't remember the stories she'd heard an hour ago, I knew it was time to go.

"Time's getting away from us," I said, looking exaggeratedly at my watch. "This has been wonderful, but we really do have to go."

"We just got here," Bess said. She didn't slur her words, but there was a little giggle hiding in her throat and threatening to erupt.

"We have two more visits, Bess, and we do have to be home for the mail."

"Oops. Gotta go. Gotta go." If all Bess could say about the mail was *oops,* she was worse off than I thought. I put down my snifter and took Bess's from her. Then I gently pulled her off the couch. She didn't miss any steps as I guided her toward the door, but she wasn't light on her feet the way Edna was. Every pace was deliberate.

When we got to the door, Bess did an abrupt about-face and ran right into me. "I've *got* to get the recipe," she said. She winked broadly as if she'd made a big joke. Edna winked back.

"We'll get the recipe later." I guided her outside into the cold air, putting her coat over her shoulders only after we were on the front step. "In fact, I have the Paradise Vue cookbook right at home. I'll give it to you myself."

Edna lost interest in us almost immediately and turned around with only a wave goodbye. I hoped she wasn't returning to the kitchen.

Bess looked ready to go home, but she wouldn't hear of it. She was the one who made appointments, and two more people were waiting for us. I opened the windows of my Blazer and drove us around in the chill air until she seemed a little more normal. The other two ladies might think Bess was preoccupied, but they wouldn't think she was plastered.

Our next appointment was just what Bess needed, although I didn't know it at the time. Karma Stooble had once been a flutist with the Boston Symphony Orchestra, but she'd left it and returned to Zion to teach. Now she kept a big flip-over sign on her door: "The flutist is in," or "The flutist is out." You only knocked on Karma's door if the sign was turned the right way.

Today the flutist was in, so Bess knocked. There was a perfectly good doorbell, but Bess seemed to need to make the physical commitment to enter Karma's house. She said she'd never visited Karma "in person," stressing the words as if she *had* visited Karma by hologram. If I'd remembered how squeamish Bess was, I would have visited Karma Stooble alone.

Karma was a compulsive organizer. She hung her clothes on color-coordinated hangers. Her shoes were grouped in the closet according to color, and then in descending order according to heel height. The food in her refrigerator was arranged on shelves — the top one for breakfast foods, the middle one for lunch, and the bottom one for dinner items. Every paper clip in Karma's house had a home.

But her compulsion ended there. Karma was the mother of six parakeets, who flew around the house unfettered and decorated furniture and floors with abandon. She also had a cat, a six-toed behemoth named Polly-dactyl. She called him Polly for short — a bird name that always had me confusing the cat with the parakeets.

Polly constantly lurched from room to room, depositing black cat hairs on the white furniture and scattering old, dried-up cat food all over the carpets. Between cat and birds, the aroma in Karma's house was overwhelming.

Karma and I had many animated discussions over who was the worse housekeeper. I thought her place should have been closed by the Board of Health, but she thought I was the slob. My house was clean but cluttered, and clutter was the unpardonable sin in Karma's book.

We found some space that was clear of bird droppings on the sofa, but the upholstery was a nest of cat hairs. When Bess sat down, they clouded up around her and she sneezed. Bess was allergic to cat dander. If she hadn't been fortified by Funny Fruit, I doubt even her Relief Society responsibility would have allowed her to sit down.

Karma brought us some limeade in finger-smudged glasses. Bess took hers reluctantly and held it in her hand without drinking it. She watched Polly suspiciously, her facial movements still exaggerated by her run-in with the Funny Fruit.

The cat spotted a roach and followed it. He staggered even when he ran, his extra toes throwing him subtly off-balance like a drunken sailor. One of the parakeets dive-bombed him, but he followed the roach obliviously. Finally he pounced and ate it in one gulp.

"Nice catch," I said. I removed a cat hair from my limeade. Bess turned her head. She looked as if she were starting to get sick.

"Polly loves roaches," Karma said proudly. A parakeet swooped over the cat again, and Polly gave it an evil glance. Karma grinned. "Polly'd eat the 'keets if they'd let him. They're too fast for him, though. They like to taunt him. Poor kitty."

Karma smiled at us conspiratorially. "I've also got rats," she confided. "They're chewing away at the sheetrock." Our neighborhood, being high on the hill in a wealthy area, had never seen a rat. But if rats ever moved to Paradise Vue, this was the place they'd come. Bird seed and cat food draw rodents like a magnet.

As Karma finished speaking, I heard a scurrying sound. Bess's head shot up like a catapult. She looked ready to hop on a chair. I got ready to move fast, in case she did it. In Bess's condition, if she hopped up, she'd fall off.

Polly heard the noise, too. His ears pricked up, and he stared intently toward the kitchen. Then he ran, limping at full six-toed speed toward the noise.

I heard a whump, then the sound of breaking glass. Karma shook her head calmly. "It's the rats," she said with an *I told you so* expression on her face. "They don't stand a chance against Polly."

Bess cringed.

When Polly reappeared, he carried a tiny snippet of a mouse tenderly in his mouth. He dropped it at Karma's feet with a flourish and sat complacently on his haunches, as if waiting for praise.

"Ha!" Karma said. "What'd I tell you? There's a rat now."

"That's a mouse," I said. "It's smaller than my thumb."

"Mice. Rats. They're all the same. I'm infested with rats."

Then it occurred to me that Karma *wanted* them to be rats. It made the story more dramatic.

"Excuse me." It was Bess. She was looking at the palm of her hand with horror. There was a white smudge on it. Bird droppings. She'd put her hand in them somehow, and now she looked ill. "I have to use the bathroom. Where is it. Please. Fast."

I wanted to tell Bess that the last place she should go in Karma's house was the bathroom, but she didn't give me time. She jumped to her feet and found the bathroom herself. I heard the water running, covering what sounded like retching. She was in the bathroom a long time. When she emerged, she was pale-faced. She was also stone sober. Karma's house was the ultimate antidote for Funny Fruit.

Bess didn't even pretend to want to stay any longer. With a few mumbled words of apology, she fled to the front door. When she opened it, a powder blue parakeet flew outside and into a frost-covered tree.

"Oh, no," I said, but Karma reassured me.

"Happens all the time," she said. "Scruffles likes to tease me. He knows I couldn't live without him."

She walked out on the front step and held her index finger horizontally aloft. "Pretty boy," she cooed, lifting her finger ever higher as Bess and I walked toward the car. "Pretty boy. Pretty boooy."

Polly the cat watched the whole scene intently through the picture window.


As I drove to our third appointment, Bess slowly recovered from Karma Stooble's pet haven. She wiped her hands over and over on her slacks and her coat. She'd just washed those hands in Karma's bathroom, but since it *was* Karma's bathroom, the soap had probably been covered with cat hairs. She acted as if she wanted to take a bath. I wanted to take a bath, too.

But the moment we knocked on Ruth Nebeker's door, Bess was all business. She had a gift for being single-minded, and her mind then was on her duty. She smiled a big Relief Society smile as the door opened.

Ruth Nebeker was the bishop's wife. She had a houseful of seven kids, but all of them were in school. She should have been sitting back, relaxing, but she didn't look like a woman in a relaxing mood.

"Do you mind if you sit in the kitchen while we talk? I have to clean the breakfast dishes." Ruth led us to the kitchen, where I took a seat at the counter and Bess pulled up a chair from the dinette. Ruth put ice in two glasses and poured orange juice from a pitcher that was still sitting on the breakfast table. I suddenly had an idea why the Relief Society presidency always saw women in groups of three — that was as long as we could go being offered Kool-Aid and juice between bathroom visits. I was beginning to feel a twinge of discomfort. I took my juice from Ruth's outstretched hand and thanked her for it.

With a loud clattering of dishes, Ruth pulled the breakfast plates and glasses from tabletops and counters. She scraped waffle leavings and syrup from the plates and ran the mess through the garbage disposal. Then she filled the sink with hot water and green dish soap. Steam rose from the sink and clouded the windows. "You look a little tense today, Ruth," I said. "Is anything wrong?"

"*Life* is wrong. When I got married, I thought I was marrying a husband. I didn't figure on marrying a bishop. Barton wanted a big family, and that was fine with me. But he didn't tell me I'd be raising it alone. I'm *tired* of it."

Ruth's lament was one that must have crossed the mind of every bishop's wife at one time or another. From sunrise to sunset on Sunday, the bishop would be over at the church. There'd be bishopric meetings one night a week, and stake meetings other nights, and personal counseling sessions in whatever time was left. It wasn't a paid job, of course — Bishop Nebeker also had his law practice. With nine mouths to feed and seven kids to send to college, he had to work long hours at that.

"How long has he been a bishop?" I asked. It seemed like forever, even to me. Being a bishop wasn't a lifetime occupation in Paradise Vue, but some of them got kept in so long it might as well have been.

"Five years. Two months. Thirteen days. Do you know how many Sundays I've had to ride herd on seven kids during Sacrament Meeting?" I started to figure the numbers in my head, but got bogged down when I tried to multiply fifty-two by five. When Ruth didn't volunteer an answer, I made a mental note to do the math when I got home.

"It's a *lot* of Sundays," Bess said fervently. Ruth nodded. That was all the calculating she needed.

Listening to Ruth, I realized why Paradise Vue bishops' wives never had ward jobs. We couldn't even get them to take a visiting teaching route, and I'd always been a little resentful of that. But *I* certainly couldn't raise seven children by myself — not just on Sundays, but on most nights, too. Suddenly I felt compassion for Ruth Nebeker, and shame that I'd judged her.

"You know what's the worst part?" Ruth asked. She washed dishes with a vengeance, ignoring the "Love at Home" sampler hanging on the wall next to her sink. "He's so *oblivious*. He doesn't even think about what this is doing to me. All he cares about are everyone else's problems."

Ruth was right. I could see it as soon as she said it. When a man's put in a hard day at work counseling people with legal problems, and then he puts in a hard night at the bishop's office counseling people with personal problems, counseling becomes work. When he gets home, he doesn't want to hear about any problems inside those walls.

I was thinking of a way to put that into words when Bess spoke up. "Ruth, I think your problem is resentment."

"Darn *right* I resent it."

"No, that's not what I mean. You don't resent the time lost with him as much as the fact that his attention's not focused on you." She took a sip of orange juice.

"That's ponder-worthy," Ruth said. It was a joke word in our ward, but she didn't sound as if she meant to be sarcastic. Ruth really was thinking about it. Her brow knitted as she scrubbed syrup from the inner tines of a fork.

"It's the difference between men and women," Bess continued. "What's the center of your life?"

"Well, *he* is."

"Right. And what's the center of his life?"

"I don't know. It depends on what he's doing. Sometimes it's work. More often it's being bishop. When he's with the kids, that's what he's thinking about. And on the rare occasions we go to bed at the same time, I guess he thinks about me."

"You know he loves you."

"Yes, he does." She said it slowly, as if remembering for the first time in years that that was the case.

"You're just not the center of his life."

"You're right. I'm not as important to him as he is to me." She took a vicious swipe at a dish. *"That's* what I resent."

"You are important," Bess said. "Men and women just have a different emphasis in life. I call it my concentric circle theory."

I looked at Bess in amazement. A year ago, I wouldn't have thought she knew a word that big. Now she had a theory about it.

"When a woman falls in love — *really* falls in love — she makes the man she loves the center of her life. Everything else relates to that center. Home, family, friends, even church — you name it. Let's use friends as an example. Before you got married, did you have a friend Barton didn't like?"

"Yes, I did. My college roommate. Barton thought she was whiny."

"And after you got married, what happened to that friendship?"

"We just drifted apart."

"Why?"

"I don't know. I guess I didn't want Barton to have to spend his evenings with someone he didn't like." Ruth looked out the window for a moment, thinking. She was starting to understand Bess's point. "But why isn't *he* like that?"

"Men aren't as single-minded as we are. They have the circles in their lives, too, but they aren't concentric. They've got work and friends and home and family and church and love and whatever other interests they have. The interests may overlap, but there's no single center. If one circle doesn't work out — if he doesn't like his job, for instance — he can still enjoy the other circles. By and large, he can still be happy."

Ruth felt around in the dishwater for stray silverware. She pulled out a handful of forks and started washing. "Well, what's my solution?"

"Right now, Ruth, there isn't one. He won't always be bishop. Things will settle down then. Until he's released, you'll just have to know he doesn't love you any less because you're not at the center of all his circles. That will help, won't it?"

"Yes, it will. In his own way, I guess Barton loves me after all."

It happened without fail. Whenever the subject was men and women, Bess had all the answers. It was amazing how quickly Bess had recovered from her earlier ordeal. Talking about life and love, she was in her element. I wasn't sure I believed a word she said, but the bishop's wife hung onto every sentence.

"You're right, Bess," she said. "I think you're absolutely right." She chewed on the inside of her cheek, thinking. Her hands dripped dishwater as they rested on the edge of the sink.

A clock chimed eleven times. Bess started. She sprang up, knocking her empty orange juice glass over on the kitchen table. "We have to go, Amy. We have to go *now*." With one look at her face, I knew what was wrong. Bess had gotten so engrossed in her advice she'd missed the mailman.

We drove home as quickly as the frosty roads would let us. I wanted to confront Bess about what she'd told the bishop's wife. As pretty as it sounded, Bess's concentric circle theory didn't make any allowances for people like me. If what Bess said was true, my life was centered around a man who'd been dead for seven years. I wasn't ready to admit that. The whole theory was preposterous.

But Bess was too preoccupied to talk to me. She leaned forward as I drove, as if her leaning would get us to her mailbox faster.


The mail was already in Bess's box, bulging out the open lid. She ran up the sidewalk, forgetting the frost-covered cement in her haste. Only her single-mindedness must have kept her from falling. I scurried behind her. She pulled out the mail with trembling hands. It scattered everywhere, and a gust of wind blew envelopes across the frozen yard. I reached down to help her retrieve them.

The second letter I picked up had a single name, *Fletcher Jacobsen,* as the return address. I wondered if Fletcher Jacobsen was sending out junk mail. Then I saw that the name was handwritten. A Fletcher Jacobsen was writing to Bess.

I was more than a little confused. There was only one Fletcher Jacobsen I could think of, and he was the Mormon equivalent of Superman. He'd won the Nobel Prize for medicine, somewhere back east, for developing a technique to do laser surgery on the pituitary.

He'd developed a whole nest of other landmark operations on the brain, most of which were publicized like a new cure for cancer.

I was a big fan of his. His greatest contribution, as far as I was concerned, were his discoveries about chemicals affecting brain function. I'd always thought depression and mental illness were physiological, and it was handy to finally have a whole bank of solid evidence to back it up. I was always quoting him when Alex and I visited unhappy housewives or post-partum mothers.

What made him famous for most Americans, though, was neither the surgery or the research, but the pop psychology book he'd written. *Be Your Own Best Friend* was in half the houses in America. In fact, it was the only book other than scripture I'd ever seen in Bess's home. Her copy was hammered, but I didn't pay any attention to that. Every copy of that stupid book that wasn't still in the bookstores was in the process of being read until it fell apart.

But Bess wasn't reading it to learn about pop psychology. Suddenly, everything was clear.

"You *know* Fletcher Jacobsen? *The* Fletcher Jacobsen? Or is this some kind of crush on a famous person?"

Bess snatched the letter from me, but it was too late. Her shoulders slumped, and she walked inside. Catalogs still lay on the ground but she ignored them, so I stooped to pick them up as I followed her in. The letter I'd found was the letter Bess stayed home every day to get.

Bess and I went inside and sat down. Then she hopped up and disappeared in the kitchen. She came out carrying two tall glasses of lemonade. I didn't want any lemonade, and she certainly didn't want any lemonade, but she was doing for me what every woman in Paradise Vue did when a member of the Relief Society presidency sat in her living room.

She was also stalling for time. She sat down on a love-seat and looked at the lemonade in her hand as if she'd never seen it before. She put it aside, using a piece of the day's mail as a coaster. Then she took a long breath and started to speak.

"I met him when Rick was in medical school," she said in a rush. "Do you believe in love at first sight? That was what it was, for both of us. He and Rick were friends, and he was over here all the time."

"You *do* know he's married," I said, stating the obvious. Every Mormon in America remembered the occasion. It's not every year a temple wedding makes the cover of *People* magazine. He'd married some fox who looked smug in her wedding pictures. And rightfully so. He must have been a zillionaire even then. By now he had a household of kids.

Bess fooled with her wedding ring. "He's miserable. We're both miserable."

I couldn't believe it. Bess lived in a perfect world. Perfect looks. Perfect house. Perfect clothes. Perfect car. Perfect kids. Perfect husband. Perfect *life*. "I don't understand this," I said. "You've never had a problem since the day you were born."

"Amy, I got married right out of high school. Rick was the only boy I ever dated. You know how it is. From the moment we're born, we're taught about temple marriage. It's all we look forward to. We get married when we're nineteen or twenty. Maybe we've had a year or two of college. We're young. We're foolish.

"Here we are getting married for eternity," she continued, "and what do we look for in a husband? He has to be a returned missionary. It helps if he's athletic, or he has a nice car or a good singing voice. If he's got the right look — if he's handsome, or if he's bishop material or even more — , we think he's perfect. We meet someone who fits all those qualifications, and if he likes us we marry him. It doesn't matter who he *is*. We're too young then to know who *we* are."

She kept twisting her ring, worrying it with her thumb. I wondered if the skin underneath it was getting raw yet. It would be soon if she didn't stop. "Rick isn't a bad person. I am. I promised to love him forever, when I didn't know anything about love. I didn't fall in love with Fletcher on purpose. I prayed to *stop* loving him. But now that I know what love is, and what I'm missing, I can never be happy with Rick again."

"Are you going to divorce him?" I worked hard to keep my voice non-committal.

"I'm married for eternity," she said. "There's never been a divorce in my family, or in Rick's family. There's never been a divorce in Fletcher's family, either. There's never even been a divorce in Fletcher's *wife's* family."

I didn't know what to tell her.

She pulled the ring off and held it. Her finger was indeed red and raw where the ring had been, but she wasn't looking at her finger. "I don't know what to do. I owe it to Rick to make him happy. But if Fletcher asked me to marry him, I think I could walk out on Rick and the kids and never turn back. It scares me. That's why I keep having children — it's the guilt. The more kids I have, the more Rick and I are tied together."

I took a long sip of lemonade. The ice had melted and watered it down. I put the glass on an end table, where it sweated on the polished mahogany. I didn't have any advice for Bess, so I watched droplets run off the glass and bead up on the wood. Bess didn't hop up and wipe off the table, the way she always did. She just sat there, clutching her wedding ring.

"The thing I don't understand is why this happened," she said. "There's got to be a purpose in this."

"I don't agree. We can't blame God for everything that happens."

"I *have* to believe it. Fletcher and I knew each other for two years. One day we both looked at each other and fell in love. It was love at first sight, because that day both of us saw the other for the first time. If there hadn't been a purpose, why did it happen to both of us at the same time?"

She dropped the ring on her lap. Then her thumb went back to worrying the ring finger as if the ring were there. "I keep looking for reasons. I loved Rick, or thought I did. I was happy with Rick. I didn't want to be in love with Fletcher. I still don't. This has ruined my life, and there has to be a reason for it."

"What about *his* life?"

"Rick's, or Fletcher's? Rick doesn't know anything's wrong. It makes me angry. I work so hard to try to hide it, and then I get angry when he can't tell. Isn't that crazy?"

Bess wiped a tear off her chin. "Fletcher is miserable. He and his wife should never have gotten married, but you don't throw away a temple marriage just because you're unhappy. Fletcher was born for great things — not just in medicine, but in the church. You hear him speak, and you think he could be president of the church one day. If he left his wife, he wouldn't even be a bishop."

"Is that a consideration?"

"Not for him, but it is for me. He can change the world, but only if he's never been divorced." She jammed the wedding ring back on her finger and clenched her hands together in her lap.

"So what's the reason you love each other?"

"I hoped you'd tell me."

"Maybe it's something he needs, to know that somebody loves him. Maybe loving you and not having you will give him compassion to lead others."

"Maybe it's a cosmic joke, without any purpose at all."

"I don't think it's a joke," I said. "God doesn't have a sick sense of humor."

The front door opened. Bess's daughter Stephanie ran in from kindergarten, covered with fingerpaint. Right in front of me, Bess became a different person. The tears were wiped away before Stephanie had shut the door, and she hugged the little girl, fingerpaint and all, with enthusiasm. Here was the Bess I knew — the one who'd never had a problem in her life.

Stephanie was acting peckish. "I want a samwich," she said, without even looking at me. "I want a *sam*wich."

Bess nodded apologetically and followed the little girl into the kitchen to make a sandwich for her. She stopped at the sink first to wash her hands. Bess washed her hands like Lady Macbeth.

I let myself out, preoccupied with the image of Bess scrubbing herself clean at the sink. Bess barely knew I was gone, but the water ring on her mahogany table would remind her later. I wished I could have done her any good.

# 13
# Separated
# at Birth

I waited for Bess to bring up the subject of Fletcher Jacobsen again, but she didn't. It was as if she'd never told me about him. I tried to reconstruct every conversation we'd had, looking for hidden meanings in everything Bess had said. The meanings were all there, but only for somebody who had the eyes to see.

Externally, her life went on as always. Bess looked like the happiest person in the world. She and Rick held hands during Sacrament Meeting, just like newlyweds. Her children had the secure demeanor of children who grow up encircled by love.

But whenever I watched her in church, surrounded by her husband and children, I wondered who else in the ward needed help. I looked at all the ladies of Paradise Vue with new eyes. On a cold winter's day, another facade crumbled.

I got an unexpected vacation from Relief Society visiting one winter morning, when Alex called me with the sniffles. After offering condolences, I went outside to the workshop to throw a pot on the wheel. I hadn't been out there since the last storm, and the snow was iced over. Once I got to the workshop and turned on the heater, I stayed there for hours.

Finally I looked at my watch and realized it was nearly two o'clock. I hadn't had anything to eat all day. More important, I hadn't fed Samson. Samson, unfed, usually retaliated by ingesting my houseplants.

I washed my hands and wiped them on my coveralls. Then I put on my boots and walked back to the house in the snow, following the footsteps I'd made earlier in the morning. It was a nasty afternoon, and Utah's soupy winter air made my lungs burn. I decided to stay inside for the rest of the day.

When I got to the kitchen, the phone was ringing. I thought it might be Alex, looking for sympathy. As I hurried toward the phone, I decided to order her a pizza to cheer her up. A pizza seemed like a safe option since I didn't want to go over there myself and risk catching her cold. If Alex wanted to visit, we could do it by telephone.

But it wasn't Alex, and at first I couldn't place the voice. Then I realized it was one of the Parker Twins. Eve, probably. Eve was the one who started the sentences for Eden to finish.

Eve didn't even identify herself. "I've been calling you for hours," she said breathlessly. "You need to come over here now. It can't wait."

I forgot all about sending Alex a pizza. "I'll be right over," I said. "Sit down and try not to panic." I ran outside without even getting a coat. My advice was too late — Eve was already panicked. The only thing that could upset her so much, I thought, was if something had happened to Eden.

I jogged the three blocks to the Parker house, running in the street because it was clear of ice. I almost got bowled over on the way by Edna Gompers, who always drove smack up the middle of the road in her Cadillac. Edna waved at me as she passed, as enthusiastically as if she were cheering on a runner at the Pioneer Day Marathon. I waved back and kept sprinting.

When I arrived at the Parker house, I was relieved to see there wasn't an ambulance or a fire truck on the street. I slowed my pace, but Eve Parker appeared on the front porch and waved me on. I redoubled my efforts and staggered up the front walk a minute later.

Eve dragged me up the front steps. Her bony hand grabbed me like a pair of calipers and almost pulled me off my feet. Age hadn't robbed Eve Parker of any of her natural strength.

I leaned against the door frame until I had the strength to totter inside. There I sprawled on the carpet, waiting for my heart to slow down. Eve knelt next to me. She was clearly concerned, so I panted, "I'm all right," one word at a time. And then, "Where's Eden?"

"Hurry. I have to talk to you. She'll be home soon." Eve was so upset she couldn't even wait for me to catch my breath. "There's a temple excursion. Letha Cannon's sister came to town. She took my place in the car. They'll be back anytime. Where *were* you? I've been calling you for hours."

Without waiting for me to answer, Eve went on. "Amy, you have to help me. I hate my sister."

The whole time I'd been running to the Parker house, I'd imagined every conceivable crisis. Eden had had a stroke. Eden had had a heart attack. Eden had fallen down the stairs. Eden had just up and *died*. All the while, I'd wondered how in the world Eve could live without her twin sister. Now Eve was telling me her sister was fine, and she hated her.

I pulled myself up to a sitting position and leaned against the couch, still panting as I collected my thoughts. Eve leaned down so her face was only a few inches from mine. "Did you hear me? I hate my sister."

"I heard you, Eve. I'm just trying to comprehend it. I thought you and Eden were two halves of the same person. How can you hate yourself?"

"We're not one person. We're completely different. I thought *you* could see that."

"You're so much alike. She even finishes your sentences."

"The sentences she finishes are rarely the same sentences I start. I used to correct her, but it hurt her feelings that she didn't know what I was thinking. Finally I realized it was easier to let her talk for both of us."

Having said that much, Eve decided she had time to tell the whole story before Eden returned from her temple excursion. Leaving me to sit on the floor, she went to the kitchen for some water. I drained the glass in one gulp and held it out for more, but Eve took it and set it on an end table.

A drop of sweat rolled in my eye, and I rubbed it to get rid of the salt sting. "How long has this been going on?"

"All my life, it seems. Everybody thinks being a twin is peaches and cream. It's almost a status thing, and I don't know why. Nobody made me a twin on purpose, but my parents spent their lives deciding who'd get the credit for it."

That struck me as funny. "Who won?"

"My father thought he did. He'd parade us around, showing his friends what a man he was for producing twins. If we'd been *boy* twins, he would have been unbearable. My mother stopped arguing about it, but when she told people Eden and I were twins, she acted like she'd planned it ahead of time."

"And you didn't like it."

"I didn't like any of it. I had to compromise on clothes, because Eden and I had to dress alike. She had to read the same books I did — and have the same hobbies, and go the same places. We even got identical presents at Christmas. I had to share everyone's affection — nobody dared love one of us more than the other." She lowered her voice. "And it even got worse than that."

From Eve's tone, I knew she was getting to the heart of the matter. I reached out and put her hand in mine. She squeezed my wrist with long, pincerlike fingers.

"She took him. She didn't know how to start anything on her own, so she waited for me to fall in love and then she took him away from me. She stole Abel. I'll never forgive her for that."

Suddenly, everything made sense. Eden, who always waited for Eve to lead the way, waited for Eve to have a boyfriend and then finished what Eve had started. She'd married the man Eve loved, and had his children.

"Was Abel in love with you first?" I had to learn if the love affair was real, or only real in Eve's mind. "How did he meet you without meeting Eden?"

"It was the church," Eve said. "The bishop couldn't give us ward jobs together forever. Oh, he tried. We were team teachers in Primary, and pianist and chorister for the choir. But finally he ran out of ideas, and I got called to a job in the stake. That's where we met."

She pulled her hand away from mine and reached to a picture of Abel on the table. It was an old black and white photograph of a man who'd died before I was born. He'd lived long enough to beget four children with Eden Parker, dying in a railway accident before he was thirty. The man in the picture had a young face, as innocent as the men in the 1940s movies.

Eve handed me the photograph, and I traced the face in the frame with my fingertip. "I don't understand, Eve. How did Eden get him away from you?"

"I'm not sure how it happened. I didn't even tell him I had a twin, and I kept him to myself for a long time. We'd go out for ice cream after a stake meeting, or stop off at the movies. Then I'd tell him I'd left something over at the stake center, so he'd drop me off there. I didn't want to tell him where I lived."

She paused for a moment to catch her breath, so I nodded and waited for her to go on. "One night I opened the front door, and there he was. He was angry with me. Somebody had told him I was a twin, and he couldn't understand why I kept something that important away from him. He found out where I lived, and he wanted an explanation."

"Well, how did he fall in love with Eden?"

"Eden was there. She was always there. She invited him in, and she was so sweet to him. She looked like me, and she talked like me, and she acted like me, but she hadn't deceived him. Before I knew it, they were married."

"Didn't Eden feel guilty?"

She shook her head. "Why should she feel guilty? Eden *always* took over what I started. It was a family joke. They even laughed about how I had to break Abel in before Eden could have him."

I couldn't believe her family was that insensitive. "It's ironic," I said. "You lost him because you tried to keep from losing him. What would have happened if you'd introduced the two of them from the start?"

"I wonder about that. Maybe it was kismet, and she would have had him anyway. But maybe if I'd trusted him, I would have kept him."

I could understand why Eve was so upset, but I couldn't understand what had brought the situation to a head so many years after the fact. "If this has been going on so long, why the sense of emergency today? I thought Eden had died."

"This is the first time since I've moved in with Eden that I've been alone to talk to anyone. She's here when I wake up in the morning, and she's the last thing I see when I go to bed at night. We even raised her children together, after Abel was gone. I can't watch something on television or read a book without her watching the program or reading the same book as soon as I put it down. I can't talk on the telephone without her picking up the extension."

She looked downward and then said, as if confessing, "Amy, I almost wish she *had* died. She doesn't know how to do anything but be a twin, and I don't want to be a twin anymore."

I got off the floor and sat on the couch next to Eve, putting my arm around her shoulders. "After all these years, why are you telling this to me?"

"I always liked you. You know how to keep a secret."

Then I remembered Alex was sick. Eve had probably tried to talk to Alex, and Alex had referred her to me. I said, "Eve, what can you do about all this?"

"I don't know. I was hoping you'd tell me. You always have an answer for everything."

I didn't have an answer for Eve, but I didn't need one. Just as I tried desperately to think of some solution for her, Eden pushed the door open and entered the house with a burst of Utah smog. She saw me sitting with Eve and rushed over to her sister. Kneeling on the floor in front of her she asked, "What's wrong? Are you sick?"

Eve, fortified by my presence or her new resolution, said, "I can't live like this anymore."

"Like what? You can't live like what?"

"I can't be your twin. I want a divorce."

The idea was so alien to Eden that she burst out laughing. Then, seeing her sister was deadly serious, she sobered fast. "You can't just change the birth certificate. We've been twins for seventy-three years. We can't live without each other."

"You're wrong, Eden," Eve said. "I can live without *you*. I love you because I know I'm supposed to love you, but I don't like you. I don't like the way you've wormed yourself into my life."

"How could I do that? We're twins. We do everything alike."

"That's a lie. You know that's a lie. You only pretend to do everything like me."

As soon as the words were spoken, I knew they were correct. Eve and Eden had never done anything synchronously; Eden was always a half-second behind her sister. Eden's eyes were constantly on Eve, ready to follow a gesture with her hands. She was always more attentive to Eve's conversation than Eve was herself, anticipating Eve's thoughts so she could end her sentences.

I could picture Eden stalling at the closet every morning while her sister chose the day's outfit — and then "coincidentally" choosing the identical clothing. I could also see her waiting until Eve had taken each bite of food at breakfast, and then eating a bite of the same food.

Betty Jo Jennings's cockeyed story about the Parker Twins was truer than she knew. Everyone thought of Eve and Eden as one person in two bodies, but they'd been separate individuals all along. Just like Chang and Eng Bunker, the original Siamese twins, Eve and Eden chafed at the prison that tied them together.

At least, Eve did. As I looked at the two sisters together, Eden kneeling on the floor in front of her sister, I saw that Eden was devastated. I took my free hand and put it on her shoulder, forming a bridge between the two women. I wanted to think of something profound to say, but no words formed. All I could think of was a trite old saying, "It is better to be a has-been than one who never was." Somehow, that didn't apply.

"Eve," I said, "Eden, the two of you have a hundred and forty-six years of history between yourselves. Things will never be the same as they were when you woke up this morning. But that only means you have a chance to build a new relationship on the ashes of the old one."

I looked at one and then the other. Eve shrugged in an I-don't-know gesture. Eden started to make the same gesture, and then she stopped. "I don't know," she said. "It's too early to tell."

I stood up. "It's time for me to go. You have a lot to talk about, and you need to do that without me."

Both sisters stood with me. Except for the silk rose at Eve's throat, they were dressed alike. I didn't think they'd be dressed alike tomorrow.

"I knew you'd understand," Eve said, kissing me on the cheek as I left. She left a watermelon-red mark on my face that I didn't discover for hours afterwards.

Eden, who watched me go in silence, looked as if her life had fallen out from under her.

# 14
# Searching for Clues

**M**y favorite part of Relief Society each Sunday was sitting in the front of the room, facing out toward the ladies and thinking about them. We learned to read a lot from their expressions, and often the visits Alex and I would make during the coming week would be chosen from whose face in Relief Society looked troubled — or whose face we didn't see at all.

One winter Sunday, the crowd was particularly heavy, with standees lining the rear wall of the Relief Society room. In that sea of upturned women's faces, Myra Boddle caught my eye. I recognized her by her wispy gray hair. She held a book squarely in front of her nose, peering owlishly at the words through Coke-bottle glasses. I squinted to read the title on the slip-jacket and made out the words, *A Marvelous Work and a Wonder*. I'd read the day's Relief Society lesson, and LeGrand Richards's classic gospel book was the focus of it. I smiled, thinking at the number of ladies who had the lesson memorized every week so they could answer questions in class.

The lesson was on the eternal family. It was a subject that always sent my mind on a tangent, and not five minutes into the lesson my thoughts were far from Relief Society.

I was brought back to Paradise Vue abruptly, when I realized the room was silent. Even the babes in arms were quiet, as if the very room were holding its breath. Everyone looked expectantly toward the back of the room. Janece Whitney, the teacher, fixed a patient stare on someone in the back row.

Finally she broke the silence. "I just want you to read a little passage from *A Marvelous Work and a Wonder*," she said in a wheedling voice.

"I'm not a good reader." It was Myra Boddle, staring right back at Janece over her copy of the book.

Janece was not to be intimidated. "That's fine, Myra. We all love you. If you miss a word, we'll help you."

"My glasses are fogged up."

"We'll wait for you to *unfog* 'em." Janece was being unusually persistent. "I've left my own copy at home. You're the only one here with a book."

"Then *I'll* read it," said LuDean Hervey, snatching the book from Myra. Myra tried to grab it back, but LuDean was too fast for her. "Where exactly do you want me to start?"

"Right in the middle of page two-oh-two," Janece said. "I don't have my book, so I can't tell you how the passage begins."

"*Right* in the middle? Here goes." LuDean started reading:

> "*What about the rest?*" said Connie.
> "*The rest? There is no rest. Only to my experience the mass of women are like this: most of them want a man, but don't want the sex, but they put up with it, as part of the bargain...*"

Janece reddened in embarrassment. She riffled frantically through her lesson notes as LuDean read the text.

Alex nudged me. "Is that the book I think it is?"

"I don't know, but I'm sure it isn't *A Marvelous Work and a Wonder*."

Ladies across the room were buzzing like curious bees, but LuDean plodded on. She read in a sing-song voice, the way people who are asked to read aloud often concentrate on the individual words without comprehending the context.

*"...The more old-fashioned sort just lie there like nothing and let you go ahead. They don't mind afterwards: then they like you. But the actual thing is nothing to them, a bit distasteful."*

"THAT'S NOT WHAT I ASKED YOU TO READ," Janece boomed. She had finally found her voice.

"You wanted page 202, the middle of the page? Well, this is it." LuDean inspected the text as if waiting for the words to change.

Janece consulted her notes. "What I wanted you to read was under the heading, 'The Family Unit in the Millennium.'"

"Well," said Edna Gompers in a stage whisper, "LuDean's reading about how the family unit gets *started.*"

Alex buried her face in both hands. She was chewing on her lower lip, but I couldn't tell if she was trying not to laugh or if she was just embarrassed. Myra Boddle grabbed her book back and slammed it shut. She took it so fast that the slip-cover stayed in LuDean's hands.

I caught a glimpse of the cover as Myra hid the book away. Alex was right — things could have been much worse. LuDean had read one of the tamer passages of *Lady Chatterley's Lover.*


When church ended, Alex took me to her house instead of dropping me off at home. I thought she wanted to talk about poor Myra Boddle, who had climaxed her humiliation by tripping and falling in her haste to get away after Relief Society. If not that, I thought we'd discuss the *faux pas* of LuDean Hervey. LuDean was a paranoid soul, and if she didn't already think the whole Relief Society episode had been set up to embarrass her, she *would* think it before nightfall.

But Alex's mind was far from *Lady Chatterley's Lover.* She warmed us up a can of soup and served it with some stale saltines.

Alex couldn't cook worth a darn, but she did like to eat. If soup and crackers was her idea of Sunday dinner, she had something on her mind. I sipped my soup and nibbled on crackers, biding my time until Alex decided to speak.

"Amy, I can't go on like this."

"Go on like what?" My mind was still on Relief Society, and I thought she was telling me she was tired of her job as president. "You mean you want to quit already?"

"What do you mean, *already?* I've been married more than half my life."

"Of course you have. What's that got to do with Relief Society?"

"Who's talking about Relief Society? Relief Society is the only thing that keeps me going." She pushed her bowl aside and put her elbows on the table. Then she dejectedly put her chin in the palms of her hands. "This Ethan thing is eating me alive. Here it is Sunday, and he's gone again. He was gone all day yesterday, too. Where's he going? He's not at the office. He's not at the club. Even I won't believe he's playing golf in the dead of winter — the ground is frozen solid. What's he doing?"

"Maybe he goes for long drives. If I had a car like his, I'd spend a lot of time in it."

"Nope. I've thought of that. I checked the odometer yesterday before he left and after he came back. He only put nine miles on the car all day. He wasn't in the car."

I laughed. "You don't have to drive the car to spend time in it. The best times I've ever spent in a car happened when the car wasn't going anywhere."

Alex laughed too. For a minute she looked like the old Alex. Then she sobered again. "Wrong again. We're talking about Ethan here. Cars are too confining for him. He won't even sleep in a queen-sized bed."

I moved my own bowl away, and in unconscious imitation of Alex I put my head in the palms of my own hands. "I thought things had been better for you since Christmas. You seemed so happy then."

Alex bit the skin around her thumbnail. She took too big a hunk out of it, and it started bleeding. Then she gazed at her thumb as if it held the answers to all her questions. "No. At Christmas I realized that whatever else is going on, Ethan loves me. I thought that would be enough, but it isn't. I have to know more."

"You may never know more, Alex. Ethan isn't going to tell you."

"Not of his own volition, anyway. Amy, what do you think of snooping around?"

"Not much. Everything I've found by snooping was something I never should have known. I read my roommate's journal in college and learned she hated me. When I was a little kid I eavesdropped on my mother and found out she was dying of cancer. I didn't need to know any of that. It didn't make me any happier."

"You're right. I know you're right, but I can't help it. I have to know. Will you help me find out?" She looked at me with such an anguished expression that I couldn't say no. I could never say no to Alex.

"I'll look. We shouldn't do it, but I'll look. We probably won't find anything. Actually, I hope we don't find anything."

"*I* almost hope we don't find anything," Alex said. "No — that's not true. I hope there's nothing to be found. But if it's there, I want to find it. I have to know."

"Even if it ruins your marriage?"

"It won't do that. No matter what I find out, I'll never let Ethan go."

Alex stood up and gathered the dishes. She had such a resolute look on her face that I thought she'd get right to work searching for clues. But once the decision had been made, she seemed to want to postpone it. She washed our few lunch dishes and then decided she wanted dessert. She made us each a hot fudge sundae, lingering over the fudge and whipping the cream up fresh. The ice cream tasted much better than the canned soup and stale crackers, so we both ate two bowls of it. Then, Alex again cleaned the kitchen and washed the dishes.

I watched the whole performance from a chair. "You know, we don't have to do this."

"Yes, we do. I'm just making my plans. I don't think Ethan would hide anything in the bedroom. I read too many books for him to hide anything in the library. It's got to be in his office, don't you think?"

I held a long lock of hair in front of my face, inspecting it for split ends. Instead I found a gray hair, which I pulled out to keep other gray hairs from getting any ideas. Finally I said, "Isn't the office too obvious?"

"If it's obvious, that's where it is. Are you ready?"

I wasn't ready. I'd never be ready to learn anything bad about Ethan. I looked at my fake Rolex watch — the one he'd given me for Christmas. The hour was still early enough that Ethan wouldn't catch us, and I couldn't think of any other excuse to leave Alex to search alone. "I'm ready. If it's what you want, I'm ready."

"Thanks, Amy. I really appreciate this. I know you don't want to do it. Let's get it over with." And with that, she dusted off her hands and went upstairs to Ethan's office.

Ethan's office was straight out of a Sherlock Holmes novel. There wasn't a violin, or a cache of cocaine, or even a pipe. But otherwise, the large room reeked of Victorian splendor. The bookshelves were lined with old, leather-bound classics. An antique world globe sat on the floor. The desk was massive and dark, and the portraits on the walls were of anonymous, neckless ancestors. The only thing missing from the office was the musty smell of antiquity. Alex's housekeeper kept the room as clean as a suite in a luxury hotel.

As soon as she walked in the room, Alex went to the bookshelves. Starting at the top left, she methodically pulled every book from its place and inspected it. I shook my head; nobody would hide anything important in a book, I thought. Nevertheless, I did run my hands along the underside of the lower shelves in case anything had been taped there.

The globe was in one piece: nothing could be hidden inside it. Nothing was secreted inside the picture frames or on the walls behind the pictures. And the house was too new to have any secret passageways or compartments that Alex didn't know about.

Ethan had a big brass container full of antique walking sticks. He'd been collecting them for years. Each one opened to reveal a hidden treasure — a compass, or a pair of dice, or a spyglass, or some other device. I sat on the floor in front of the big brass pot and opened each walking stick in turn, almost forgetting I was on a mission for Alex. I was surprised to see that one cane hid a tiny pistol. The walking stick had been built around the pistol more than a hundred years ago, so the gun didn't look threatening on that winter afternoon.

All the while I looked, Alex inspected books. She opened the covers and riffled through the pages, but she found nothing.

After I put Ethan's cane collection away, I examined the furniture. The overstuffed chairs and sofas yielded no evidence to convict Alex's husband. I even scrutinized the lamps and fixtures, but there was nothing to find.

At last there was nothing in the room untouched but Ethan's desk. I didn't want to look through it: that really *was* unethical. Peeking under sofa cushions was one thing, but I had no right to look in a man's private papers.

"I'm finished," I said. "All that's left is the desk."

Alex looked up from *The Red and the Black*. "Well, look in the desk." She said it a little impatiently, as if saying *of course* I had to look in the desk.

I didn't argue. Frankly, it was because I didn't think I'd find anything. Hiding something in a desk was as obvious as hiding it inside a book. It was like hanging a neon arrow above a treasure chest, pointing the way to secret riches.

Methodically, I looked through Ethan's personal files. I inspected his checkbooks and his charge card statements. I read the file marked "letters," but all I found were letters from Jean and Clementine and love notes from Alex. I checked health records and insurance policies. All I found was the normal effluvia of a man's life.

After I'd read the files and looked inside the drawers, I removed the drawers to look underneath them. Alex saw me take out a drawer and check the underside. She shook her head. "He wouldn't hide anything there."

"Well, he hasn't hidden it anywhere else. Alex, we're not going to find anything. Let's give up."

She blew the hair out of her eyes in annoyance. "You can give up if you want. I have to look. We're almost done. Just finish the desk and let me finish the books." She pulled down a fat volume, *Canterbury Tales*, and opened the flyleaf, dismissing me. Even though I knew Alex was trying to make me feel guilty, I let her succeed.

"All right. I'll finish looking in the desk. But why wouldn't Ethan hide anything under the drawers?"

Alex put *Canterbury Tales* back on the shelf. "Let me tell you something about secrecy. The best place to hide something is out in the open. That's not just true of *things*, either. If I've got a secret that means a lot to me, the way I hide it is to tell everyone. They all think I'm kidding, and no one ever finds out."

"Sounds logical to me. Tell me, is that Ethan's philosophy too?"

"I don't know. You know men. Maybe you'd better keep looking where you are."

Alex was partially right: I didn't find anything taped to the underside of the desk drawers. But when I felt around inside the desk after the drawers were removed, I found a piece of paper taped to the roof of a compartment. I pulled it out and saw it was only an American Express bill. I must have been wrong about it being taped there, I thought; it must have just been stuck.

But when I read the bill, I saw the evidence Alex had been looking for. It was a page from December's statement — the part that contained a photocopy of each separate purchase. American Express was unique in that respect. Most charge card companies sent statements telling how much money you spent, and where, and what was the date. American Express sent an actual photocopy of each transaction, as itemized as the sales clerk chose to do it.

The sales clerk at Arent's had itemized Ethan's purchases well. Ethan had bought Alex's mink jacket at Arent's. But the sales receipt showed he'd bought a second jacket, identical except in a smaller size, at the same time.

In what had to be a case of clerical overkill, the clerk had also written the delivery addresses right on the billing statement. One mink jacket had been sent to Alex. The other jacket, the smaller one, had gone to an address up Emigration Canyon.

As I stared at the receipt, trying to comprehend it, Alex walked up behind me. There was no time for me to hide the receipt. She was reading it before I knew she was there. A tiny moan escaped her lips, as she tore the paper from my hands and looked at it as if to memorize the words. Finally she said, "Ethan's secretary lives up Emigration Canyon," and she gave me back the bill.

Alex watched as I carefully taped the evidence back where I'd found it. Then she silently left the room, turning back once to give the office a last miserable glance. I realized later she was checking to make sure we'd left the room as we'd found it, but right then it seemed as if she wanted to go back in time — back to the moment she was inspecting *Canterbury Tales,* when she still believed there was a chance she was wrong about Ethan.

If Alex was sick at heart, I was devastated at finding the evidence that caused her misery. If any proof would be found, I'd assumed Alex would find it. I was just supporting Alex while she did the looking. Finding the evidence wasn't my role; it wasn't my place.

I followed Alex to her bedroom, where she lay down on the edge of her side of the bed. She shut her eyes, but tears escaped the tightly closed lids.

I didn't know what to say. "I'm sorry, Alex. I'm so sorry."

Alex was quiet for a long time. She was so still I thought for a minute she'd fallen asleep. Finally she said in a low voice, "He'll never know that I know, and I'll never leave him. I could never live without him."

"Don't say never, Alex," was all I could answer her back. "We don't know what tomorrow will bring."

✳

I walked home from Alex's house, leaving her to worry in solitude about the proof we had found. As I picked my footing along the icy sidewalks, I was in a somber frame of mind. All I could remember was the way Ethan had been with Alex at Christmas, less than six weeks before. Even then, when their marriage seemed so strong and secure, Ethan was thinking of somebody else. I wondered how any person could hide his true feelings so well. Then I thought of Bess, and of Eve Parker, and I wondered how many other lives were hidden behind masks of complacency.

I was concentrating so hard on my thoughts that Verna Liddell had to call me several times before I heard her cries. When I looked up, she was hailing me like a New York taxi at rush hour. I smiled at the picture of Verna flailing her arms on her front stoop, but then I saw Verna's face. Verna wasn't in a smiling mood. She wasn't saying hello to Amy; she was hailing a member of the Relief Society presidency.

I turned up Verna's walk and headed precariously toward the old lady. Verna, like so many Salt Lake residents of all ages, only wanted to shovel the snow when it was springtime and there wasn't any. During the winter months, it was too much trouble to deal with snow shovels and the cold wind, so the accumulation from every storm turned to ice before the winter sun finally melted it away. I didn't fall down on Verna's front walk, but I did slide dramatically for several feet once before regaining my balance.

Verna had something on her mind, but she didn't tell me what it was until after she had heated up some apple cider for me in the kitchen. I took the drink and sat with my hands around the mug, warming my fingers as I waited for Verna to tell me what had her so upset. Finally she produced a letter from her apron pocket. She didn't read it to me, but held it in her hands, crinkling the stationery as she worried it with her fingers.

"I got a letter today."

I raised my eyebrows. It was Sunday, and there wasn't any mail delivery.

"I was down in Heber City, and I just got home this morning. There was the mail, a-waiting for me." She opened the pages, and I expected her to read from them. Then she shut the letter and went back to crinkling the stationery.

"It's from Cora Peabody. Do you remember Cora?"

"No, I don't. She must have moved before I got here."

"Well, do you remember the Pearson family — Delwin and Saralee and the three little ones?"

"I remember a Joyce Pearson. She lived somewhere in the neighborhood."

"Joyce was Delwin's niece. She lived in the house for a few years after Delwin and Saralee left. She sold it to the Crowthers, and they sold it to that Baptist family, and that Baptist family sold it to that nice young Peeples couple. Jason Peeples is a nice boy, isn't he?"

"Yes, he is." I couldn't place Cora Peabody, but at last I knew where the woman had lived. Her family home was now owned by one of the many oglers of Emma Austen.

"Well, Cora told me all about Theressa Munch. Do you remember Theressa?"

I sighed. I was so worried about Alex that it was hard to worry about people who were strangers to me. "No, Verna, I sure don't."

"Theressa was married to Hugo Munch, who was the bishop back in '46."

"Paradise Vue wasn't even a *ward* in '46."

"Well, Hugo was bishop of whatever ward Paradise Vue was called back then. His counselors were Hal Howard and Colin Forbes."

"Sorry. I didn't know them, either."

"Well, Hal worked at Cream o' Weber. That was later on, of course. And Brother Forbes had a job with the Post Office."

"No, I can't place either one of them. Must have been before my time."

"Brother Forbes lived in the old Massey house. That's the one was bought up by the Cuthberts during the War."

"World War II?"

"No. Korean." She fixed a brief look of impatience on me, but I wasn't deliberately being obtuse. "The Cuthberts sold to the McConkies, and the McConkies sold to the Hyman family. They lived in it a long time and sold it to Juanita Coulman. Then, when Juanita went to the rest home, she sold it to the Wilkersons."

"I know the Wilkersons!" Finally I was on firm conversational ground.

"Of *course* you know the Wilkersons. *Everybody* knows the Wilkersons. Well, they're living in the old Massey home — the one Brother and Sister Forbes lived in."

"So what did you find out about Sister Forbes?" I was anxious to get Verna's thoughts back on track.

"I didn't find out anything about her! Who's talking about her? She's been dead and buried for twenty years. I'm talking about Theressa Munch, who was married to Hugo Munch, who was in the bishopric with Colin Forbes who lived in the old Massey home."

"Oh, I understand." Actually, I wasn't sure I did understand. But Verna's train of thought had been thoroughly derailed, and agreeing with Verna was my only hope to steer us back to the point.

"Well, she's gone." Verna came back to the point with a bang. She dropped the letter in her lap, and tears formed in the corners of her eyes. "I'll never see her again."

I moved over to the couch next to Verna and put my arm around her. "I'm sorry," I said. "I didn't know Theressa, but I'm sure she lived a long and full life. I'll bet she's happier up in heaven with her loved ones."

Verna shook my arm off her shoulder and shot me a withering glare of disgust. "Who the hell said she's dead? Theressa's moved to Chicago." Then she sighed and slumped in her seat. "But she might as well be dead to me."

After commiserating with Verna about the loss of her friend, I finished my apple cider and left. I wasn't as successful going back down Verna's front walk as I had been coming up it, and I fell solidly on the ice in my church clothes. Verna called her sympathy from the safety of her doorway, leaving me to limp home alone.

I spent the rest of the day in bed, where I had plenty of time to think about Verna's friendship with Theressa, as well as all the other things that were dying without the formality of a burial.

# 15
# Vindication

For the rest of my life, Valentine's Day is going to remind me of beef stew. And no matter how long I live, I'm going to owe a pretty big debt to Welfare Square in general and beef stew in particular for keeping me there on a snowy February fourteenth. If you've got the sign-up sheet for a canning assignment at Welfare Square, count me in.

When that Valentine's Day welfare assignment came, however, I wasn't nearly so happy about it. The stake had probably had the date marked on their calendar for three months, but in true stake fashion they didn't tell us about it until Sunday — two days before the assignment.

As a veteran of ward sign-up sheets, I know how easy it is to get people to commit to something that's three or four months down the road. Then you can hold them to it with guilt when the time comes.

But tell someone she's wanted to go to Welfare Square two days hence, and it's amazing how busy she is. Cupboards need to be cleaned. Colds are coming on. Luncheon dates spring up like weeds on a roadside. After all your pleading, you're sitting around with an empty sign-up sheet.

As luck had it, I conducted Relief Society that Sunday. I pulled out all the stops, making the announcement with pathos and drama. I did everything but dance on the table, and I would have done that if I'd thought it would help. I had the whole Relief Society laughing halfway through the announcement, and several of them were in tears. But when the sign-up sheet came around, only Alice Barnes had put her name on the list. Alice Barnes always signed up. I blessed her name.

Alice's gesture still left us with six blank spaces on the sign-up sheet. Alex looked at Bess and Emma and me and wrote our names down, too. That left us with two holes to fill, which was something it was Emma's job, as secretary, to do. I smiled sweetly and passed the sheet along to her, glad to be rid of the problem.

But Emma scribbled something on the sign-up sheet and passed it right back to me. She'd scratched her own name off the list, and she added a note saying she couldn't possibly soil her hands at Welfare Square. She and Leo Byrd had gotten engaged the night before, the note said, and they were going to announce it Wednesday night at a family dinner. She planned to spend Valentine's Day at some beauty salon in Provo, getting her hair tinted with blonde highlights that would match the ones in Leo's hair.

She leaned over Bess and said innocently, "I wouldn't be caught dead in that stinky place. You don't expect me to risk breaking a fingernail the day before my *engage*ment party, do you?" She gave me a winning smile. "And I just don't have a spare minute to call anybody else. This is an important time for me. *You* understand."

The whole left side of the Relief Society heard Emma, and it shamed three of them into volunteering right there. That was gratifying. I may have been the only one in the world who didn't like Emma, but everybody else knew they had to make allowances for her.

When I awoke on Tuesday morning, it was pitch black outside. I peeked through the blinds and was disgusted at life. It had been snowing all night, and now there was an ice storm. I dreaded the thought of seven Paradise Vue ladies skidding down the hill to

Welfare Square three hours hence. I guessed I'd better drive them. I took the stake welfare leader's name in vain and rolled over for a nap.

The telephone woke me. I thought it would be somebody cancelling the Welfare Square assignment, and I couldn't have blamed them if they did. At this hour, I wasn't going to be able to get a replacement. We'd be short on our quota, and the bishop would be furious.

But it was only Emma. "Hi, Amy," she gushed. "Isn't it a *beau*tiful day? I just *love* the snow. It's *so* Christmasy." I cringed when I heard that. Emma had that you're-my-best-friend-in-the-whole-wide-world tone in her voice, a tone she only used when she wanted something major. I steeled myself.

Emma finished the formalities and got a plaintive wheedle in her voice. I could see her scrootching out her mouth in a pout the way she always did when she used that pleading tone. Emma must have thought the pout made her look irresistible, but I thought it made her look like Roddy McDowell in full *Planet of the Apes* makeup.

"You've got to help me," she said. "I'm desperate." I kept my mouth shut, waiting for the crisis. "Janna Lee Simonsen was going to drive me to Provo today for my hair appointment, but now she won't go. I've just *got* to get there. Janna's so *unreasonable*. *I* wouldn't be afraid of a little snow, and I'll bet you aren't either."

"You lose," I said. I loved to prove Emma wrong. "She'd be a fool to drive to Provo in weather like this." The truth was, I loved to drive in the snow. My Blazer could navigate anything, and I enjoyed the challenge. But I wasn't about to let Emma manipulate me. And today I had a good excuse to tell her no.

"I have to can beef stew this morning," I reminded her. Uncharitably, I didn't let it go at that. "It's true I'll just be breaking the heck out of my fingernails, but somebody has to do it."

"Well, you obviously don't care anything about Janna *Lee*," she sniffed. Emma sounded hurt. "Now she's just going to have to take me, and she'll be afraid all the way. She won't be any fun at all. This is an important day for me, but you don't care. Your stupid assignment is only an excuse. My day is ruined, and it's all your fault. I *knew* I could never rely on you."

She fell silent, waiting for me to apologize and tell her I'd drive her to Provo. When I didn't, she gave me a saccharine, "Well! Have a *nice* day," and hung up.

I forgot about Emma as soon as she was off the phone. Remembering it was Valentine's Day, I crawled back in bed and daydreamed until it was time to get up. Only when the alarm clock rang did I get dressed and eat breakfast. Then I cleared snow off the Blazer and collected the Relief Society ladies for our trip to Welfare Square.

I picked up Alex first. She got in the car silently and nursed a Diet Coke morosely until we picked up Alice Barnes. I knew Valentine's Day would be hard on Alex, and I wanted to try to cheer her up. But it had to wait until after Welfare Square. When Alex was being Relief Society president, she sublimated her own problems and concentrated on others'.

Her disposition improved, at least externally, when Alice Barnes got in the car, but Alex was on my mind for the rest of the day.

Next we stopped for Bess, whose trip to Welfare Square represented a bigger sacrifice on her part than anyone else in our group suspected. As nervous as she was about the mail any other day of the year, she must have been frantic on Valentine's Day. She got into the car timorously, with several sidelong glances back at her house.

Before Bess could say a word, I said, "Look at the snow! It's so deep today I'll bet the mail doesn't get through until four o'clock."

Alice Barnes chimed right in. "Nope! With all the Valentine's mail, I bet it'll be later than that. I'd hate to be a mailman on Valentine's Day." Alice rambled on for a minute or two about Valentine's Day and snow and mail and mailmen. She dearly loved to talk. But looking at Bess in the rear-view mirror, I saw that my strategy had been successful. Bess appeared considerably less uneasy. She gave me a grateful smile in the mirror as I turned a corner.

Our next pick-up was Joanna Wheeler, one of the young mothers in the ward. Joanna was a cipher to me, because she had just moved into the ward. She made a big impression today, however, by slipping on the top step outside her door and falling all the way to the ground below. The deep snow cushioned her fall, but Alex was out of the Blazer and halfway across the lawn before Joanna hit the ground. Joanna was unhurt, but the accident was almost as successful at distracting Alex from her own problems as I'd been at distracting Bess.

Our last stop was to pick up the Parker Twins. Despite their falling-out, the habit of doing things as a couple was so ingrained in them that they'd both volunteered to go to the cannery. But when they came out to the car, it was almost as if they did everything the opposite of one another on purpose, to show the world — and each other — that they were two separate people.

Eve appeared at the front door. Eden came out the back door, even though it meant a long walk in two-foot snow to get to the car. Eve wore slacks. Eden wore a dress. They sat apart from each other in the car. And when Eve started a sentence, Eve finished it.

All this was a little disconcerting for me, but it seemed even more unnerving for Eve and Eden. Eve would start to say something and then hesitate, as if waiting for Eden to barge in. When Eden didn't interrupt, Eve seemed to have to gather her thoughts before finishing what she wanted to say. Meanwhile, Eden looked out the car window. Her mouth formed a tight, straight line. As soon as I saw the two of them together, I knew the day would be a long one.


Canning beef stew was just as disgusting as I remembered. The potatoes were lumpy. The onions were strong and made us cry. The carrots were a little woody, and the knives were dull. How such an awful environment could produce a stew that tasted pretty good was beyond me.

The cannery floor got slippery from the gravy, and Alice Barnes fell down twice. The second time she bruised her elbow. She didn't complain, but I could tell it hurt her. I finally put her upstairs on the can line to give her a rest.

After skinning and chopping and mixing and canning, we had to wait about a million years for the stew to process. All the time, we got to smell the heavy odor of beef stew cooking in the processing vats. Beef stew, processing, doesn't smell nearly as good as beef stew simmering on a stove. It smells more like beef stew boiling in dishwater — a nauseating combination. I wanted a Pepsi to bolster my spirits, but the Welfare Square vending machines didn't contain any caffeine but chocolate.

When it was cold and snowy outside, the steam inside the cannery got frigid. It was easy to get chilled from it. I caught myself sniffing and realized I was on my way to a cold. It put me in a foul mood, and once I even wished I'd driven Emma to Provo. But everyone did her job without complaint. Despite the chill in the air, the day passed quickly.

Our work was so successful that when everything was finished, Alex took us all to Don Antonio's for a late lunch. We reeked of beef stew, and people who passed our table wrinkled their noses.

Like the rest of the day, lunch was jarred by the demeanor of the Parker Twins. They didn't sit next to each other at the meal; nor did they sit at opposite ends of the table to present a bookend effect. They didn't order the same food, either. Eve ordered enchiladas, but Eden just ate a taco.

I wondered if Eden was secretly relieved to be ordering what she wanted to order for the first time in so many years, but she didn't look happy about it. Following Eve's lead in every decision for most of her life should have been constricting to Eden, but I don't think she looked at it that way. Suddenly, Eden was making choices. It made her life more complicated.

Despite the uneasiness between Eve and Eden, the warm restaurant and the hot food gave us all renewed energy. Alice Barnes monopolized the conversation, telling us all the cute little things her husband Ralph had done for Valentine's Day over the years. Joanna Wheeler had a few comments of her own, and Alex and Bess looked interested. But I kept noticing Bess looking at her watch, and eventually I suggested we leave. Bess flashed me another grateful look as we got our coats and left for home.

I dropped Bess off first. She heaved an audible sigh when she saw the mailman's truck on her street as we pulled up to her house. Alice Barnes had been right: even though it was after four-thirty, Bess hadn't missed the mail. When she waved goodbye to us, she was more cheerful than she had been all day.

I couldn't say the same for Alex. Every time someone else got out of the car, Alex seemed to deflate a little more. When the two of us were finally alone, she heaved a large sigh and lowered her head to the dashboard. When we got to her house, I went inside with her.

We walked in Alex's back door stiffly, because the beef stew on our clothes was getting dry and hard. The first thing we heard was Alex's answering machine, beeping at eighty decibels. We didn't have time to turn it off, because Man o' War and Chesapeake smelled the beef stew and went into a frenzy. Alex, who always dropped her clothes the moment she walked inside, got two bathrobes from the hall closet. We slithered out of our clothes, and the dogs went crazy. Man o' War grabbed my sweatshirt and circled the kitchen with it, looking for someplace to bury it. Chesapeake wrapped herself in Alex's stewy jeans and writhed on her back, whimpering.

I looked at those dogs and wished Alex had never bought them for Ethan. They'd turned her home into a kennel. But even more than that, I resented the way they riveted attention on themselves whenever they were in the room. I was embarrassed to admit I was jealous of two animals.

After we put on the bathrobes, Alex ignored her answering machine long enough to pour me a Pepsi and herself a Diet Coke. I grabbed a handful of Oreos from one of Alex's cookie jars. Only after our hands were full and we'd had a sip of our soft drinks did Alex rewind her answering machine.

Alex had six messages. Grace Hunter wanted her to call about a visiting teaching problem. Alex wrote down the message and the number on a notebook and waited for the next one. Clementine called from Boston to wish her happy Valentine's Day. That brightened her spirits a little.

The next call was a hang-up, and the dead line hummed loudly across the room until the message machine recycled. Alex and I took simultaneous sips of our soft drinks. Alex looked at her watch and sighed.

The next message was from Ethan. As soon as Alex heard the hearty tone in his voice, she seemed to shrink. "Hi, Hon!" he boomed on the tape. "Happy Valentine's Day. I was going to take you to The Five Alls for dinner, but I've got a client in town. We'll have to put it off. I'll make it up to you another time." The phone went dead.

"I'm sorry, Alex," I said.

Alex shrugged. She acted as if she'd been expecting this. In the winters, when Ethan couldn't "golf," he "played tennis" or "had clients."

"Want a hot date tonight?" Alex asked. I answered yes, but the word was drowned out by the fifth call: another hang-up.

The last message was from Bishop Nebeker. As soon as Alex heard the tone in his voice, she sat at attention.

"There's been an accident," he said. He must have been calling from his car phone, because there was static on the line and the words were hard to make out. "Emma Austen and Janna Lee Simonsen got hit by a truck at Point of the Mountain. Emma's been flown to University Hospital, and I'm going there now." There was a pause on the line, and he cleared his throat. "I'm sorry to tell you this on an answering machine, but Janna Lee is dead."

I don't remember much of what happened over the next few hours. We went to Janna Lee's house first. Relatives were just starting to arrive there. Alex hugged Stan Simonsen and sat for a few minutes holding his hand. The two of them discussed funeral arrangements, while I played with the children on the floor.

The three children were too young to understand what was going on, and they proudly showed me the day's accumulation of Valentines. When relatives arrived, they acted as if it were all part of the holiday. None of them asked about their mother.

Afterwards, Alex and I drove to University Hospital. The snow had frozen on the roads after sunset, and even my Blazer had trouble getting traction on the black ice. When we got to the hospital, there was little news. The bishop was there, and Emma's mother. Emma was in intensive care. She would live, Bishop Nebeker said, but her face would be badly scarred.

When we'd done all we could do at the hospital, I dropped off Alex at home. She had to make telephone calls about food assignments for the Simonsen family. I offered to help her, but she said she wanted to do it alone. Alex was good at delegating easy tasks, but the horrible ones she always kept for herself.

I was exhausted when I got home. I wanted to hold Samson for awhile and then go to bed. But no sooner had I turned on the lights in my house when the doorbell rang. My next-door neighbor, Mrs. Antonelli, was at the door, radiating good cheer.

"You'll never guess what happened today," she said. "You got flowers! Two batches of them!" Mrs. Antonelli, who wasn't a member of our church, never could understand why I hadn't married again. Now I apparently had not one boyfriend, but two. She was ecstatic.

She produced a bouquet and a rose box from the side of the doorway, where she'd hidden them to heighten the drama. She walked inside with the flowers, expecting to share my good fortune. I couldn't turn her away, so I tried to act as excited as she was.

The bouquet came with a card that was still sealed. Inside the Valentine was a note that said, "Thanks for setting me up with Emma. I will never forget what you did for me." Leo's note was written in clumsy block letters, and he wrote the word *setting* with one *t*.

But Mrs. Antonelli was so excited I couldn't tell her the truth about the flowers. "This one's from a secret friend," I said confidentially. "I can't tell you what the note says, but the flowers are beautiful, aren't they?"

"Oh, yes." She bobbed her head up and down. The secret made the flowers even more exciting.

She handed me the box. The note that came with the single red rose hadn't been sealed, and the paper flap was bent as if it had already been opened. But the note was just what Mrs. Antonelli wanted to see: "Thinking of you on Valentine's Day. Reynolds Cleese." I pretended Mrs. Antonelli hadn't already read the card, and I passed it over to her to read. She beamed.

"You like this Mr. Cheese?" she asked.

"He's a nice man. Thank you so much for bringing these over to me."

Mrs. Antonelli stood to go. I took a pink carnation out of Leo's bouquet and handed it to her with a flourish. "This is for you," I said. "Happy Valentine's Day."

The little old lady accepted the flower with childlike glee. "And happy Valentine's Day to you," she said. She turned around several times as she walked toward her own house, pointing to the carnation and waving her thanks.

When Mrs. Antonelli disappeared, I turned out the porch light and returned to the living room. I read Leo's message again, knowing how happy he must have been when he wrote the words. I put the bouquet on my dining room table.

Then I threw the single red rose in my kitchen garbage can and went to bed.


Emma was in intensive care until Friday, when she was wheeled to a private room with a *No Visitors* sign out front. Anybody in Utah can tell you *No Visitors* doesn't apply to the bishopric or the Relief Society presidency, so on Saturday morning Alex and I went down the hill to the hospital to see her.

I had a bunch of long-stemmed red roses for Emma. All women love roses, but Emma was always more gung ho over the trappings of womanhood than anyone I knew. Red roses were almost as important to Emma as lipstick, and lipstick was more important than scripture.

Emma didn't know it, but Alex had discovered a florist on 13th East who sold roses for $40 a dozen when they were buds, but twenty-five cents apiece if the flowers had started to open. Alex and I went there whenever somebody in the ward was sick, and the people who got the flowers never knew they weren't the $40 variety. The florist would even wrap the roses in green tissue paper with a few sprigs of baby's breath, which was some bargain for three dollars.

Alex carried a box of See's Bordeaux chocolates, which Emma liked even better than Cummings's. "You're awfully quiet today," Alex said as we got off the elevator and headed toward Emma's private room. "I know what you're thinking. You don't think Emma will share the chocolates with us. I know you and Emma have your problems, but please try to be nice to her in the hospital."

Actually, I hadn't been thinking about chocolates at all. I was wondering about something far more important. Alex and I were on our way to visit a person whose vanity had killed Janna Lee Simonsen, leaving three little children motherless. I'd read enough books to know such a tragedy had to change Emma's life. She'd realize how selfish and shallow she'd been all these years, and she'd be miserable. For the first time I felt sorry for Emma, and I wondered how I could help her.

The blinds were drawn and the curtains closed on top of them when we entered the private hospital room. Emma was silent from her bed, but she wasn't asleep. I could feel, rather than see, her eyes on us. Alex went over to pull the curtains and let some light in the room. It was a cold, clear day. A fresh snowstorm on Friday had washed the smog out of the air, and the sun bouncing off the snow made Salt Lake City a winter palace. It was such a great day to be alive I felt sorry that Emma was in a sickroom.

"Shut that window and get out of here!"

Alex whirled around so fast she dropped the box of chocolates upside-down. Two of them got squashed when Alex took a step forward to steady herself, and another piece rolled under the hospital bed. Little chocolate sprinkles scattered everywhere, and I fought a crazy impulse to sit on the linoleum and eat the sprinkles off the floor. Twenty years ago I would have done it, but today I set my flowers aside and bent down to help Alex pick up the chocolates that were still good. When we got them all, she rearranged them in their white See's gift box so the box looked full again.

Alex ignored Emma's outburst and sat down benignly. She got that Relief Society president look on her face — a kind and loving look that a year ago Alex couldn't even make. I *still* couldn't do it, but I wasn't the Relief Society president. And Emma wasn't looking at me.

Emma's head was wrapped in bandages. Only her mouth, her right eye, and part of her nose were uncovered, but it was enough to show that Emma's face was nearly twice its normal size under all that gauze. Her left arm and leg were immobilized with casts, and big Frankenstein stitches criss-crossed her hands. Emma must have shielded her face with her hands as she went through the windshield of Janna Lee's car. From the look of her face, it didn't help.

"I guess you're not going to leave," Emma said. "That means you're here to gloat. Well, I hope you're happy, Amy. You've ruined my life."

"I what?" This wasn't the tender hospital scene I'd had in mind. Alex looked at Emma as if she had gone crazy, but I'd known Emma long enough to know she wasn't crazy at all.

"You know exactly what you did." Emma's voice was pinched and angry. "You were too selfish to drive me to Provo. *Janna Lee* had to drive me to Provo. Janna Lee was too stupid to get me away from that truck, and now my face is ruined. I'll never be beautiful again."

"Janna Lee is dead, Emma," Alex said quietly.

"It's her own fault. I told her three times to pass that Camaro. If she'd listened to me, we wouldn't have been stuck behind it and the truck wouldn't have hit us and my life wouldn't be ruined."

"Janna Lee is *dead*, Emma," Alex repeated, a little more firmly than before. "We buried her yesterday. She left three little children. Your face is only scarred. It's hardly comparable."

"That's not true. She's better off than I am. Well, isn't she? I'd rather be dead than alive and ugly. *Look* at you! How do you go through life looking like that? How can you face yourselves in a mirror?"

Alex and I weren't beautiful, but I'd never thought of us as ugly. We just didn't look like Emma, and Emma couldn't accept things that weren't exactly like she was.

"We don't spend much time looking in a mirror," I said. "It's not that important to us."

"Then you're stupid. If you can't live with yourself, what's left?"

Alex looked straight through the mass of bandages. "We can live with ourselves, Emma. You don't need to like what you see in the mirror to like yourself. The way you live is more important than the way you look."

"Only an ugly person believes that," Emma said bitterly. And then, "Now *I'm* an ugly person. What am I going to do?"

"You'll live your life the way everyone else does," Alex said. "You'll get by. Think of it as the law of natural selection. The people God makes extremely beautiful, He doesn't need to give them any other gifts. Beauty is all they need. People love them, follow them. They don't need intelligence. They don't need character. People follow them anyway.

"The ugly people have character in spades. God gives it to them as compensation. Character helps them survive knowing they aren't beautiful."

"*I* have character," Emma said. "Who says I don't have character? I'm intelligent, too. I have a *law* degree, if you'll remember."

I couldn't argue the intelligence. Emma was stupid because she chose to be stupid, which was infinitely worse than being born that way. Emma's sin was smallness of heart. It crippled her more than scars on her face would ever do, but she couldn't look beyond the mirror. I felt an alien emotion then. It was compassion for Emma Austen. She'd been handicapped all along. The accident had just made her face look the way she already did on the inside.

I realized then that there wasn't going to be a happy ending. The accident wasn't going to change Emma, in any important sense. She was incapable of remorse. Janna Lee meant no more to Emma in death than she had in life. She'd lived and died as a commodity, and the friendship she'd tried so hard to buy from Emma hadn't been purchased at all.

But at least Janna had lived her life trying to make other people happy. Emma lived just for herself. Emma was right about one thing. As sorry as I felt for Janna Lee, I felt worse for Emma. Janna Lee's troubles were over. Emma's stretched on into eternity.

"Just get out," Emma said, with weariness in her voice. "I don't have anything to say to you."

Alex and I left quickly, leaving the flowers and candy on Emma's bedside table without even putting the roses in water. When we shut the door behind us, Alex leaned against it as if for strength. Her face was pale, and for a moment I thought she was going to faint. But instead, she straightened herself up and started walking down the hall.

"You were right about Emma," Alex said, shaking her head. "You were right all along."

What Alex saw for the first time there at the hospital was Emma's utter heartlessness, the way Emma's personal interest clouded everything but self. I'd seen that all along, hidden out in the open the way the rhinoceros was hidden in the blue sky of my cityscape.

After all these months I was vindicated, but I didn't feel jubilant about it. I was sorry I'd been right. Maybe I'd seen Emma's flaws so clearly in her because I recognized them in me. I'd spent half a year trying to develop compassion for the Relief Society members, but I'd never thought of feeling compassionate toward Emma. I picked the objects of my love as surely as Emma did.

Alex asked if she could take me to lunch but I couldn't eat. Emma's words had brought home to me the fear and the guilt that had been hidden deep in my heart ever since the accident. There was something I had to do.

I was silent as Alex drove me home. Emma was right, I thought. I was supposed to be driving that car. I was the one who should have been killed.

Janna Lee had had a purpose in life. She had a husband and three little children. I didn't have a family, or even a reason to live. I was just taking up space.

I had an even darker guilt. I'd thought of driving Emma to Provo and sending Janna Lee to Welfare Square in my place, but I didn't do it. Now it occurred to me that perhaps that thought had come to me as inspiration. Maybe the Lord wanted me to be with Tim again. But because I didn't want to spend that time with Emma, because I was so selfish, Janna Lee was taken from her family and I remained apart from mine.

When I got home, I didn't even stop to take off my coat and my boots. I knelt by my bed and asked God's forgiveness for ruining everything.

Suddenly I heard a voice in my mind. It wasn't a voice of comfort, but a voice of chastisement. "Don't tell me when to call my daughters home." Then, silence.

Chastened, I leaned against the bed and pondered the words until I fell asleep.


Emma didn't go back to work, even after the bones were knitted and the swelling was gone. She ordered food and medicine and incidentals from stores that delivered. The only time she left the house was to visit a steady stream of plastic surgeons. The doctors' appointments slowed down after a while. There were a lot of plastic surgeons in Salt Lake City, but none of them told Emma what she wanted to hear. Emma would never look like Emma again.

She accepted visitors, unless she saw me at the doorstep, but she drove them all away with anger and bitterness. Nearly every woman in the ward visited Emma once, but few of them saw her more than that.

Alex continued to see Emma, as did Leo. Alex visited her every day, first in the hospital, and later at home. Emma never thanked her for coming, and she never warmed toward Alex. She wouldn't let Alex mention my name.

As time passed, Alex expected Emma to return to church. She called somebody else to be the new spiritual living teacher, but she held the secretary's job in abeyance, waiting for Emma to walk in the Relief Society room on a Sunday afternoon and pick up where she left off. Emma never arrived.

Alex and Bess and I took over the secretarial duties, each doing what we could. Eventually, the mark Emma left on the Relief Society was filled just as seamlessly as ocean waves smooth the sand on a beach. By the beginning of May, Emma's name was seldom mentioned in the ward.

# 16
# Melted Dreams

The big spiritual holiday of the Paradise Vue year approached relentlessly that spring. When the day finally arrived, it dawned cold and snowy. It was unseasonable weather for May, but as far as I was concerned, it was perfect weather for Mother's Day.

I sat in front of the fireplace all that Sunday morning, looking out the window between sections of the *Deseret News*. I hoped there would be so much snow on this worst day of the year that church would be cancelled, but I knew it was futile. I remembered one year that Christmas had fallen on a Sunday. There had been so much snow then that *Christmas* had been cancelled, with almost everyone I knew celebrating instead on the twenty-sixth. But church at Paradise Vue had gone on with the regularity of an Ex-Lax factory.

Even worse was the time back in 1986, when the asbestos insulation had been removed from the Paradise Vue meetinghouse. The workers showed up in yellow suits that covered every square inch of their bodies. They spent the week breathing through gas masks as neighbors watched in amazement from across the street. They only got half-finished by Friday, and on Friday afternoon they put a yellow cordon around the whole building so people wouldn't cross the line until the job was done.

Everyone rejoiced. We all liked church, of course, but nobody ever objected to a holiday. I made plans to spend the whole day painting, and I stretched a six-foot canvas to keep me occupied from dawn till dark.

But at 5:30 A.M. on Sunday, our hardworking stake president marched over to church and took down the yellow cordon. He removed all the signs that told people not to enter the building until the work was done. We didn't just have Sacrament Meeting that Sunday. We had our entire three-hour block of Sacrament Meeting, Sunday School and Relief Society. And before and after church, the bishop held the regular contingent of meetings and appointments that made Sunday the busiest day of the week at Paradise Vue.

Shortly before midnight on that occasion, Alex and I watched from the parking lot as President Neugent drove up in his black Buick and unloaded the yellow cordons and signs and traffic cones from the trunk. Quietly, he set them up just the way they'd been before dawn that morning. When the asbestos workers arrived on Monday, in their gas masks and protective suits, they had no idea that more than three hundred people had spent up to twelve hours apiece inhaling asbestos fibers at Paradise Vue the day before — with no more protection than their Sunday go-to-meeting clothes.

With a history like that, there wasn't a prayer that church would be cancelled on Mother's Day. I dressed in funeral black, right down to a pair of black sunglasses for Sacrament Meeting. I didn't want to get snow-blind on top of everything else on Mother's Day, so the sunglasses were even more important than they were when we only had to deal with sun.

When the time came, though, I couldn't walk out the door. I called Alex, and when she answered the phone I made my voice sound weak and gravelly. "Aaaa-lex?" I asked, with just the right amount of tremor. She couldn't help but think I was at death's door.

"Won't work, Amy. If it were any other day of the year, I might fall for it."

I sighed. "I don't *want* to go this week. Can't I just take one day off?"

"I can't decide for you, Amy. Mother's Day is hard on a lot of people. We'll need you at church today, but if you can't go, I guess we can do without you."

Alex had used the one tactic that always worked on me — guilt. But she didn't seem to be enjoying it as much as she usually did. She seemed just a little depressed. I realized then that if nobody else needed me in church that day, Alex did. I suppressed another sigh.

"What time should I pick you up, Alex?"

"The regular time will be just fine. Thanks, Amy. Let's just get the day over with."

When we got to church, the chapel had been decorated to the heating vents. Two florists with competing shops lived inside the Paradise Vue boundaries. Sam Carbine and Gretta Rodgers were arch-rivals, always trying to outdo the other. They took turns decorating the chapel on important Sundays, and each arrangement had to be better than the one before.

One day, years ago, we'd walked into church at Easter, only to find a large card reading "Flowers by Carbine," sitting among the orchids and the Easter lilies. The card hadn't lasted through Sacrament Meeting, but now there was a little acknowledgment in the program, telling people who donated the day's floral sprays.

If truth were told, the acknowledgment wasn't necessary. Their handiwork was as distinctive as their signatures. Today's flowers were Gretta's doing. Gretta's idea of beauty consisted of dyed carnations and gladiolus, tied with big ribbons in formal sprays.

On days Gretta felt creative, she'd throw in some baby's breath or daisies. Usually she'd add a chrysanthemum or two, especially the spindly ones that looked like spiders. But dyed carnations and gladiolus were Gretta's meat and potatoes. Gretta's main business was funerals. No matter what she did to flowers, she made the chapel look like a coffin was about to be rolled to center stage.

On this day of all days, Alex found a seat for us right near the front. The funeral smell of the floral displays made my nose itch, and I fixed a malevolent stare on the closest spray of them. The salmon-colored ribbon clashed with the mauves of the Paradise Vue chapel, and I wondered why Gretta had done the room in salmon and cream instead of the customary shades of purple.

Alex poked me. "Look at the ribbon in that flower arrangement."

"I *was* looking. Pretty bad match, isn't it?"

"I wasn't referring to the match. Look *through* the ribbon."

I stared harder. The tail of the salmon-colored bunting was highlighted by the sun behind it, and through the satin I could see what looked like a letter. I studied it for a moment, until finally I recognized a backwards *e*.

Alex bent over close and whispered. "Those are glitter-letters — the kind the florists use. I'm pretty sure the back of that ribbon says 'Rest in Peace.'"

Once she pointed it out, I could see backwards letters in all the ribbons. One message said, "Till We Meet Again." Another said, "Not Forgotten." If Alex hadn't noticed them, I never would have seen them. Once she brought them to my attention, I couldn't *not* see them. Sure enough, we'd been plopped down in the middle of recycled funeral flowers. I was glad I'd worn my funeral black.

I didn't have to open my program to know what lay before us. After the Sacrament, there'd be a few tearful tributes to Mother. One year I'd sat in front of DeAnn Wilkerson. When we got to that part she said, "It's a damned *Martyr*'s Day." DeAnn's observation summed up Mother's Day for me.

Sometime during the program, you could count on having to sing all four warbling verses of *Love at Home*. *Love at Home* was written for out-of-tune violins, and to me the cumulative effect of a roomful of aged, heartfelt voices singing the old song was the musical equivalent of a roomful of cats in heat.

The only redeeming social grace of the program was seeing the Primary kids get up and sing a few children's songs. They'd crowd up on the stand, waving at their parents in the audience, and the sight of all those little kids grouped in front of the stained glass window was touching. When the Primary children were at the podium, I could envision what Paradise Vue's architect had in mind when he designed the chapel.

But just as the children would put me in a good frame of mind about Mother's Day, their part of the program would end. They'd march off the stage, and the women of the ward would be subjected to hell on earth — the distribution of wilted geraniums to every mother in the ward.

I didn't have anything against mothers. If my own mother had been alive, I would have been proud to give her a wilted geranium. But Paradise Vue never figured out how to distribute the geraniums to the mothers without hurting the feelings of women who weren't.

Do you give geraniums to pregnant women who haven't had a baby yet? Do you give them to married women who can't have children? Do you give them to old maids who would be mothers if only someone had cooperated and married them? Paradise Vue compromised and gave geraniums to every woman of childbearing age, or every woman who'd ever been of childbearing age. Thus they honored the mothers — and gave the rest of us a vivid reminder of our pitiable state.

As the meeting progressed, I got steadily more nervous. The scent of the funeral flowers was cloying enough, but the looming geraniums made me almost physically ill. Even when four-year-old Bucky Pedersen got nervous during the Primary part of the program and tinkled in his knickers, it didn't distract me from the coming humiliation.

When the geranium distribution was announced by a beaming Hiram Jeppsen, I made my decision. "I'm not going to stand up," I said to Alex. "I'm not a mother, and I'm not going to take a geranium."

"It has nothing to do with motherhood," she hissed. "It has to do with plumbing. You're a woman, aren't you? Then stand up and get your flower." Alex pulled me to my feet. I sat down. She pulled me up again and held me there. I hated geraniums.

Resolutely, like ants attacking a picnic, the Young Men and Young women marched down the chapel aisles with the obligatory geraniums. But they weren't geraniums. They were flat rectangular boxes glazed with frost. TV dinners! Some bozo had bought the mothers TV dinners for Mother's Day.

A box was thrust in my hand, and I sat down with it. It was frozen meat loaf, with peas and carrots and mashed potatoes. I inspected the prize. It was a budget brand, and it looked lethal. The list of ingredients was three inches deep on the box, and most of the words had been made up in a chemical factory. Monosodium glutamate was only one of the treats inside the brightly colored package. I wouldn't even feed this stuff to Samson. Looking at it, I thought I'd rather eat a geranium.

Alex sat down with her own frozen dinner, giggling like a teenager. She could afford to giggle: she'd gotten turkey. It was the first time I'd seen her look happy all day.

"Isn't this rich?" she whispered. "It's Hiram's idea. He announced it in correlation meeting last week, and I've been dying to tell you ever since. He said mothers cook all year, and he wanted to give them a day off on Mother's Day. I couldn't *wait* for you to see this."

Hiram Jeppsen stood at the podium, proud as the NBC peacock. People said he wanted to be bishop when he grew up. Hiram himself told people he would have been bishop long ago if he hadn't been so short. He was always cooking up new schemes so the stake president would notice him. Every one fell as flat as one of my cakes.

"Mothers cook all year, and we men in the ward wanted to give them a day off on Mother's Day," he said, gathering himself up to his full height as he started the same speech Alex had heard in correlation meeting a week ago. He smiled importantly and took a breath while he checked his notes.

From the back of the chapel I heard a disgusted, "*One* dinner? Great. What's *he* going to eat on Mother's Day? Is *he* going to cook it?" It was Hiram's long-suffering wife, speaking in what she thought was a whisper. Her words echoed around the chapel, and several women clapped. Hiram shot his wife a look of horrified betrayal. His face reddened, and he continued his speech. He lost his place in the text, and he started over. "Mothers cook all year, and we men in the ward wanted to give them a day off on Mother's — "

"BRIMSTONE AND TURNIP GREENS!" Clela Sanders, one of the blue-hairs, sprang to her feet. "That TV dinner is melting on my fox fur!"

Her frozen dinner flew through the air like a guided missile and landed on the carpeted aisle near me. Roast beef, I noticed. Why had *I* gotten meat loaf?

Hiram stopped in mid-syllable, shot down in his moment of glory. Across the chapel, several dozen other women started wailing that they, too, were being thawed on by their Mother's Day presents. At least my meat loaf was frozen solid.

Bishop Nebeker, who hadn't gotten to be bishop by sitting still in a crisis, elbowed Hiram away from the podium. "Don't panic," he told the audience. "The Elders Quorum will collect the frozen dinners and put them in the ward freezer. The Relief Society presidency will distribute them again after meetings."

The bishop put his arm around Hiram and drew him to the podium. "It was a fine gesture," he said heartily. "I'm sure all the women know what you were trying to say to them." Hiram, unconvinced, nodded soberly. His shoulders slumped, and he took his place on the stand. He never did finish his speech. I could see him watching his dreams of glory melt around him, in the form of thawing roast beef and turkey and salisbury steak.

Mother's Day or not, I resolved to catch Hiram later and tell him he'd done a good job. Sometimes a lie can be good medicine.

Only two or three women picked up their TV dinners after Relief Society. Alex and I took the rest of them to the Salvation Army for the soup line. As we drove downtown with a trunkload of frozen food, I asked, "What did Ethan give you for Mother's Day?"

"Nothing. He says I'm not his mother. He's off for the day — 'golfing.' He'll have a hard time keeping track of his golf ball in the snow, don't you think? Jean and Clementine will call sometime today. The rest of the day I'm alone."

Alex's words were cheerful, but she was troubled. As much as I hated Mother's Day, it was a big deal to some people. Trying to cheer her up, I said the first thing that came to mind: "Want to share a TV dinner?"

"No, but I've got some steaks in the refrigerator. We can barbecue."

"In the snow?"

"There's no law against it, is there? Besides, the snow's almost stopped. We'll use the snow scraper on the grill and barbecue like crazy." She gave me a solemn wink. "And afterwards, we'll lie out and get a suntan."

With that thought in mind, we unloaded nearly two hundred frozen meals from Alex's trunk, shivering from the cold of the dinners as well as from the falling snow. Midway through the delivery, Alex stopped to inspect a fried chicken dinner. She held it closer and closer to her face, as if transfixed by the picture of three pieces of mystery chicken.

Just as I was wondering what to say to break her reverie, she said, "I know who'd appreciate some of these."

"Alex, *nobody* would want these things who could afford to eat anything else. The only person I can possibly think of is Gardenia Whittaker. Her taste buds died years ago."

Alex slapped the chicken dinner on the palm of her hand. "Gardenia is exactly who I had in mind. Do you want to go say hi?"

Actually, I didn't want to say hi. I also had a nervous suspicion that Alex hadn't even thought of Gardenia until I said her name. As long as Alex had been Relief Society president, we'd never visited on Sunday except for condolence calls and hospital visits. Gardenia didn't fit into either category.

I almost protested, but then it occurred to me that Alex was stalling. She didn't want to go home. As long as she was away from home, it wasn't Mother's Day.

Twenty minutes later, we were wading through ankle-deep snow toward Gardenia's front door. Our tracks were the only ones in the snow, and I made a mental note to ask why the priests hadn't been here to give Gardenia the sacrament. Alex shuffled ahead of me, carrying an armload of TV dinners like precious cargo. From the curtained window, Gardenia's daughter Hester watched our progress up the walk. I waved at her, and she waved back with wild swoops of her arms. She looked like a woman on a life-raft who'd just been spotted by the Coast Guard. Hester's face made me glad we'd stopped in for a visit.

Gardenia Whittaker was the matriarch of Paradise Vue. She'd celebrated her hundred and second birthday several months back, with a big open house in the cultural hall. Gardenia didn't look a day older than a hundred and eighty-six. Her skin was papyrus, and her eyes looked like sockets in a skull. Her corkscrew wig, which was henna red, was so sparse you could see every web of the netting underneath the dime store hair. Inside her wrinkled mouth, her teeth were flawless, thanks to modern dentistry and Poli-Grip.

Gardenia's mind had departed Planet Earth years ago. Wherever it lived was a happy place, and Gardenia's perfect dentures were always framed in a leathery smile. But taking care of the old lady's earthly tabernacle was a sore trial for Hester. Hester, who was pushing seventy-five, hadn't planned to spend her golden years changing her mother's Depends.

As soon as she opened the door, Hester enfolded Alex and the frozen dinners in a giant hug. When she broke the embrace, Hester's chest was wet. After I embraced her, I reeked of frozen gravy.

"Happy Mother's Day!" Alex said, with a great show of cheer. "Has it been a good day for you?"

"Just *special.*" Hester rolled her eyes as she said the words. "Mother's got a little case of the gas today." Hester spoke the truth. The house smelled like a methane plant. Once I placed the smell, it was almost unbearable.

The offender sat in a rocker in the corner of the room, smiling benignly. Two cats were draped over the old lady's carcass. One of them had a bent tail from where Gardenia had rocked over it years before. The other cat appeared to be in the early stages of mange.

"Is that you, Daddy?" Gardenia asked plaintively, when Alex leaned over to tell her hello. Alex hugged the old lady, squeezing her arm gently before she retreated. I raised my eyebrows questioningly at Alex, but she shook her head: Alex's arm-squeeze revealed no sign that Gardenia was on her way out.

I hugged Gardenia, too. Just as I bent over her, she broke wind with a loud blatting sound. I hugged her just as lingeringly as I hugged everyone, trying not to look like I was holding my breath. While we were still in the clinch, Gardenia confided to me, "Cantaloupes are everywhere." I nodded pleasantly, hoping my face didn't look purple yet.

"Are these nice dinners for Mother and me?" Hester changed the subject hopefully. Alex, who'd apparently forgotten she was holding four thawing meals, surrendered them to the old lady. Hester claimed them as if they were first prize in the Publisher's Clearing House sweepstakes. "Oh, look, Mother! A nice chicken dinner. And there's a turkey and dressing one for you, too."

Gardenia broke wind again. From anyone else, it would have been an editorial comment on Mother's Day and TV dinners and the state of the world in general. For Gardenia, it was a way of life.

Alex told Hester all about the Mother's Day program, including Gardenia in the conversation as if the old woman could hear her. Meanwhile, Gardenia's mind orbited Saturn. She'd sporadically interject a bit of nonsense into the conversation. Hester reassured her after every comment, and Gardenia smiled in her reverie.

"I hope you can make it out to Homemaking meeting on Tuesday," Alex invited Hester. "The nurse will be here to take care of Gardenia, won't she? We're having an international tasting table, with foods from Greece and Thailand and Afghanistan. Then we're having a demonstration on how to cook cheesecake."

Hester, who still hadn't forgotten the TV dinners, brightened at the mention of food. She opened her mouth to say something, but Gardenia interrupted her.

"Such a big organ! *MY!* how nice."

"Yes, it is a big one," Hester agreed.

Alex peered around the room as if she'd missed something. When she didn't see any organs, large or otherwise, she shrugged and told Hester more about Homemaking Day.

Alex prolonged the visit long after we should have left. When I finally caught Hester casting longing glances toward the kitchen, with its cache of frozen dinners, I stood up quickly and said it was time to go. Gardenia pooted loudly in agreement. Alex looked at me as if I'd been the one who committed the indelicacy, but Hester didn't protest. No sooner did we hug Hester goodbye at the door, than she bustled off in the direction of the kitchen. I knew from the spring in Hester's step that no frozen pea or carrot would escape her enthusiastic fork.

Alex wasn't so cheerful. She drove us to her house like a cattle rustler waiting for the hanging. She opened her door as if she were a visitor there, calling Ethan's name before she even crossed the threshold. When nobody answered, she looked both disappointed and relieved.

Our barbecue should have been a merry event. It started snowing again in earnest, and the two of us stood bravely outside over the barbecue grill, cooking steaks in the snowstorm. But Alex was strangely melancholy. We watched the smoke waft up from the meat and out of sight, blending with the falling snow. I stuck my tongue out to catch some snowflakes, but I felt silly and stopped. I looked at Alex, but when I saw her staring at me I quickly returned my gaze to the rising smoke.

"You're trying hard to cheer me up. I'm sorry it's not working."

I wanted to ask Alex what was wrong, but she always told me things in her own time. I turned the steaks and moved them away from the fire. Alex, who liked meat as rare as I did, moved hers back to open flame. The steak singed and charred.

Alex took a deep breath. "I told Ethan what we found."

I looked up quickly, surprised. It was the last thing she should have done.

"I promised myself I'd keep the secret, but every time I looked at him, I knew he'd been with someone else. It hurt so much I wanted to hurt him as badly as he'd hurt me."

"Did you?"

"I think I did. He started crying. He said he loved me, but then he left. He stayed away all night."

I wanted to put my arm around her, but we were separated by the barbecue grill. "You should have called, Alex. I would have come over. You shouldn't have been alone."

"I couldn't call. I kept hoping he'd come back, and I needed to be alone when he did. When he didn't come, I finally fell asleep."

I took the steaks off the grill. Alex's was overcooked and shrunken. I left the fire to burn itself out. When we got indoors, I put Alex's steak in the dog dish. The two big dogs fought over the scraps. Man o' War won. He carried the prize downstairs, with Chesapeake in hot pursuit.

I cut the remaining steak in thin slices and arranged the pieces on two plates, while Alex watched. It was a pitiful serving, but neither of us felt much like eating. When the silent meal ended, most of the food also went to the dogs.

As we were washing the dishes, Alex said, "Emma called this morning. Leo took back his engagement ring."

"He did? I thought he was crazy about Emma. I would have expected more from him."

"He was crazy about the person he *thought* was Emma. Everyone was crazy about the person they thought was Emma. Everyone but you."

I shook my head, thinking how ironic it all was. Before the accident, I was the only one who hated Emma. Now that everyone was forgetting her, I wanted to be her friend.

"Leo told Emma he didn't realize how ugly she was until after the accident."

"That was an unfortunate choice of words," I said.

"It sure was. Emma thinks he was talking about the way she looks. She's devastated, of course. She thinks everyone has deserted her because she's ugly."

I didn't say anything. I was scrubbing barbecue leavings from the grill, and I pretended it took all my concentration.

"I had a dream last night." Alex didn't seem to realize she'd changed the subject, as smoothly as a disc jockey segues to a different record. "I was wrapping boxes, and they kept coming untied. I asked Ethan to hold his finger on the ribbon while I tied the knots, but he wouldn't do it. He took the ribbon, and he walked away, and all the boxes fell apart."

# 17
# Resolution

When Ethan wasn't home by nightfall, Alex couldn't spend the night there alone. After all those years, the house was too big for her. Always before when Ethan wasn't there, she knew he'd be home tomorrow. Now there was no tomorrow, and every creak of the floorboards told Alex she was alone.

At about nine o'clock, she called me. "I can't do this," she said with a tremor in her voice. "Can I come over and spend the night?"

I said sure and hung up. I changed the sheets on the guest bedroom and locked Samson in the basement, where he yowled in protest. I also cleaned the bathroom and got rid of some clutter, but it didn't help. What Alex needed wasn't me; it was Bess. I called Bess, and the two of them arrived at the same time.

As if they'd planned it, neither Bess nor Alex was dressed. Bess wore a nubby bathrobe, and Alex had on a pair of flannel pajamas. I wore the surgical scrub suit I'd inherited from Tim; it was what I wore to bed every night. It was an unseasonably cold night for mid-May, so I built a fire in the fireplace, and Bess made us all some hot chocolate.

Alex's eyes were red from crying. She held her mug and watched the marshmallows melt together. "Last night, before Ethan left, he told me the vow that binds too tightly snaps itself. What does that mean?"

Bess blew on her chocolate to cool it. "I think it means he's looking for an excuse to play around. He's chafing against his marriage vows, and he's blaming the vows instead of himself."

"But we were married *forever.*"

"At the beginning of forever, you can't comprehend how long that will be. Ten or twenty years into it, with eternity stretched before you, forever can be a frightening concept."

Bess wasn't talking about Ethan; she was talking about herself. But Alex, who didn't know Bess's secret, found truth in her words.

"Bess," she said, "you're so lucky. Everything happened right for you. When I see you in church, surrounded by your children and the man you love, it hurts to watch you. I'm jealous of you because you're so happy."

Bess took a slow sip of hot chocolate. She looked as if she were giving herself time to choose the right words to say. I thought she would tell Alex what she'd already told me, but she didn't mention Fletcher Jacobsen.

"You only see what you're supposed to see, Alex. I don't belong in that family. I shouldn't have married Rick. I never should have been a mother. That's not my real life. That's not what I was put on earth to do."

Bess shifted position in her chair, shaking her head as if her neck hurt. Then she looked pointedly at me. I remembered telling her once that she'd been born to be a mother, and she'd bristled at the idea even then. But she hadn't told me on that occasion what she was born to do, and she didn't tell Alex now.

"Don't be jealous of me because my life looks perfect to you," she said. "You have no reason to be jealous of me. But if you *are* jealous of me, at least it means I'm doing my job as well as I can."

Alex waited for Bess to explain, but she'd confided enough for one night. The three of us stared at the fireplace for a long time in silence.

Bess didn't stay all night. She was cryptic about it, and nervous. I wondered why she was so uneasy, but I decided she was just worried about Alex. I was worried about Alex, too.

I put Alex in the guest room and said good night to her, but five minutes later she was knocking at my bedroom door. She peeked inside and said, "Amy? Can I sleep in here with you? You've got a big bed, and I'll only take part of it."

She sounded so sad, in a little voice that was so unlike her normal one, that I told her to come in. She crawled in Tim's side of the bed and put her head on Tim's pillow. In all the years since Tim had died, nobody had lain on that side of the bed; no head had rested on Tim's pillow. But every night for nearly seven years, I'd held that pillow in my arms as I slept.

I felt uneasy for a moment, until I realized Tim would have approved. I lay on my side of the bed, listening to Alex breathe as I stared at the ceiling in the dark.

"It's so easy for you," she said finally.

"*Nothing's* easy for me, Alex. What are you talking about?"

"I'm not like you. I can't let go so easily."

"Alex, it only looks as if I've let go." There was silence for a minute. Only the gentle sounds of Alex's breathing told me I wasn't alone in the room.

"You tease me because I spend so much time in bed," I continued. "I don't get dressed all day if I don't have to go anywhere, and I'm usually in bed by eight o'clock at night. But when I'm asleep, Tim's still alive for me. It's the mornings I dread. Every morning I lie in bed with my eyes closed, because when I open them he won't be here."

Alex said, "Oh," in a little voice and reached for my hand in the darkness. "I'm so sorry," she said. "I didn't know."

After a few minutes Alex said, "Maybe Ethan was right. If I'd trusted him, maybe he wouldn't have left me."

"We all have *ifs*, Alex. If I could have had children, Tim would have stayed home instead of getting that job in Denver. If I'd moved to Denver, he wouldn't have had to commute. If Thanksgiving hadn't been so important to me, Tim wouldn't have flown home in a snowstorm. Forget the *ifs*, Alex. *Ifs* won't bring Ethan back."

I held Alex's hand in the darkness until she fell asleep. When I awoke in the morning, she wasn't there. I dressed quickly and hurried to her house, driving to save the five-minute walk. The back door was open, and when I went inside something seemed wrong. There was some disarray I couldn't immediately understand. Then I realized the dogs weren't barking, the way they always did when anyone came to the door.

I looked on the kitchen floor for their food and water dishes, but they weren't there. There were only some bits of dry dog food scattered on the floor to indicate that dogs had ever lived in the house.

As I walked through the house to the stairway, I realized that other things were missing. Here and there, a light spot on the wall marked the place where a painting had been removed. Ethan's easy chair was gone from the den, leaving only marks on the carpet where the feet had rested.

I ran up the stairs to Alex's bedroom, afraid of what I'd find. Ethan's closet was open, and all his clothes were missing. He'd taken everything that was his, including the pillow from his side of the bed. Alex wouldn't even have that to comfort her. But Alex wasn't there.

I looked for her in all the rooms, but all I found was a house that looked torn apart. Ethan's half of her life had vanished, leaving only marks on the floors and coat hangers left askew in the closet and empty places in the house to show where he had been.

After looking everywhere else, I went down to the basement. Alex sat in her workshop, lowering the innards of a clock into a finished case. She didn't say anything, so I watched her quietly as she picked up a small screwdriver and slowly tightened the works into place. When she finished, she placed the hour hand, then the minute hand. She screwed them down, one atop the other, with a steady turn of her wrist. She hung the clock on a nail and wound it. Nearly an hour passed, but in that room time stood still.

Then Alex took the pendulum and put it on its hook, where it moved back and forth with a gentle rhythm. Finally she moved the minute hand forward until the clock chimed. Everything worked perfectly, and she sat back to inspect it. Only then did she speak.

"This will be my last clock," she said, wiping her hands on her blue jeans.

I couldn't imagine Alex's fingers unstained by varnish or free of splinters. She'd been building clocks for such a long time. "Why? You've been doing this as long as I can remember."

She wiped a smudge off the glass of the case. "I don't know why. I just know this part of my life is over."

"But what will you do next?" I persisted.

"I don't know that either. It's just time to move on with my life."

I didn't answer, because I didn't know what to say. Alex started putting tools away, each in the slot on the wallboard designed for that particular tool. The tiny clockmaker's screwdrivers she packed away in a plastic case.

"Do you know what was my big mistake? My big mistake was wanting the proof. All along I thought if I only had proof, I could live with the knowledge. I looked for the truth for years." Then she laughed bitterly. "But why am I telling *you* that? I made you look for the proof with me.

"What I never realized was the truth didn't matter. Ethan loved me. He didn't want to leave me. He just didn't know how to love one person."

A hammer fell to the floor with a clatter. Alex retrieved it and put it away. Her hand was shaking, and she had to try twice before she placed the hammer squarely on its pegs. "I think what Ethan needed was for me to have faith in him. My priesthood blessing said that when we got set apart. If I'd believed in him, maybe he would have lived up to the trust. But I never trusted him, not for a minute. I had to look for the proof, and once I had it, I couldn't let it go."

Alex stood up and dusted herself off. We walked upstairs to the kitchen, and Alex opened the refrigerator. She gave me a Pepsi and took a Diet Coke for her. Then she looked at her drink and put it back. We walked out on the porch and sat together on the front step. The sun had melted the snow off the concrete, leaving snow in patches in the yard. The steps were still wet, but Alex didn't seem to notice. She pulled a cluster of needles off a pine tree and braided them aimlessly. Then she threw them down on the snow.

"Reynolds Cleese called this morning," she said. "He can't understand why you won't return his calls. I can't understand it either. I think you should call him."

"I don't *want* to call him, Alex. I don't want to date him; I don't want to marry him." I watched a bug cross the sidewalk, threading its way around lingering patches of snow. When it got to the edge, it turned around and went back to the other side.

Alex pulled another cluster of pine needles. "He didn't tell me he wanted to marry you. I think he just wants a friend."

"Why me? Why can't he just leave me alone?"

"It could be he thinks you'll understand him. You've both been through the same thing, losing someone you love. Besides that, people confide in you."

"Not more than anyone else."

"You're wrong, Amy. Why do you think I called you as my homemaking counselor? You certainly don't have a talent for homemaking."

I waited for Alex to go on.

"People trust in you. They tell you things they haven't even told themselves. You never laugh at them, and you never break a confidence."

Alex stared at me so intently I looked downward to break the gaze. "When we go visiting," she continued, "I'm the one they tell their friends about. 'The Relief Society president dropped by,' they tell their kids. I don't have a name; I'm an office. But you're the one they talk to, after they've served me the biggest glass of juice and the nicest cookie. You're the one they look at. You're the one they hug the hardest when we leave. You're the one whose visit matters."

I'd wondered why Bess told me her problems, and why Eve Parker called me instead of Alex when she was in trouble. I assumed I'd just been in the right place at the right time. I hadn't realized that people wanted to confide in me. Even Emma. Why else was I able to see through her when no one else could? She had always confided her secret nastiness to me without even realizing it. When she was alone with me, she let her true self show through.

Maybe they all did, at least a little. Sitting on the steps with Alex was the first time since I'd been called as homemaking counselor that I saw a purpose in my being there.

Alex put her arm around me. "You're always trying to find a way to help people compassionately," she said. "But you seem to think that only applies to Relief Society members. If Reynolds Cleese were a Relief Society member who wanted you to call her, wouldn't you do it? Wouldn't you help her when she was alone?"

I nodded. Alex was right: I never would have ignored his calls if he'd been a woman. And it wasn't always women who needed help.


I left Alex's intending to drive awhile and sort my thoughts, but when my car turned on Brigham Circle I knew I was going to see Bess. There was a car in the driveway as I pulled up. Company, I thought, doubting the prompting that had taken me there. But slowly, the car backed out and drove away. As it passed me, I saw the ascetic, pockmarked face of the man inside. It could only be Fletcher Jacobsen, larger in life than the black and white pictures in *People*.

Bess was leaning against the frame of her front door with tears streaming down her face. I sat her down and fixed her a glass of water, but what she wanted was comfort. I sat with my arm around her as she cried. Fletcher had flown to Utah to ask Bess to leave Rick and marry him. Bess had told him no.

"I'm not the saint you think I am," she said. "I'm doing this for me. If Fletcher married me, one day he'd grow to hate me. The day would come when he'd realize what he'd given up, and he'd spend the rest of his life wondering what his life could have been without me.

"I'll never marry Fletcher. I'll never have his children, and I'll pray each day not to resent my own daughters every time I look at them and know they aren't his. But by giving him up, we'll always love each other. That will have to be enough."

"What are you going to tell Rick?" I asked.

"Nothing. He'll never know. That's my penance for not loving him."

"That, and children."

"Yes," she said, and smiled. "It's time to have another baby."

Then I remembered the fortune teller. "When you wrote down *F* for the palm reader, you weren't asking about Rick, were you?" She shook her head. "And all the time I thought you were being clever. What did that woman say? He'd give up everything for you, and you'd live happily ever after. That's bizarre."

"Amy," she said, "did you believe that fortune teller?"

"No, Bess. No."

Bess looked stricken. "I think they do have a power, but it's not a good one. It comes from the wrong source. But you can't believe a fortune teller any more than you'd believe Betty Jo Jennings. They aren't bound to tell the truth."


I went home and went to bed, the place where I did all my thinking.

The fortune teller hadn't told us the truth. She told us what we wanted to hear. Alex suspected Ethan was being unfaithful, and she wanted confirmation of that. She got her confirmation, but when she lost faith in Ethan it ruined her marriage.

Bess needed to believe she and Fletcher would live happily ever after. She knew it could never happen, but she wanted it more than she'd ever wanted anything in her life. When she heard what she longed to hear, it gave her hope enough to forget her duty until she could accept it.

And me — I wanted to know I was doing the right thing, shutting myself off from life to remember the past. Tim would always be a part of my life, but for now he was as much in the past as Alex's clocks.

I thought of Alex, and how hard she had held on to what was hers, and how unhappy it made her. Then I thought of Bess and all her misery. Married to one man and loving another — but loving enough to let him live his life the way it was supposed to be lived, without her.

It was time for me to let go. I got out of bed and got dressed, throwing my surgical scrub suit down the laundry chute. I got down on my knees and stuck an arm down the chute after it. When I retrieved the top and the bottom, I threw them both in the garbage. That scrub suit was a ratty old thing. I should have retired it years ago.

Then I found the ward directory and looked up Reynolds Cleese's telephone number. After a moment's hesitation, I picked up the phone.

*Sterling & Chantilly, Virginia*
*21 July 1989*

# About the Author

**K**athryn Helms Kidd was born in New Orleans, Louisiana, in 1950 and grew up across Lake Pontchartrain in Mandeville. As a child she planned to be a paleontologist until she was told that she couldn't be a Christian and a paleontologist at the same time. She changed her plans at once, deciding to be, in turn, a herpetologist, an Egyptologist, a U.S. senator, and a baseball broadcaster — which led her to major in communications at Brigham Young University.

Why did a non-Mormon Louisiana girl end up attending college at the Mormon school? Her mother had read in a magazine article that BYU didn't allow cigarette smoking, and Kathryn at once announced that that's where she wanted to go — in large part because both her parents were chain smokers and she didn't think they'd let her. To her surprise, her parents agreed at once and Kathryn's whimsical choice became her alma mater. She didn't mind, though — she wanted to get away from Louisiana, and Provo, Utah, seemed culturally as far away as it was possible to go.

At BYU, Kathryn soon became involved in Church activities, but it took her three years to gain a testimony. By that time her mother, a dyed-in-the-wool Episcopalian, had leukemia; for her sake, Kathryn waited to join the Church. Soon after her mother's death, when Kathryn was twenty, she was baptized, and received her patriarchal blessing eight days later.

One day in the Harris Fine Arts Center she saw a posted notice of a test for an internship at the *Deseret News*; the test was scheduled to begin five minutes from the time she saw the notice. So she promptly took it, passed it, won the internship, and changed her career plans from broadcasting to journalism. When she graduated she went straight to the *Deseret News* and ended up, among other assignments, as religion editor, which meant she covered the news of all religions *except* Mormonism.

She met Clark L. Kidd, then computer systems programmer for First Security Bank, through the singles branch in the Emigration Stake. Her first words to him were: "You're growing a moustache. That's disgusting." They immediately became inseparable. On 18 November 1976, she and Clark were married in the Salt Lake Temple and took up residence on Princeton Avenue in Salt Lake City.

They lived there until they moved to Sterling, Virginia, in November 1987, where Clark is a software developer for Legent Corporation and Kathryn writes political fund-raising letters for clients from London to Australia. They read Dave Barry's column, watch *Married with Children*, and produce the ward newsletter for the Sterling North Ward. Kathryn paints and keeps a journal. Clark makes stained-glass windows. And Clark still has the moustache.